*Before he can take a ___
he needs lesson___* ⟶ P9-BYV-354

A Date at the Altar

"There are a half a dozen birds around London who men would be jealous to see you with, Your Grace. Why me?"

"I require someone who will not be foolish," he said. "I do not want bastards."

He was smart. Baynton was wealthy. He would be honor bound to support any child he bred. The mother could find herself set for life.

"I also need someone whose discretion I can trust."

"And you believe that is me?" Sarah asked, incredulous.

"As a matter of fact, I do. You actually do have principles."

"Thank you, I think."

"You think?"

"Yes, you have me confused," she said. "You wish discretion and yet you obviously plan on letting everyone in London know we have been lovers. What game are you playing?"

"No game. I need help and you are the only one I can trust."

CATHY MAXWELL

A Date at the Altar

MARRYING THE DUKE

AVONBOOKS

An Imprint of HarperCollinsPublishers

A DATE AT THE ALTAR. Copyright © 2016 by Catherine Maxwell, Inc. All rights reserved. Printed in the United States of America. No part of this book may be used or reproduced in any manner whatsoever without written permission except in the case of brief quotations embodied in critical articles and reviews. For information, address HarperCollins Publishers, 195 Broadway, New York, NY 10007.

First Avon Books mass market printing: November 2016

ISBN 978-0-06-238865-0

Avon Trademark Reg. U.S. Pat. Off. and in Other Countries, Marca Registrada, Hecho en U.S.A.
Avon, Avon Books, and the Avon Impulse logo are trademarks of HarperCollins Publishers.
HarperCollins® is a registered trademark of HarperCollins Publishers.

16 17 18 19 20   QGM   10 9 8 7 6 5 4 3 2 1

For Geri Krotow
Step by step, word by word . . .
I am wealthy in my friends.

The SIREN Returns!

The Glorious Creature who captured London
and then Disappeared will once again
Grace the Stage.

THE BISHOP'S HILL THEATRE

Tuesday, July 7, 1812
An Evening tailored to Gentlemen with Refined Tastes
and for their *Special* Enjoyment

⊢——— *Come see* ———⊣

THE NAUGHTY REVIEW:

A *Clandestine* Performance

This is a return Engagement of London's once
most Talked about Evening in the Theatre,
having been received with Roars of Laughter,
Applause, and Great Appreciation.

For ONE night ONLY
Lovely ladies, Song, and Frolic!
Special boxes close to the stage available.
An event NOT to be missed.

Discretion would be kindly advised.

Chapter One

$\mathcal{S}$arah Pettijohn had vowed she would never play the role of the Siren again . . . and yet here she was, tucked high above the stage behind the proscenium arch so that the audience could not see her, dressed in practically nothing, waiting her turn on stage. From her perch, she watched the teeming mass of male bodies in the audience below and knew they did not bode well for her.

The owners of the theater, Geoff and Charles, were masters at creating a stir. The house was packed with men from every walk of life. The rich, the poor, the old, the young, and the stupid had all paid their four shillings because, as Geoff said, men could never have their fill of "tittie" watching. "No matter how much it costs them, they like to look."

Sarah was not showing her "titties." She wore a nude shift beneath her diaphanous costume.

Granted there was little beneath the shift, but she was well covered compared to the other women in the company. She'd insisted upon it. She knew from the last time she had been compelled to play the Siren, six years ago, the male imagination could fill in the details, whether seen or not.

Keeping her identity a secret was important, just as it had been in the past. To that purpose, Sarah wore a bejeweled mask and mounds of face paint and powder to create a fanciful, feminine creature with long lashes and golden skin. A black wig plaited into a thick braid hid her red hair. She'd also refused to attend rehearsals, preferring to practice her act in secret. She was not proud of what she was doing. She had a reputation to protect.

After all, she wasn't just an actress. She was a playwright.

She'd agreed to play the Siren because Geoff and Charles promised to stage her play.

Her play.

For years, Sarah had rewritten and edited the work of men who used her talent and gave her none of the recognition. This past summer, Colman at the Haymarket Theater where she'd been part of the company for years, had promised to produce one of her plays but when the time came, he'd reneged and put one of his own on the schedule instead. *One Sarah had rewritten for him.*

Sarah had walked. She'd left his company with her head high, and her pockets empty.

That is when Geoff and Charles had approached her.

They were talented theater men who had staged the first *Naughty Review* in order to raise the funds to build the Bishop's Hill Theater. It had been a one-night event, just as this was. At that time, Sarah had been desperate for money so that she could provide a home for her half-sister's orphaned daughter. She didn't expose her "titties" then, either, but she would have done that and more to protect Charlene.

What no one had expected was for the Siren to become almost legendary in men's minds. Even Sarah was astounded and she was thankful that she'd been disguised so no one knew who she was. For months after that first *Review*, personal notices were run in the papers from men either begging the actress playing the Siren to contact them or looking for information about her. Fortunately, those few people who knew Sarah never betrayed her.

Now, after years of running their own theater, Geoff and Charles were deeply in debt. They were in danger of losing the Bishop's Hill and hoped that if the *Review* worked once, it would do so again.

"Everyone wants the Siren," Charles had said.

"You do this for us and we will stage your play. We'll all have what we want."

Sarah had reluctantly agreed. She'd had no choice, really. She didn't have the means to stage the play herself. Charlene was now happily married and living in Boston, an ocean away. The time had come for Sarah to live her own life.

If dancing and singing almost naked would bring her what she wanted, then so be it. A woman alone had to do what she must to survive—and if Sarah was one thing, she was a survivor.

She shifted her weight on the narrow shelf and tightened her hold on the silken rope that would be used to lower her to the stage. The Siren would be the last performance of the evening. She'd secreted herself an hour before the curtain.

Below her, two female gladiators with swords shaped like phalluses left the stage. William Millroy, an Irish tenor, came out and began singing about being cuckolded by his wife. The audience wasn't paying attention. They had come for women. Someone threw a cabbage at Will but he ducked. More vegetables and a few fruits were thrown to the delight of the crowd, especially when they hit their target. William scampered off stage to the sound of cheers.

"Where's the Siren?" someone called out. A chant began. "Siren! Siren!" Sarah shook her head. Men could be so ridiculous. They had been doing this all evening. Her nerves were frayed.

A group of bare-breasted dancers costumed as sheep came out onto the stage and the men forgot their chanting and roared their approval. One gent leaped from one of the boxes upon the sheep nearest him. Sarah knew the girl. Irene. She screamed and pushed his hands away from her breasts just as the bullyboys Geoff and Charles had hired rushed forward to toss the man into the pit. Laughter and ribald comments met his comeuppance.

The music started and the sheep pranced around while a shepherd ran among them poking them in the bum with his staff. Every time he touched a sheep, she'd cry "Baaa" and the audience started mimicking the sound with an obscenity in place of the "Baa."

Sarah had an urge to go down on that stage and lecture the men on manners. If they kept up this rowdiness, her performance would be a short one.

In fact, she *would* make it quick.

She would sing one song, escape this theater without anyone being wiser to who she really was, and then she could start living the rest of her life the way she wished. She'd cast her play, *The Fitful Widow: A Light Comedy Concerning the Foolishness of Men*, and prove that her talent was equal to any male playwright's—

Her fierce determination came to an abrupt halt as she recognized one of the men in the very expensive boxes to the side of the stage.

Uncertain she could believe her eyes, she leaned forward as far as she dared on the platform for a better view, balancing herself by holding on to the rope.

It was *him*. There was no mistaking the broad shoulders or that arrogantly proud tilt of the head.

The Duke of Baynton, that Pillar of Morality, the Nonesuch, the Maker of Ministries *was at the* Naughty Review.

Sarah sat back, stunned, and then drew a deep breath.

Who knew? Baynton was mortal after all.

Or perhaps he had wandered in by chance? Oh no, he wouldn't.

She distinctly remembered him coolly informing her that he did *not* attend the theater. *Well,* he had added, *save for the occasional Shakespeare.*

This was no Shakespeare.

And it was intriguing to see him here.

The duke had once wooed her niece Charlene. When Charlene had run off with another, his twin brother, no less, Baynton had gone after them and Sarah had insisted on accompanying him so that she could protect her beloved niece.

In the end, Baynton had not won the lady.

Charlene had married the man she loved and the duke had been somewhat gracious about it—that is, to everyone save Sarah. Apparently he did not appreciate outspoken women.

She had little admiration for him as well. Two days of traveling to Scotland with him had convinced her that no other man on earth could be more insufferable or self-righteous than Baynton. At their parting, she had prayed to never set eyes upon him again—except this was *good*. This was a moment to be relished.

Watched only Shakespeare. The hypocrite.

If she'd had a shoe on, she would have thrown it down right on his head. Let him think it was the judgment of God Almighty for being in such an immoral place. Sarah would have adored seeing the expression on his handsome face . . . and he *was* handsome. Sarah was not blind to his looks. It was the words that came out of his mouth she didn't like.

But gazing at him, well, that was pleasure.

In truth, she'd been overjoyed when he'd first called on Charlene. She'd wanted what was best for her niece and the Duke of Baynton was the best London had to offer. He was wealthy, respected, honored, and Char would have made a lovely duchess.

Sarah could even recall the last words she'd

heard the duke speak. Baynton had paid Sarah's way home from Scotland by private coach rather than endure more travel time with her. He'd mentioned within her hearing that it had been "money well spent. She is too opinionated by half." Words that Sarah had found surprisingly hurtful, although she'd had her fill of him as well.

The sheep were almost done with their act. It had gone on overlong. The crowd no longer yelled crudities or baaa'ed. They grew restless. That was the problem with this sort of entertainment. It could never capture the imagination—not in the way a well-written play could.

The Siren was up next.

Had Sarah thought to make her performance quick and be done with it? *That* had been before spying the Duke of Puffed Up Consequence in her audience.

She stood and wrapped the silken rope around her hand, readying herself to step off the platform the moment the dancers on stage finished. She felt strong, powerful, and inspired to give the performance of her lifetime.

If Baynton thought his matched set of grays were high flyers, wait until he witnessed the Siren.

Chapter Two

$\mathcal{I}$f not for his concern for his friend Rovington, Gavin Whitridge, Duke of Baynton, would have walked out of the *Naughty Review*.

Oh, he liked looking at women's breasts as well as any man—and they were all on display here. Big breasts, little ones, and everything in between jiggled and bobbed to the point that, after a while, it became rather tiresome.

Well, at least for him. The other men in the theater could not seem to have enough. They crowded together, pushing against the pit where the musicians—two violins and a pianoforte— played, trying to close in on the stage and all those dancing breasts.

And what a crowd it was! Since the theater was lit by what seemed to be a thousand candles not only on the stage but over the audience, Gavin could count no fewer than three judges of the High Court in attendance and what seemed to be every member of the Commons. The octogenarian Lord Bradford was present in a sedan chair and enjoying the show with his carriers. Fathers were accompanied by sons. Sailors milled about by the shipload and lords, gentlemen, knaves, and obvious criminals exchanged catcalls and quips with gusto.

Serving lasses, their own bosoms barely covered, wove through the crowd with mugs of ale that they charged *a half-guinea* apiece for, and the lads happily paid.

Oh, yes, it was a great night at the theater, reminding Gavin why he could barely abide it. He detested crowds. Then again, he wasn't here for entertainment.

No, he was here because he believed his trust in Rovington, in whose private box he now sat, was being betrayed.

Several months ago, Rov's wife Jane had approached Gavin for help. Rov had always fancied himself a gambler except now, he had apparently been playing too deep. Jane claimed he was cleaned out, done. Ruined. He'd turned to the moneylenders and would start losing his unentailed estates. Since his father, also a gambler, had not been wise with his responsibilities, there were a number of them.

Gavin counted Rov as one of his oldest friends. They had known each other since school. Of course he wanted to help and had pushed for Rov to be named to the lucrative position as Chairman of the Committees in the House of Lords.

He did it for several reasons: First, Rov had a bit of a touch with the Common Man and this position called for good communication with the House of Commons. The Chairman of the Committees could dictate the importance of all legislation in Parliament. And that was the second reason Gavin had placed him there. Gavin expected Rov to carry out his suggestions. In turn, the income from the position would relieve Rovington's money woes.

Unfortunately, the decision was not a successful one.

Yes, Rov did well with the members of the Commons—as could be seen by the number of them who had stopped by their box this evening. But he was not controllable. He ignored Gavin's recommendations and handled matters his own way . . . and Gavin was starting to suspect Rov might be involved in double-dealing, even in accepting bribes.

Nor had the income helped. Rov's gambling was even worse now. Jane had come to Gavin only that afternoon, begging him to help. Apparently

Rov had placed wagers all over London that he would bed a woman known as the Siren.

"He's besotted with her," Jane had said. "He saw her in performance years ago and has never forgotten her."

"But to place a bet on bedding her?" Gavin had said in disbelief.

"See for yourself. My husband is a fool."

She'd been right.

With a bit of investigation, Gavin had learned Rov had placed a fortune on the bedding wagers. He'd also paid five hundred pounds for the private box right next to the stage, an exorbitant amount even if there had been some decent acting presented.

And Rov was as bold as you please about his wager. All evening, men had stopped by to up their wagers or badger Rov about his "swordsmanship." Gavin knew Rov was fond of actresses. He liked Jane and hoped she never found out about Rov's many mistresses, who probably had received more of her husband's money than she did.

All in all, Gavin realized he had made a bad decision in trusting Rov. He could hear his father mock him. His father had always warned Gavin to stay away from gamblers. Then again, his father himself had made more than one bad investment, and wasn't that a form of gambling?

Other members in the box with Rov and Gavin included Admiral Alexander Daniels and Lord Phillips, who was a member of the Chancery. Both were well into their cups, Phillips being the worst of the two. There was also Rov's cousin, Sir John Harmond, a well respected mathematician who twittered like a girl at every act. There were also two sly fellows who were quite obvious sharps, confirming the disturbing rumors Gavin had been hearing about his friend.

"This is Harris and Crowder," Rov had introduced them offhandedly.

"Your Grace," Crowder had said for the twosome, but not with the deference Gavin was accustomed to receiving. They acted as if they'd seen too much of men, of the underbelly of the beast, to be humbled just by his mere presence. Rov was nothing more than a mark for them, a man caught up in his spending ways and, if friends did not become involved in the situation, they would eat him alive.

Gavin didn't have many close companions—male or female. His title was a barrier as were the duties that took up the majority of his time. His father had impressed upon him that a man of substance must hold himself to a higher standard than those around him.

So, while his peers were going off on larks and

entertainments, Gavin worked. He had a sense of obligation to his country. He used his considerable political influence to support the right causes, to be the sort of duke his title bade him to be. He prided himself on being the kind of man who stood head and shoulders above others.

It kept him busy and left little time for personal friendships and perhaps that was why he'd trusted Rov too much. As he watched half-naked sheep dance on stage, his mind chewed on the problem of how best to keep his friend from ruining himself—

A sharp jab to his arm almost caused him to spill the swill in his mug. "I told you this was going to be something, eh?" Rov asked, his eyes bright, excited. He was a tad shorter than Gavin and thinner, with blond hair. Lines of dissipation from long nights and hard drinking were beginning to show on his handsome face. "I said *this* is what you have been needing, Baynton, instead of poring over reports to Parliament and Whitehall. A man needs to play. You need to unleash the *wolf inside.*" He emphasized the last words by bouncing his fist off of Gavin's shoulder. "Especially before you leg-shackle yourself."

He referred to Gavin's hunt for a wife.

"If I had a wife like yours, I'd be home playing," Gavin said pointedly, trying to keep his tone mild.

Rov laughed. "Jane's a good lass, but a man can

get bored eating the same meal night after night. There comes a time when he realizes he is growing soft, aging . . . and he wishes for something more. You don't know how fortunate you are to have escaped the parson's knot—"

"What ho, what are we discussing here?" Admiral Daniels said boozily, leaning between them. "Is His Grace still trying to find a wife?"

"I tell him it isn't worth it," Rov answered.

"It isn't," Daniels said. "Better a mistress than a wife. I liked that yellow-haired gal up there on the stage. Nice bit she was. More than a handful." He made a squeezing motion in the air as if he held a breast in his palm.

Rov laughed and Sir John twittered and Gavin wished he were somewhere else. He hated that his personal affairs had become public knowledge. Of course, after being jilted by two women, there would be gossip.

And advice.

And marriage offers.

Everyone was tendering their daughters, sisters, cousins, even aunts to him, along with the promise that *their* candidates for his wife would go through with the marriage. Meanwhile, Gavin sensed those same young women were wondering what was wrong with him that *two* women had bolted. Humbling.

But he wasn't about to take advice from the likes of Daniels.

Before he could give a tart response, a serving girl with rosy cheeks entered their box with drinks that had been ordered. Lord Phillips reached right across Gavin to slam his empty tankard on her tray.

"Careful now," the girl chided.

Phillips looked taken aback. "Do you know who I am?"

"A drunk," she shot back as if she'd seen too many of his kind this evening. "Here's a full one." She offered the full tankard she'd carried over to him.

Phillips took it, but then gave the girl a leering smirk and poured the contents down her frightfully low bodice before Gavin even realized what he was about.

Ale splattered everywhere including over Gavin. Phillips then followed this antic by lurching forward and diving his face into her cleavage. He shook his head wildly in her bosom, wrapping his arms around her waist.

The girl screeched for him to let her be. She hit his back with her tray and struggled to escape. All around them, men roared with laughter. Some stood on the benches or their chairs in the boxes for a better look. They thought this a great stunt and shouted encouragement loud enough to drown out what was happening on stage.

Gavin thought it criminal. He stood, grabbed Phillips by the collar and the seat of his breeches and yanked him up. "Run," he said to the girl, and he didn't have to tell her twice.

Swinging Phillips around to meet him, Gavin said, "You are chairing a committee meeting on the morrow with the Regent. Sober up."

Phillips looked into Gavin's face, grinned like the sod he was, and burped. Offended by the odor, Gavin let go of his hold and Phillips dropped to the floor at Harris and Crowder's feet where he did not move.

"I told you he'd be the first to pass out," Rov announced to Daniels. "Pay up."

"You'll have my marker on the morrow," the admiral answered, unconcerned.

"Do you wager on everything?" Gavin asked his friend in horrified surprise.

"Only when I know I shall win," Rov assured him, sitting back in his chair and crossing his legs. "For example, I've a wager that I shall bed the Siren before any other manjack in this room."

"That is a ridiculous bet," Gavin answered, pleased to finally be able to express his opinion on the matter.

"Is it?" Rov asked, unperturbed. He took out his

snuff box and took a pinch. "Perhaps you would like to place money against me?" He sneezed.

"I don't waste money on immoral women," Gavin answered.

"The Siren is more than just any woman," Daniels said, speaking as if Gavin was a simpleton. "Don't you know who she is? Why are you here if you don't?"

"No, Baynton doesn't know," Rov said. "I'm certain he wasn't in attendance when she appeared in London years ago."

Daniels chortled his thoughts. "Well, you are in for a treat, Your Grace. Loveliest creature in the world. Captured every male heart and then disappeared."

"Disappeared?" Gavin asked.

"Aye," Rov said. "When they had the *Naughty Review* years ago, she was the queen of the evening. God knows I had never laid eyes on anything more magical than her. There wasn't a one of us in the theater who didn't want her."

"Aye, that is true," Daniels said.

"But she vanished and no one, including the theater managers would tell us who she was or where she went. I know because I spent a pretty penny trying to learn the information. But tonight, she is back and she won't escape me, not this time."

"Do you intend to hunt her down?" Gavin said.

Rov laughed. "Absolutely, Baynton. She's an actress. She's fair game. It is what her kind expects."

"You aren't stalking a deer. This is a person."

"A lovely one," Rov agreed, unrepentant. "Wait until you see her. You'll want to stalk her as well—oh, wait, you won't keep a mistress."

This had been an old squabble between them. Rov didn't understand why Gavin didn't use his ducal title to wallow in female flesh. "You are suspiciously like a monk," he was fond of saying, only half in jest.

If he knew the truth, he'd truly roast Gavin . . . because Gavin had yet to "know" woman, as biblical scholars were fond of saying.

It wasn't that Gavin didn't wish to. He was hungry for sex. He longed for the softness of a woman, a wife, a helpmate.

However, as a duke, it was important that his wife be a virgin. Otherwise, as his father had stressed on several occasions, how would he know her offspring were his?

And if Gavin's wife must be a virgin, should he not be one himself? 'Twas said that knights of old remained celibate until they'd taken their vows and the idea had captured Gavin's imagination, not that his father had allowed him any time to go whoring with Rov and the others. His father had been a tireless taskmaster in preparing his eldest son.

Furthermore, when Gavin had made his decision to wait for marriage, he had not believed it would be such a long wait. After all, he'd been betrothed since boyhood to the heiress Elin Morris. He'd expected to marry her when she'd turned of age but his father's death and then the loss of her beloved mother had delayed those nuptials for years. Too many years, and then she'd married another, his youngest brother Ben. Theirs was a true love match and Gavin could not in good conscience hold her to her promise to him.

So, here he was, now three-and-thirty and untried . . . in a room where every man claimed to know the secrets to women, or at least that was what they were shouting at the female "sheep" dancing on stage. Meanwhile, Rov was so confident of his manhood, he was betting on bedding the Siren.

No wonder Gavin felt alone. He wanted to believe that there was something sacred to the marriage bed, to the binding of body and spirit between a man and a woman. "What if you don't win your wager?" he asked his smirking friend.

"I'll win."

"But if you don't?" Gavin pressed, wanting Rov to consider the error of his ways.

"There are always ways to find money," was the cryptic answer, and Gavin knew then that he must see Rov removed as Chairman of the Committees. He also knew it would not go over well. Not only for Rov but also for Jane. But how to handle the matter delicately?

The sheep finished their dance by bending over so that everyone could see their bare buttocks beneath the silly costumes. The male crowd hooted their appreciation and then fell into an expectant silence.

"'Tis time for the Siren," Daniels whispered, leaning forward. Even Harris and Crowder also sat up.

Phillips roused himself from the floor and said groggily, "Have I missed her?"

Several voices around them shushed him and Gavin couldn't help but be caught up in the moment.

The Siren. A woman of mystery. No one knew her identity and yet all in this theater waited for her. They were also aware of Rov's boasting wager. It added an edge to the evening.

Then, in the stillness, a woman's voice, as clear and strong as a songbird's, sang out. The sound filled the theater.

Gavin looked around for her, expecting her to come from the stage.

Instead, a thick, silver rope lowered. Wrapped around it was a glorious golden creature with raven-black hair. Her translucent dress was light as air. It clung to her well-rounded curves, pulling across full breasts. She wore a mask of sparkling jewels. Her lips were ripe and red. Her legs could be seen through her skirts and her feet were bare.

Gavin's reaction to the Siren was immediate and demanding. He did not believe he'd seen a more beautiful sight in his life.

He had to stand. He could not sit, and he was not the only one. Rov was clapping, holding his hands in the air as if doing homage. Sir John was twittering and the other men around them including the sharps were equally in awe.

She was no mere actress.

The Siren was a goddess and true to her name had the power to lure men wherever she wanted them. *Now*, Gavin understood why the theater had been packed. *Now*, he believed that having once seen her, he would never forget her.

The rope slowly turned.

She raised her leg, bending it at the knee. One arm curled around the rope, a gesture of pure feminine grace. The rope began to swing back and forth. Her diaphanous skirts swirled around her, revealing shapely calves and a glimpse of thigh and, perhaps, something more? Something so tantalizing a man would sell his soul for it?

And all the time she sang.

Gavin didn't hear the words. All he grasped was the sound of her voice, a voice that called to the deepest part of his soul . . . a voice that actually sounded somewhat familiar—?

The thought was startling. It gave him pause.

She leaned back. Her skirts slipped between her thighs. A man could imagine his hand there, himself there. Her black, black braid whipped around her and she turned and looked right at Gavin.

Her eyes were green.

It was actually hard to tell, even though Rov's box practically sat on the stage, but Gavin *knew*.

In fact, he knew *who she was*.

The impact of recognition was both startling and jarring. The Siren was *Mrs. Sarah Pettijohn*.

He sat, jolted by the realization.

Sarah Pettijohn was the most obnoxious, opinionated, headstrong woman of his acquaintance. The last time they had been together, he couldn't wait to escape her.

She was the aunt of Lady Charlene, the last woman to jilt him, with Sarah's blessing, of course, because that was how contrary Mrs. Pettijohn could be.

And now here she was, wearing barely anything and flaunting herself in front of the male population of London.

Then again, Mrs. Pettijohn was an actress. Actresses put themselves on display for a living, although Gavin could never have imagined the proud woman he'd parted company with in Scotland would parade so much of herself. He couldn't take his eyes off of her.

She twirled the rope, holding the last note of her song and Gavin crossed his arms, waiting for the black-haired wig to fly off her head. Then the world would know their glorious goddess was nothing more than a surly shrew with fiery red hair.

But she did look good.

Dangerously good. The sort of good that makes a man prickly and hungry. Even a man like himself who prided himself on his control and tried *never* to have the thoughts he was having now.

The spinning rope slowed and lowered her to the stage. The jewels around her mask sparkled in the candlelight. Her arm extended with grace as she brought her song to a close. She turned, looked once again directly at Gavin, and smiled with a smug little lift of the lips as if she felt she'd put him in his place.

Lust died a quick death.

Knowing her as he did, how could he have even responded to her in that manner?

Of course, the audience had no such hesitations. They went wild in their enthusiasm, crying, "The Siren," as they pounded the floor with their feet. They clapped. They whistled. They shouted for more—and she preened in their adoration.

She waved, accepting their adulation, pointing her bare toes in a dancer's graceful stance as if she knew how strenuously Gavin disapproved, as if she performed for him. In fact, it was all he could do to not jump onto the stage and either throw his coat over her to hide her nakedness or carry her off to his bed—

Gavin might not have jumped on the stage, but Rov did.

In a blink, before anyone could react, he leaped from the box and rushed to Mrs. Pettijohn. He grabbed her around the waist, swung her around to face him, and attempted to kiss her. The black wig fell to the floor and now everyone knew her secret as the deep red hair she'd been hiding tumbled down to her waist.

Gavin reached for the edge of the box, ready to fly to Mrs. Pettijohn's aid and rip Rov's lips off of her body. However, she did not need him. Her knee came up, and with a robust, unerring movement, caught Rov squarely in a very sensitive place.

Indeed, if Rov was like Gavin at this moment, he was probably fully aroused so her well-placed attack had greater impact.

Rov doubled over in wheezing pain.

There was a moment of shocked silence and then the audience burst out into laughter, one beat before mayhem broke out. Everyone decided to follow Rov's example. Men jumped onto the stage from expensive private boxes or clambered over the musicians' pit and pulled themselves up. They all had one desire and that was to put their hands on Mrs. Pettijohn.

She saw what was coming for her and had the good sense to run.

Chapter Three

Stupid, she had been so stupid . . .

Sarah didn't know what man had accosted her. She'd been focused on Baynton—the proud, mighty duke sitting in his box watching her with his arms and legs crossed as if in judgment.

Oh, she'd wanted to shout at him to look at her now! All of London was at her feet. She had power, too. She also had talent and even though she was considered old for an actress at four-and-thirty, men now acclaimed her. She was the Siren!

That had been her last thought before she'd been flipped around and bussed on the lips by the lout who had accosted her. She hadn't even known who he was, except that he sat in the duke's box.

Had Baynton put him up to attacking her? Was this his way of delivering a comeuppance?

If it was, she was sorely disappointed in the duke. The kissing attack was far from original.

Fortunately, having spent the last few weeks trying to keep her identity a secret so as to not harm her reputation, Sarah knew every hidey-hole in the theater. She dashed backstage, heard the pursuit of a horde of men behind her and, with quick thinking, knelt and began feeling for the line of the trap door located in the floor. Digging her nails into the wood, she lifted the door and jumped into the darkness below, closing it behind her.

No call of alarm went up. And within the span of four racing heartbeats, there came the sound of heavy boots and shoes overhead. Men shouted at each other. *"There she went,"* one called.

"Who grabs her first, has her first," was the buoyant answer and the pounding feet stormed over her head.

Sarah crouched, covering her ears, not wanting to hear any more. What if they realized they were following the wrong trail? Would they return to the theater and hunt her down?

And what would they do once they caught her? She dared not think on it.

Her hand brushed against her mask and she was surprised she still wore it. She took off the fanciful thing and threw it. She would never play the Siren again. Ever.

On the floor above, there were more footsteps, more running around. She could hear muffled voices but they were too far away to make out the words. She began to believe she might be safe.

She kept still, her mind going places she rarely let it venture. After all, how many times in her childhood had she hidden this way? Curling herself into a ball so as not to disturb the men who visited her mother? She'd once been quite adept at tucking herself away where she couldn't be seen. Or pretending to not be where she was.

Dark memories . . . they marked the passage of time until the theater above her seemed quiet. She allowed herself to breathe. She rose and lifted the door. All was dark except for a light that came from the back door entrance. In the distance she could hear movement but they were the sounds of the theater being closed. That must mean that her pursuers had left.

Sarah pushed back the door and climbed out. Her muscles complained and she felt every one of her years. Most of the pins had fallen from her heavy hair. She gathered it up with one hand and pulled it behind her.

For a second, she debated just going home but then realized she couldn't run around London in this dress.

As she walked across the backstage, she held

out her hand to keep from tripping over anything in the dark. Apparently even Geoff and Charles must have left. She knew she needed a candle before going to the dressing rooms. Otherwise she'd never manage the labyrinth of corridors and old stage pieces. She moved toward the light where she knew Old Ollie the back door watchman sat. His last act of the evening before locking the door would be to blow out his lantern.

All the other cast members appeared to be gone. Sarah hoped no one had been caught up in the craziness of the riot and that none of the other actresses had been harmed.

She heard the sound of sweeping. Reaching the rear entrance, she saw Ollie using a broom to set things to rights in his area. Ollie had worked around most of the theaters in the London area and knew Sarah by sight. He smiled when he saw her.

"Hey there, I wondered if you'd escaped them. Hot after you they were." He set his broom aside.

"Men are strange, Ollie."

"Aye, we are."

"Was anyone hurt?"

He shook his head. "Nah, the girls they know how to take care of themselves. I shouted that you'd gone out the back door and the lads went running after you. We cleared this theater out quick."

"I have never seen anything like that in my life. Was there much damage done?"

"Mr. Geoff and Mr. Charles were shouting about the curtain being torn but all is in decent shape. They were actually more interested in this night's take." He referred to the seat sales.

That was a relief. If there had been extensive damage, Geoff and Charles might have blamed her and refused to put on her play; then all she'd done would have been for naught. "May I take a candle to the dressing rooms? I must change."

"Of course you may, miss." He reached for a candle stub for her and lit it off his lantern.

"I hope you know I'm trying to keep my identity a secret, Ollie. Geoff and Charles said they would stage a play I've written if I would do this for them. However, I would rather be known as a good playwright than as the Siren. Can I trust you?"

But it wasn't Ollie who answered.

"I'm afraid your secret is out, Mrs. Pettijohn," a male voice said. The blond man who had attacked her on stage stepped out of the darkness. "And if I were you, I would be proud of my performance. You captured my attention."

She frowned at Ollie, knowing he must have a hand in betraying her. "I hope he paid you well."

"I'm sorry, Sarah," Ollie murmured and moved off into the darkness.

The man walked toward her, his intent clear. "Don't be upset, Mrs. Pettijohn," he said. "I know how to make a woman very happy, especially," he added, letting his heated gaze roam over her body in the thin costume, "a woman as lovely as yourself. Let me introduce myself. I'm Rovington."

Sarah had heard of Rovington. He had a taste for actresses and considered them free for his taking. Stories she'd heard about him teased her memory. He was not one of the favorites. He had a temper—and she knew about men and rages . . . knew better than she wished.

"You and I are going to become very good friends—" he started to promise, reaching out as if to capture her, but Sarah had a different idea.

She grabbed the high desk where Ollie usually sat by the door and threw it down in front of him before whipping around, opening the backstage door, and running.

Rovington cursed at being thwarted and then he laughed, the sound strange behind her. Evil.

Sarah's bare feet flew down the steps and out into the alley. She heard Rovington behind her. She expected him to give chase.

Instead, he stood by the door and shouted almost happily, *"Take her.* The first man who grabs her will receive a fiver."

More men?

Three men stepped out of the alley's shadows, coming at her from different directions.

Panic brought her to a halt. She could not believe she was being attacked in this manner—and then the sound of running hooves echoed in the alley.

An ordinary hack charged forward, forcing one of the men to jump out of the way or be run over. It slowed as it reached Sarah. The door flew open. *"Climb in,"* a rough male voice ordered. A hand was offered to her.

She knew that voice. *Baynton.*

He was the *last* person she wished to associate with, but she feared what would happen if she stayed. Rovington was not the sort to take her refusal lightly and she could not run forever. Performances took energy and she was now beyond fatigued.

She leaped for the strong, capable hand and let him pull her inside, the hack barely slowing down. The still open door swung widely as the hack careened around the corner of the alley and into the street. Behind them, men shouted threats to stop. The driver, thankfully, kept going.

Holding her so that she didn't topple out with the bouncing and swaying of the vehicle, the duke reached across her body and yanked the door shut. His movements brought them face-to-face.

"Hello, Mrs. Pettijohn."

For a second, this close to him, Sarah found it hard to breathe, let alone think. He had an arm around her waist. She found her chest practically against his, her hips resting against his thigh. Their bodies rode the hack's rolling movement together and she had no choice but to cling to him for balance.

It was not such a bad experience, being this near to him. In fact, she felt safe, but then, as soon as she could collect her wits, Sarah pushed the heel of her hand on his shoulder. Baynton did not release his hold, not immediately.

Instead, in the light of the hack's small interior lantern, she detected a glint in his eye, an interest. Her breasts tightened in awareness. Her heart still raced from the madness of escaping the theater and Rovington and yet, there was a skip to the beat. She hadn't pushed away as hard as she could . . .

By anyone's account, the Duke of Baynton was a very handsome man. Dark-haired, blessed with sharp blue eyes and the sort of lean, square jaw that spoke of character, he would attract any woman's attention. Furthermore, he exuded masculinity. It was in the air around him, enhanced by the spiciness of his shaving soap and just the being of his person.

However, no one, simply *no* single person in the world could annoy her more than this fellow with his arms around her waist. He was the most contrary of souls—even if he did just rescue her from a fate she'd dare not consider.

She broke the moment between them. "I know what you are thinking, and you can't have it."

"And what is it I'm thinking?" he challenged in his deep voice, as if he could deny the obvious truth.

Sarah let her hand come down between them, lightly touching the erection pressing against his breeches. The man was hard, boldly so.

Baynton let go of her as if she'd scalded him, turning away. "It is not what you believe."

There was that contrariness again. In the cab's hazy light, she even thought she saw a dull red rise to his face.

Her mind had to be playing tricks. Few men blushed, especially if they were as morally rigid as the Duke of Baynton.

She laughed quietly. "Oh, yes, it is," she answered him. "If there is one thing I know, it's men."

He stiffened, but did not respond.

The hack had now slowed to a reasonable gait. Sarah straightened in the seat, edging toward the door, putting space between herself and his uncomfortable presence. Her bare feet were responding to the escapades and abuses of the evening. She wished for shoes, and a few more articles of clothing would have also been warranted.

As if reading her mind, he took off his jacket. "Here," he offered.

"That is not necessary. I'm fine."

"Put it on."

"I don't wish to," she responded coolly. "I am not chilled." She belied her words by crossing her arms. Now that she was out of the range of his body heat, gooseflesh ran up and down her. She even shivered, a response, no doubt, to the wildness of the evening instead of the night air . . . or her companion in the hack.

"Perhaps I wouldn't be so—" He paused a moment as if searching for the right word and chose a polite one, "*Uncomfortable* if you were not naked."

Now it was her turn to have heat rise to her cheeks. She lifted the shade over the window so that she could see out of the vehicle and avoid him seeing her embarrassment. "I'm not naked," she informed him. "I am fully clothed. I have on an underdress. You saw nothing." She had to add, "You may have thought you saw something, but it was only the nonsense going on between your male ears, not anything you could see with your eyes."

"Your feet are bare."

She pulled her feet together, placing one foot's toes on top of the other as if she could hide them. "They are only feet." The scenery they passed was beginning to seem familiar.

"Your legs are bare."

Yes, he would have noticed that during her dance on the rope. She crossed them away from him. "They are only legs."

"Makes me wonder what else is bare."

A new resonance, a suggestive one had entered his voice. A tone that she'd not imagined the haughty Duke of Baynton possessed, and it set off a tingling warmth in some of her other bare places.

Sarah tried not to squirm. Or to look at him. She didn't want to see the interest in his eye or think of Baynton as a . . . lover.

Oh no, she didn't. Well, her brain didn't. The naked parts seemed to have thoughts of their own.

He shoved his jacket almost in her face and shook it at her. "Put on my coat."

There was no denying the order.

Still, when she accepted it, she did so because right now, she needed protection from her own reactions. She didn't like this coil of feelings, especially around him. It had been a long time since she'd slept with a man or felt his strength moving within her. The last time she'd experienced this piercing hunger, it had almost destroyed her. She mustn't forget. She need *never* forget—

Of course, Baynton's scent was in the folds of his jacket, circling her, teasing her—

The hack came to a halt. Sarah was surprised to see they had stopped before the house on Mulberry Street where she had lived with Charlene. A house that held almost all the very best memories of her life . . .

And then she realized, of course, Baynton would bring her here. He believed this was her address. He had no idea of what had befallen her, and she wasn't about to let him know.

Without waiting for the driver or the duke, she opened the door and started to let the jacket slip off her shoulders.

"Leave it on," Baynton ordered. "I don't want you parading around your neighborhood in that dress. Your neighbors might not realize you are 'not naked' beneath it."

"At this hour, my neighbors will be asleep." Sarah stepped out of the hack but she kept the jacket. He was right about the wisdom of her racing around the streets of London dressed as she was, especially where she was going. Once again she wished she wore shoes. She had a ways to walk.

But for right now, her purpose was to rid herself of Baynton's troubling, overbearing presence.

"Thank you very much, Your Grace, for the rescue and the ride." There, she'd done the pretty but she was speaking to air. He had exited the other side of the hack and was coming around toward her.

Baynton fully dressed was a formidable presence.

However, Baynton in shirtsleeves and brocade vest and hatless, especially in the dim lamp of the hack's coach lamp, was something else entirely. He appeared relaxed. At complete ease—while the tension inside her from this night threatened to break like the string on an overplayed violin.

"Where are you going?" she demanded.

"Seeing you to the door," he answered.

"There is no need. It is only steps away. Good night, Your Grace. Thank you for your help. Move on now."

He stopped, a mere foot away from her. "I shalln't leave until I see you properly inside."

Her chin came up. "I know your gambit. 'Safely inside,' eh?"

The duke frowned. "What else do you think I mean?"

She cocked her head with a meaningful glance to that juncture between his thighs.

***

From the second Sarah Pettijohn had appeared on the stage, Gavin had gone as hard as an iron pike, and he'd stayed that way.

Being in the hack with her had been the worst. He was aware of her every gesture, of her breathing, of the defiance in the lift of her chin, the arch of her brow, of the subtlest movement of her lips. Even the act of snatching her away from those men chasing her had added to the almost animal tension thrumming through his veins. When she'd been bold enough to touch him, he'd almost embarrassed himself.

However, he was not one to give in to impulse.

He was the Duke of Baynton. He had a will of steel. He controlled himself. He did what was honorable—except he would like to take her in his arms and bury himself to the hilt in her body.

Didn't she realize she didn't have to be naked in that dress to unleash the wildness in a man's blood?

It was the legs, he decided. The bare legs and feet. How could she be anything but vulnerable with her toes showing? And Sarah Pettijohn vulnerable was a very attractive bit. He wanted to lift her up in his arms. Protect her.

And in turn, she'd probably spit on him. Certainly she wouldn't thank him for it.

Ah, yes, Mrs. Pettijohn had a sharp tongue. He was the fool with the cock who conveniently forgot how independent she was. Damn it all.

"I'll see you to the door and no further," he bit out. "I understand you find my company loathsome. You needn't worry I will force myself upon you." With those words, Gavin started toward the house, but she didn't follow.

Of course not. *That* would be simple.

He faced her. "Are you coming?"

"I don't find you loathsome," she answered.

He blinked, uncertain what she meant until he remembered his own heated words. He cut the air with the movement of his hand, denying her denial.

"I don't," she insisted, approaching him. A cat would envy the shape of her eyes, or the way the dark lashes framing them added to her every expression. She rested those eyes on him now. "Indeed, I appreciate your help this evening—" She stopped herself, even raising her palm as if to stem the flow of words.

Taking a moment to release her breath, she gathered his coat tighter around her shoulders and started again, "I don't dislike you. I am aware I may have given that impression, but it is because of my own flaws, not yours, Your Grace."

Back when they had spent days together chasing her niece, she had rarely addressed him by his title, and when she did, not politely.

Her use of it now put him on guard—and yet, she sounded contrite. Or, as contrite as her outspoken nature would allow her.

"You should remember," she continued, "that I was the one who championed your suit for my niece's hand. I thought you would be a good husband to her."

"That's not how I remember our argument at this very house when I set out to stop her from eloping with my brother Jack."

"You were furious. I needed to protect her. Certainly you can appreciate that desire?" She lifted her shoulders to indicate his coat he'd forced upon her.

"I would not have harmed her."

"But your brother?"

Her question resonated in the air. Jack was more than just Gavin's brother; he was his twin. The elopement had kept the gossips going for months afterward.

"In the end, I gave them my blessing," he pointed out, noncommittally.

"Yes, you did. I recognize that could have been difficult."

This time it was his turn to shrug.

Her answer was a shrug back, and then she

held out her hand as if they were equals, as if she were a man. "Let us set tensions aside between us. I do not find you loathsome, or think ill of you in any way."

Even of my arousal? He swallowed the words.

The faintest hint of a smile crossed her face as if she'd read his mind. She had. "Or your manhood," she confirmed.

For the second time that night, he felt heat creep up his neck. No one had the skill to disarm him. *No one*—except her. Which was unsettling. It was actually best they did keep apart. Especially since Gavin preferred dealing with people who knew their place, whom he could control.

Thankfully, the hack driver interrupted them. "Do you wish me to continue to wait, sir?" he called, a reminder that he had other fares to earn.

"A moment more," Gavin said. He looked to Mrs. Pettijohn. "Well, I suppose we're done."

"Yes," she agreed, a bit of a rueful note to her voice as if she was possibly a bit disappointed he was taking his leave of her. "Thank you again," she added with a bit more cheer.

"You are welcome." He waited for her to go inside.

She didn't move. "You may go now. The driver is anxious," she informed him.

"We will leave after you have gone inside. It doesn't appear that Lady Baldwin is awake."

Lady Baldwin was a close friend to Lady Charlene and Mrs. Pettijohn. Gavin understood that she lived with them. He had been quite accustomed to thinking of the three of them together.

"She is probably asleep. You don't have to wait. I'll watch you drive off."

"And leave you standing on the step? Especially after the near riot at the theater? And the attack in the alley? Once you are safely inside, I shall go."

"I'll go inside once *you* leave."

Exasperation replaced bonhomie. "Mrs. Pettijohn, go in your house."

She didn't even bother to consider. "After you drive off, I will."

Gavin frowned. Was there ever a more pigheaded female?

He went onto the step and began knocking on the door.

That sparked a reaction out of her. *"What are you doing?"*

"Waking Lady Baldwin."

Mrs. Pettijohn reached for his arm to yank his fisted hand away from the door. "She's not there," she said, speaking in a furious whisper. "She was only visiting when you saw her with us in the past. She actually lives with her daughter."

"And yet, now you are whispering," he observed, "as if you do not wish to wake *someone*."

Even as he said that last word, he was surprised by a jolt of jealousy. *Who* did she not want him to meet? Why else would she be so anxious?

He pounded the door this time, her hold unable to stay his arm now that he was determined to see the matter through. The wood-and-lacquered door jumped with the strength of his fist. He had to know who she was hiding.

"Stop it," she ordered in a furious whisper. "Stop now—"

The door opened. The house inside was pitch black but two elderly faces, ghastly pale in the hack's lamplight, peered out at them. The man wore his night cap; the woman's hair was braided.

"Yes?" the man asked, his voice creaky with alarm.

Gavin brought his brows together, conscious that Mrs. Pettijohn had stepped back off the step into the darkness. He had the good grace to bow and said calmly, "I'm sorry to wake you. I only wished to return Mrs. Pettijohn to her home."

"Mrs. Pettijohn?" the man asked, craning his neck to peer out into the night.

"Yes," Gavin said, feeling awkward. He turned to draw her up onto the step, but she wasn't there lingering in the night beyond the lamplight. He looked to the hack.

"She went that way, sir," the hack driver kindly offered. "Running as fast as one can barefoot."

Gavin faced the couple. "Mrs. Pettijohn doesn't live here, does she?"

"No. There were some women who lived here before us but we don't know their names."

"Excuse me for bothering you," Gavin apologized to the couple. To the hack driver he said, "Follow me."

"This will cost you a pretty penny, sir."

Gavin almost roared that he was the Duke of Baynton. Cost did not matter to him.

But common sense warned him, he might not want this night's escapade to be bandied about. He started to reach for his coin purse and then realized it was in his jacket. Damn it all.

"I'll pay your fare and double," he informed the driver. "But first, I need to catch that woman."

There was a beat of silence as if the driver weighed whether or not Gavin would be true to his word, which was a novel experience. Few questioned his word.

The driver came to the right decision. "Come along then, sir. We'll catch up to her."

Gavin stepped up onto the hack's step without opening the door. He put his arm through the window to hold on and was ready to jump off at the first sight of Mrs. Pettijohn. "On with it, man."

"Yi-up!" the driver said to his horse and they took off in hot pursuit.

Chapter Four

Sarah knew it was a fool's errand to run away from the duke, but she had to try.

She had not wanted to face him once he found out she no longer lived at Mulberry Street. Or to have him ask questions in that high-handed manner of his, questions that were not his right to ask.

What she did with her life was her business. He might believe that because Charlene had married his brother he had the right to interfere, but he didn't. Oh no, not at all.

She slid her arms into the sleeves of his jacket and kept moving, her feet feeling and stumbling over what only the Lord knew was on the road. When she reached home, she was going to scrub her feet raw—

A horse's steady clop and the rolling of wheels across uneven stones warned her that Baynton was not going to let her go.

Drat the man.

And yet she'd known the duke would follow. He was tenacious, a quality that went along with being overbearing.

The hack pulled up beside her. Baynton was standing on the step and easily stepped down beside her before the vehicle pulled to a halt. He moved to block her path.

Sarah had to stop but she was determined to sidestep him. However, before she could, he boldly opened his jacket, slipped a hand inside the pocket—located uncomfortably close to her breast. The back of his hand brushed against her as he pulled out a small coin purse.

He tossed it to the driver as she jerked the jacket closed around her. "Good?" he asked.

The driver opened the purse and gave a low sound of appreciation. "There's more than we bargained for, sir."

"Just stay with us, but not too close," the duke ordered.

"Aye, sir."

Sarah shook her head with annoyance and started walking again. He matched his stride to her limping one.

"You should leave with the driver," she informed him. "I'm not climbing back in that hack with you."

"You needn't. I'm happy to walk. After all, I'm wearing boots."

"You can walk to hell for all I'm concerned," she muttered under her breath before giving a little hop as the bottom of her heel landed on something sharp.

His hand came to her elbow with a light touch as if to help her to balance. "Is that where we are going?" he asked, unconcerned. "To hell?"

She shook his hand off. "Where *I* am going is none of your business."

"But it is. I'm the head of my family. It is my responsibility to take care of everyone, including extended family. Your niece is married to my—"

"*I knew* you were going to make that claim," Sarah said, whirling on him. "And *you are wrong.*" She emphasized each word with a pointed finger. "I'm my own person. You have no control over me whatsoever. So, you can climb into the hack and drive off wherever you wish."

Instead of the insult or anger she had anticipated in response to her declaration, Baynton looked a bit contrite. "I can't," he said. "I've hired the driver for this night and have probably paid him enough for the next seventy nights. I won't leave you alone in the dark wearing nothing of substance but my jacket. We can either hobble around London together or I can see you home safe. Look at that," he added, perking up a bit. "You have a choice. Hobble or ride? What shall it be?"

Her feet hurt. Her legs under the costume's filmy skirts were cold. Exhaustion threatened . . . and right now, all she wanted to do was climb into her bed, pull the covers over her head, and worry about what Geoff and Charles would say about her starting a riot in their theater on the morrow.

Besides, Baynton was being kind instead of bombastic.

"I would like to ride."

No triumphant or smug I-knew-you-would look crossed his face. He merely signaled for the hack to join them and opened the door for her. He held out a hand to help her in.

She placed her fingers on his. For the briefest second, she could swear she felt the heat of his blood beating even in that light touch. Then again, she'd always been too aware of Baynton. Too, too attuned to him.

However, Sarah had learned that, while she understood what men wanted from her, she was not a good judge of them. Oh, how she'd learned that lesson . . .

The duke climbed in behind her and said, "Where do you live, Mrs. Pettijohn?"

"On Bolden Street."

"Bolden? I've not heard of it."

"The driver will know."

Baynton opened the door so he could lean out and say, "Take us to Bolden Street."

"Are you certain, sir? No good comes from going to Bolden Street."

"Is it that bad?" the duke asked.

"Worse than the devil's cave," came the answer.

The duke seemed to hesitate a moment, then knocked on the roof. "Let us go pay a call on the devil then." He lowered back into the cab, shutting the door behind him.

The driver muttered something to his horse that Sarah could not hear, but the wheels began turning forward.

She and the duke sat side-by-side. Sarah tried to ignore him, which was difficult with his thigh right against hers and his body taking up most of the space in the hack's narrow confines.

She expected questions. She knew he had them. He was Baynton, after all. The Supreme Being of the Truth. She knew exactly how she would put him in his place.

He didn't ask.

Minutes stretched between them.

He shifted. The seats were hard leather but there seemed to be a dip beneath hers. She slid a bit closer to him. She tried to hold her breath so she wouldn't drink in the scent of his shaving soap. She actually liked the scent. She'd forgotten how good a man could smell.

The duke seemed pleased to travel in silence, something she'd told herself she dearly wished for—except, his silence was unnerving. He had to have questions. Insisting on knowing what was going on was just part of who he was.

And finally, she could not take the stillness any longer. She turned on the seat to him. "I lost Mulberry Street. I was in arrears for the rent. And before you start nosing about for more information, Lady Baldwin's daughter refuses to allow her to have *anything* to do with me and she must obey if she wishes a roof over her head."

Sarah faced the front of the hack. "Apparently, her daughter believed—as did many others—that Charlene's choosing another gentleman to wed was tantamount to jilting you, even though there was no true promise between the two of you as a couple. And I don't know why everyone has an opinion on the matter," Sarah continued, heatedly. "Whatever happened was between you and Charlene, not Charlene and all of London."

"Perhaps I'm popular?" he suggested.

Sarah shot him a withering look, and he laughed, the sound gruff, as if he didn't do it often.

She dropped her gaze to his jacket and fell into

a disgruntled silence. His sleeves were so long, only her fingertips showed.

"You weren't tossed out of Mulberry Street because of me, were you?" he asked, not unkindly.

"We had issues before you met Char. However, once your name was linked to hers, the landlord was willing to make allowances about the rent. He let us put it off. Then, when she married Lord Jack, there was a reckoning that did not go in my favor."

"You could have come to me for help."

"I don't take charity."

"Yes, but in a way I am fam—" He stopped short once he caught the look in her eye.

Sarah lifted the flap that was over the window on that side of the hack. "We are almost there."

The duke glanced out, too. His frown deepened. "This is not a safe place, especially for a woman."

Now it was Sarah's turn to be silent, and she was a bit pleased to see her stubbornness bothered him as much as his annoyed her.

She recognized the corner of Bolden Street and reached up to knock on the roof. The hack rolled to a stop. She opened the door and hopped out, anxious to shut the door, but Baynton blocked her action with his arm.

The hour was well past midnight. A group of loud young men, obviously in their cups, stumbled their way up the steps of a nearby building and knocked on the door. Light spilled into the street as they were laughingly admitted among female calls of welcome.

The hack's lamplight highlighted the lines of concern on the duke's face.

"Thank you, Your Grace. You may go on your way now."

Sarah started walking. Of course, he followed, and she knew she had no choice but to let him.

Gavin was more than concerned about Sarah Pettijohn's lowered circumstances. He was alarmed. Even in the dark the buildings appeared derelict. The atmosphere seemed more ominous than he could have imagined.

"Shall I wait, sir?" the driver asked, sounding decidedly nervous.

"Yes," Gavin shot over his shoulder. He hurried to follow Mrs. Pettijohn, thankful for the light material of her skirts so that he could see her in the darkness.

She rounded a corner and then stepped into an alley between buildings. From somewhere, a man moaned. Her step didn't flag and neither did Gavin's. They moved through the narrow corridor to a set of stairs at the rear of one of the buildings. She stopped and took off his jacket, thrusting it toward him.

"I live here. You don't need to follow me further."

"I'll see you to your door," he insisted doggedly.

Mrs. Pettijohn made an impatient sound but didn't put up further protest. Instead, she climbed the stairs leading to first one floor and then the next.

Gavin was aware of her graceful form moving ahead of him. Her hips were at his eye level. She did not look back.

On the topmost floor, she followed a railed walkway to a door. Two cats had been preparing to fight. They dashed off with yowls of protest as Sarah approached. She stopped in front of a door and he heard the scrape of metal as she found the key she'd hidden.

"You should keep that on your person," he warned her.

She turned to him. He couldn't make out her expression in the dark, but he had the sense she childishly stuck out her tongue at him. The key turned in the lock.

"See? I'm home," she said, the words flowing out of her in dismissal. "Thank you, Your Grace. It was a pleasure to see you again. Good night."

Mrs. Pettijohn would have shut the door, except Gavin pushed his way into her rooms. Hades could not be as dark. "I'll wait until you light a candle."

"You are *annoying*," she lashed out. But he heard her fumbling for what she needed. A beat later, a spark was struck, then another. The tinder caught flame. Her hands carried it to a candle that only she could see.

At last, a warm, yellow light brought the room into focus.

Gavin looked around. He couldn't help himself. He knew she would disparage him for it, but he was human.

He had actually been quite fond of the atmosphere in her house on Mulberry Street. It had been rather shabby but genteel and with a good amount of personality. He'd always found the house welcoming. Of course, he had been quite enamored of one of its occupants, Lady Charlene . . . but he'd also noticed Mrs. Pettijohn as well. Or at least, he had been a touch more than aware of her. Her eyes had captured his attention at first. They were the color of emeralds. Unusual eyes with the spark of intelligence.

This room was unworthy of her. It was bare save for a table, two rickety wooden chairs, and a pallet on the floor. A few bandboxes were in a corner beside a neatly stacked tower of paper that was as high as the table. There wasn't even a hearth to provide heat in the space.

Layers of hardened tallow wax spread out on

a corner of the table. She melted a portion of it with her candle and then stuck it upright there, a makeshift candlestick. The glow fell upon the meager remains of a meal: stale bread, a hunk of cheese, a small pitcher. She did not eat well. No wonder she was thinner than he remembered.

"Are you pleased now?" she said. "Will you let me be?"

"This is beneath you," he murmured, taking a step toward those papers, curious about what they were.

As if seeing where he was heading, she quickly blocked his path, even putting a hand out as if to stop him. "I am safe. You may go now."

"What are those papers?"

"My work," she said.

"Work?"

"My plays."

"*All* of that?"

The brilliant green in her eyes turned into sharp, proud glints. "Yes, *all* of that. I am dedicated to my writing. Now, *leave*, Your Grace. I'm done with you in my life."

Harsh words. He turned to her, wanting to say something conciliatory.

She would not let him. "*Go*," she ordered. "*Please*. I'm tired. I'm done."

And what more could he say?

He took a step, then another. He moved out of the door but then faced her. "Mrs. Pettijohn—"

She slammed the door in his face. A key turned in the lock.

Gavin was stunned. He was the Duke of Baynton. *No one* slammed a door on him. No one would *dare* to be that unwise—save for one.

For a second, he debated breaking the door down. It was not that strong and he was that infuriated with her.

She acted as if he meddled but she needed someone to meddle. Did she not understand what those young bucks had been about clambering up the steps to that house, that *bawdy* house?

The area was surrounded with them. Furthermore, this alley tucked away as it was, would be a haven for a den of thieves. Why, in short order he could name a half-dozen reasons for her to not stay here . . . and yet he knew Mrs. Pettijohn would not listen to reason.

Nor would she thank him for rescuing her. She was too bloody independent.

He stood staring at her door for another good five minutes until his temper ebbed. In truth, he had no course other than to leave.

That still didn't stop Gavin from taking a step away, then coming back two steps toward her, and, finally, forcing himself to go down the stairs.

His hack driver was happy to see him. Even the horse appeared relieved.

Across the street, at the bawdy house, one of the young bucks who had entered it when Gavin had arrived was now being summarily tossed out the door. The lad lay on the ground, rolling in drunken laughter. Several of the bawds opened their windows to shout insults at him.

"Drive," Gavin ordered the driver, giving him the address for Menheim, the Duke of Baynton's London house. He did not have to repeat the order. He sat back in the hack, conscious of how empty the cab seemed now, and yet her presence lingered in the air around him. She'd not worn perfume. She had no need of it. She had a fragrance all her own.

Funny how he'd never noticed that about other women. Or could it be that Sarah Pettijohn's boldness made her stand out from her sex?

I don't take charity. What an inane thing for a woman to say. Charity was how men took care of women. Seeing to their needs was a moral obligation, a code of conduct.

He could almost hear Mrs. Pettijohn snort at that argument.

Menheim was quiet when Gavin returned. A word with the footman waiting by the door gave Gavin the knowledge that his mother had come home hours ago and was safely in her bed. Well, at least, there was *one* woman in the world he could protect.

He went upstairs to his rooms to find his valet Michael asleep in a chair. Gavin roused him and sent him to bed. He could undress himself.

In truth, he was tired but he was also restless. He did not like thinking of Sarah Pettijohn alone in that place.

Stretching out naked on the clean sheets of his bed, as was his custom, he shut his eyes but sleep did not come. Instead, what came was the memory of her, spinning high above the crowd of men, her bare legs parting to control her motion. She said she had not been naked, but Gavin could easily picture what she'd look like if she had been. The image was delectable.

God, and that hair . . .

No one had hair as vibrant as hers. In his mind's eye, she wasn't wearing the black wig. No, there was no mask and her own long, glorious red hair whirled around her—

He tried to roll onto his belly to break the lust weaving images in his imagination but *that* was uncomfortable because he was once again hard and aroused in a way he'd never imagined he could be.

And it wasn't just any woman he yearned for. He wanted *her*.

He needed *her*.

Gavin climbed out of the bed and looked down at his proudly errant male part. Always before it had obeyed, but not this night. Tonight it made him keenly aware that it was past time he'd put it to use. That at his age, most men were married, with a nightly bedmate to give them the sweet comfort of release, a bedmate to ease the twin pangs of desire and, yes, loneliness.

Aye, Gavin was lonely, and he had been for some time. In fact, he had started to become bored with life, with doing the same activities every day and meeting the same expectations.

However, being with Mrs. Pettijohn this evening had been more than just an adventure. She was not afraid to meet him as an equal. There was a blunt honesty about her that he could persuade himself was refreshing. Certainly, he could never be able to anticipate what words would come forth from her lovely lips.

Yes, *those* lips. He'd rather like them with red paint. Before, he'd not truly appreciated how full they were. Now, his mind wondered how they tasted—?

Damn. He needed to stop thinking like this. He'd never sleep if he kept fantasizing about her being in his bed.

And since his mind was too busy with lust

for sleep, there were other matters he should be attending. He threw on a robe and stomped to his study. He had a stack of treatises to review before a meeting he would be holding later that day with members of the Bank of England. Nothing could bore him to sleep like reading paperwork—except even these mundane documents were no match for the lure of Sarah Pettijohn.

He read, but he didn't remember anything. Instead, the documents' flourished handwriting reminded him of the way she'd thrown her arms up at the end of her song with a grace all her own. Arms that had clung to him in the hack so that she wouldn't fly out the open door . . .

Slowly, a new idea took hold of his mind.

I don't take charity, she had said.

But what if he didn't offer charity?

What if he gave her *carte blanche*?

She was an actress. She'd been a wife, presumably. Mrs. Sarah Pettijohn. He'd been assured that many actresses invented deceased husbands because the status of widow gave women more freedom, especially in their associations . . . *their associations* . . . such as accepting a protector, one who could cherish and keep her in exchange for her favors—and Gavin wanted her favors. He ached for them.

Besides most men of his stature kept a mistress. And taking a mistress would let the world know that he *was* a lover, that he was a man. Wasn't it time to relieve himself of his *virginity*?

God, he hated the word. But it was what he was, a discontented, disgruntled virgin.

In truth, he'd never truly been discontented or disgruntled until seeing Mrs. Pettijohn's bare legs through transparent skirts as they curved around that silver rope.

Her performance had ignited a fire in him and he could not, would not rest until he'd quenched it. He wanted her. Plain and simple. Taking her under his protection would actually be the best thing for her. He could save her from men like Rov who enjoyed preying on women. He could see that she was treated as she deserved to be.

Because wasn't it universally recognized that a woman needed a man? And didn't a man need a woman? At least, that was what his mother and his great-aunt Dame Imogen kept telling him. Yes, they were referring to a wife more than a mistress but Gavin needed help to relieve this howling lust coursing through his veins or he would never be fit company for anyone.

Indeed, when he considered the matter that way, Sarah Pettijohn should feel obligated to let him protect her. It was her fault he was so damned aroused, and he would tell her as much.

Right this very minute.

She needed rescuing from her own stubbornness.

He rose from his desk and returned to his bedroom. He dressed with the energy of a man who had slept a hundred nights. With an anticipation for the day that he'd not experienced in months, he walked to the stables and saddled his own horse, a new one he'd recently purchased in an attempt to snap himself out of his own lethargy. Ares was a dappled gray with four black socks. He nickered a welcome, rousing one of the stable lads.

"May I help you, Your Grace?" the boy said, rubbing the sleep out of his eyes.

"No, I can manage, lad." Gavin tightened the saddle girth and reached for the bridle.

"Norton will have my hide if I don't help, Your Grace."

"Then it will be our secret. Hand me the lantern."

The lad obeyed. "Will you tell me where you are going, Your Grace? Norton always wishes to know where the horses are."

"Tell him I went to a meeting."

"It's not even dawn yet, Your Grace," the lad said incredulously.

"Then tell him I had a woman to see," Gavin answered, and just saying those words gave him a sense of exhilaration that he had never known. He put heels to horse.

After all, he wasn't going after just any woman.

He was going to claim the Siren and save Sarah Pettijohn from the misery of her current existence.

As he galloped through the night streets of London, the lantern in his hand lighting the way, he realized there wasn't a man of his acquaintance who wouldn't be jealous.

Chapter Five

It had taken Sarah hours to finally fall asleep.

After she'd ordered Baynton from her home, she'd had to spend a good hour pacing the floor, reliving every frustrating moment of being in his presence, and imagining quick rejoinders to put him in his place.

The worst had been when he'd been curious about her plays.

My work, she could hear herself telling him haughtily.

"Work?" he'd questioned as if women never did such a thing. Or that writing wasn't the very hardest work, which it was. In fact, it was harder than an aristocrat like himself could appreciate because he had *never* worked. He had *servants* to work for him.

And then, in her outraged mind, she could see herself stuffing pages of her play into his arrogant mouth. She'd make him chew on her words for questioning her. Yes, she would!

Indeed, she could not wait until Geoff and Charles produced her play. She'd already chosen *The Fitful Widow* because it was humorous and yet, had a poignancy to the story, especially when the hero falls to one knee and declares himself in love with the Widow.

She could vividly see the scene staged in her mind. She knew Londoners would flock to the theater after the first performance. Word would spread throughout the city of how wonderful her play was until it reached the ears of the Duke of Baynton—and he would wonder, who was this marvelous new playwright who had captivated the capital?

Perhaps he would be curious enough to seek her out?

She could picture their meeting. For some reason, she saw herself dressed in Georgian fashion with powdered hair and even a patch. Paste jewels were in her ears. She'd chosen for her imaginings, she realized, the costume that her mother had worn in her performance of *She Stoops to Conquer*, the last role she'd ever played before Lord Twyndale had made her his mistress.

The costume was perfect for Sarah to appear regal and self-assured. *That* was the attitude she wanted around Baynton.

For his part, in her mind's ramblings, she saw him in somber clothing. Drab browns. He appeared contrite, humbled. It was a very good image . . . however, she could not discount reality.

Baynton would never humble himself to her.

Furthermore, her thoughts had led her down the path of regret and of those things that could never be.

Aloneness had filled her being.

Baynton would never see her play. It was beneath his dignity. And her mother was gone. Disappointment, cynicism, and a taste for the poppy had let her drift away with only Sarah left to mourn her.

Sarah had looked around her room then, seeing it as she believed Baynton had. There wasn't anything to her surroundings. It was a shell compared to the life she'd once lived and she was fiercely glad that Charlene was gone, safe away from her. Her life was in Boston. She'd have children and love and all the good things that came with them— things that were lost to Sarah.

Her temper spent, Sarah knew she had grown

maudlin. She should put herself to bed. Tomorrow was an important day. She had a meeting to discuss her play with Geoff and Charles. She should not let the Duke of Baynton ruin it for her.

So, she'd undressed, carefully folding her Siren costume away and placing it in a bandbox. She had pulled her heavy cotton nightdress over her head and had blown out the candle. Her pallet was not comfortable but she cheered herself with thoughts of the morrow and drifted into a turbulent sleep.

Sarah had never been one to dream, except now she did. She found herself walking in a dark and dangerous place that she couldn't quite define but she wasn't alone. The Duke of Baynton was beside her, guarding her, guiding her. She was glad he was because she heard voices mocking her. She thought she saw faces and yet, it was unclear in that hazy, jumbled way of dreams.

Her only certainty was that Baynton was by her side—until the knocking started.

At the sound, he stopped, but she kept walking. She had a thought that he would catch up. He didn't. He just disappeared and she was left with the awful knocking that kept growing more and more insistent—

Sarah came awake with a start, shocked to realize she was in her bed and not walking the streets. Certainly her body ached as if she'd traveled for miles, and *she had*, she realized. She'd exercised herself very well the past evening and had received little sleep in return.

"Mrs. Pettijohn? Wake up!" The Duke of Baynton began rapping heavily on her door again.

"What in the world—?" She combed her hair back from her face. She hadn't bothered to braid it before turning in and its heavy mass was tangled. The side of her face felt as if she'd been sleeping too hard and her eyes were crusty. She rubbed them.

"Mrs. Pettijohn, *open the door*. I have a matter of great urgency to discuss with you." There was a light around the door as if it was day, but it couldn't have been.

The word "urgency" captured her attention. What could be urgent that he hadn't said to her last night? Her mind immediately went to Charlene.

What with England and the United States at war, letters between Sarah and her niece were now difficult to exchange. If anyone could receive information, it would be the mighty Duke of Baynton.

Fear for Charlene gripped her. She stumbled to the door and cracked it open just as he was about to knock again. The light around the door was from the lantern in his hand. She threw the door open wider, squinting.

"Is all well with Charlene?" she asked.

"Yes, of course," he replied as he walked right by her, inviting himself in. He removed his hat and set it and the lantern on the table.

"Then what is so urgent?" Sarah asked, confused.

But he wasn't paying attention to her. Instead, his gaze fixed on her bare toes peeking out beneath her nightdress and she remembered the warmth in his voice when he'd wondered earlier what else about her might also be naked. She tucked her toes in from his view, which only brought his interest to her tangled hair around her shoulders. Wherever he looked, it was as if he touched her, and she struggled with a desire to hide.

And then he announced, "I wish to spend the night with you."

It took a moment for those words to penetrate her still sleep-heavy brain, but when they did, she almost laughed—until she realized he was serious.

His presence, his *person*, filled every nook of her mean little room. He was too fine to be here. Too full of vitality and life.

And of his own consequence.

Standing by the still open door, Sarah said, "*That* fact was established when you mentioned my breasts tonight, Your Grace, and complimented my legs. You will not be surprised by my answer—no. Now good night, or good day to you, whichever it is at this hour." With a sweep of her hand, she urged him out the door.

He did not move. "Hear me out, *and*—" he continued as if knowing she would not be convinced, "if you still wish me to leave, then I will do so."

"*If?*" In spite of her sarcasm, Sarah had a kernel of curiosity as well. Baynton had never taken a mistress. She'd heard the gossips among the actresses and dancers who kept track of that sort of thing. He was the most eligible bachelor in London and a prize for every conniving woman.

Furthermore, she'd never received an offer of this sort before.

Yes, when she'd been younger there had been men who chased; however, since the painful farce that had been her marriage, she'd never given anyone a chance to close in on her. She rather liked being her own person. A bad husband could do that to a woman.

She closed the door. "Speak."

"You do not like me. I understand," he hurried to add. "But I am not set against you."

This was news to Sarah.

"I do find you headstrong," he added, "and wrong thinking, but I believe that is no crime."

"How generous of you, Your Grace."

He didn't react to her mild derision. Instead, he began pacing the small confines of her room, just as she'd done not more than an hour or two earlier.

"I have a problem," he said. "I must marry. I will. I have money. I'm a duke. Some woman will want me."

"Two have already said no," she silkily reminded him.

He stopped. "Yes, they have and that is part of the difficulty. You are one of the few people who knows that I've done the honorable thing to let them marry the men of their choice. It was not because they faulted me. However, the rest of the world is not aware of the full story." He paused as if wrestling with himself and then admitted, "Some see me as less of a man."

"That is nonsense," Sarah answered.

"And yet it is true."

She wanted to refute his claim . . . then again, he was right. She'd heard whispers from small minds. They wondered what was wrong with him that Charlene had chosen another? And they had prodded Sarah, hoping to glean knowledge and were disappointed when she'd kept her mouth shut. She knew the gossips were unfair to Baynton; however, what could she say to help? Who cared what an actress thought?

He took her hand and brought her over to sit in one of the chairs. He pulled the other up so that they were facing each other, their knees so close they almost touched.

"Last night, Mrs. Pettijohn, you created a vision every man in that theater wanted."

That was true. She had been a sensation. "I did not encourage them."

"You needn't. Men are covetous. They see; they want. Having you on my arm will do much to restore my reputation."

"I am not a whore."

She would have risen from the chair but he caught her hand. "This is a business proposition."

"I. Am. Not. A whore," she reiterated.

"I would never call you so. However, you have created an impression—a false one, perhaps—but people think what they will."

"And for what others think I am to sell myself?"

"Or use this moment to your advantage. What do you want that you can't have, Mrs. Pettijohn? What of security? Of owning a lovely house to call your own?"

"Attempting to take care of me again, Your Grace?"

"You have refused charity."

Sarah made a sound of annoyance. Leave it to Baynton to use her own words on her. She crossed her arms. "I have principles."

"Aye, the world is aware that Mrs. Sarah Pettijohn is no mere actress. She has principles," he replied. "She'd never stoop so low as to sing away while pumping her legs on a swing over the heads of a pack of hungry lords behaving like dogs."

For a bald second, Sarah hated him.

Nor would she defend herself.

She had good reason for participating in the *Naughty Review*. A woman alone had to do what she must to survive. She didn't need to explain herself to His Haughtiness. She'd meet his haughty and raise it with her haughty. "A pack of dogs in which *you* were a member," she reminded him archly.

"I was there," he conceded.

She glared at him, angry . . . and tired. Exhausted actually.

For a moment, the struggle of her life threatened to overwhelm her. How hard would it be to say yes and own a house, a home no one could take away from her?

She could not give in to temptation. That is what her mother had done. Still, she was curious . . .

"There are a half a dozen birds around London men would be jealous to see you with, Your Grace. Why me?"

"Why not you? Besides, I require someone who will not be foolish. I do not wish to bring bastards in the world."

He *was* being smart. Baynton was wealthy. He would be honor bound to support any child he bred. The mother could find herself set for life.

This was also an issue he needn't fear with Sarah. She wondered if he knew, but he couldn't. This was her secret.

"I also," he continued earnestly, "need someone whose discretion I can trust."

"And you believe that is me?" she asked, incredulous.

"As a matter of fact, yes. You actually *do* have principles, Mrs. Pettijohn."

"Thank you, I think."

"You think?"

"Yes, you have me confused. You wish discretion and yet you obviously plan on letting everyone in London know we are lovers. What game are you playing?"

"No game, Mrs. Pettijohn. I need help and you are the only one I can trust."

"Because," she prompted.

"Because I'm a virgin, Mrs. Pettijohn."

Sarah went still, uncertain if she'd heard him correctly.

He didn't laugh or act as if he jested. He was remarkably serious about the matter, and she realized he was speaking the truth.

She straightened her shoulders, folded her

hands in her lap and said simply, "Don't worry. It isn't a permanent condition."

He bolted from his chair as if he objected. "But it has been," he announced. "Do you think I wish to be this way? At my age?"

"Then why are you?"

"You are not the only one with principles. I believed that if my wife was a virgin then it was only right I should come to her chaste as well. Pure, so to speak."

"Why, Your Grace, you are a romantic."

He frowned confusion at her statement. "Of course I am." He shrugged and then plunged forward with his story. "However, you are aware of my wife challenges."

"I am."

"And now, if my peers should find out . . ." He let his voice trail off, filling in words with a wave of his hand, and Sarah had to stifle the urge to laugh.

Here was Baynton, handsome, noble, possessing all the qualities anyone could wish to live a fine life—and he was worried about *this*?

Sarah could not relate. She shook her head. "Then change it," she said. "Go sow your oats."

"I'm trying to," he answered, sitting down in front of her again. "I want to."

"With me?"

His brows came together. "Of course. That is why I'm here."

"No."

"No, what? That I'm not here? I am here."

"I'm not going to be the field for your 'oats.'"

"You aren't thinking clearly—"

"Oh, I am thinking very clearly—"

"—Because otherwise you would see the advantages."

"*What* advantages?" Sarah stood. She looked around her hovel of a room. "Yes, a house would be nice. Not worrying about money would be even sweeter. But I've been this route before, Your Grace."

"You have had a protector?"

"My mother did. That is what happens to women alone. If we don't become dressmakers or governesses, personal maids, nannies, or that worst of all occupations, companions to crotchety old ladies, well, there isn't much left in the way of supporting ourselves. But I want something more from my life. I don't want to just make a living, I want my life to matter."

He stared at her as if she'd spouted gibberish. "Of course, your life matters."

She returned to the chair facing his and leaned in, needing him to understand. "*You* have purpose. Well, *I* have purpose as well. My writing is my reason for being. My mission, if you have it, for walking with my head high and not earning a living on my back."

"I've insulted you," he answered, still sounding confused.

"Oh yes, you have."

Again those brows came together. A muscle worked in his jaw. "But you don't wish charity."

"No."

"I'm not offering charity."

Sarah had an inkling of where his argument was going. And it both astounded and amused her. "You believe that my being your mistress will allow you to take care of me while making me feel productive?"

He considered her words a moment. "That is my intention."

"And you don't understand why I would refuse your offer, do you?" she continued.

"Quite frankly, I'm astonished. I believe this solves several problems."

"And would you make such an offer to a lady of rank? Or one who is considered genteel?"

Now, he began to sense that he'd best be wary. His sharp blue eyes slid away from her gaze. "You know that would not be right."

"Because?" she prodded, with the primness of a governess.

"Such an offer might be considered an insult."

Sarah leaned forward. "My father is Lord Twyndale, the late one. I was born on the wrong side of the blanket, Your Grace, but how does that make me less respectable than his daughters born by his lady wife?"

"I believe you know the answer to that."

"You are right. I fought it for years. In fact, my sense of worth doesn't come from who my father was. It comes from who *I* believe I am." Proud words. Bold ones. They wrapped themselves around her.

Baynton heard them. He might not believe them, but between them passed a moment of complete understanding.

And she expected him to apologize. She was ready to hear him babble on about how he mistook her situation. She was even ready for him to ask forgiveness, which would please her very much. She doubted if he spoke those words very often.

Instead, he sat silent, his expression unfathomable—and then he leaned toward her, cupped his hand around her face before she realized what he was about, and kissed her.

Shock paralyzed her mind.

His hands were warm against her jaw. His lips upon hers hot.

It was not the kiss of an experienced lothario. There was no demand to it, only naked yearning and a sense of wonder.

In spite of her best interests, Sarah responded.

She couldn't remember the last time she'd been kissed. Years ago it was. She would not count the sloppy kiss of one of the young actors who had caught her in the wardrobe room. Baynton wasn't groping her. He was speaking to her, and wasn't it lovely to be spoken to in just this language? To have a man offer to worship her? To envelop her in his arms? His body?

She'd forgotten so much but his kiss made her remember.

Her lips parted, softened. She found she didn't wish to hold back. She discovered a desire for something more.

The duke caught her movement and mimicked it.

Baynton was a novice at seduction. He didn't know exactly what he was doing. His kiss was earnest, honest, and, surprisingly, delightful.

For one sparkling moment, Sarah breathed him in and it was good.

Very good.

One of them sighed. She realized the soft sound of pleasure was from her. The duke was too busy placing his arms around her, drawing her closer.

For a span of time, she could see herself and

Baynton in the room. See them kissing and the growing heat. If she wasn't careful, his hand would be on her breast—

His hand went to her breast and Sarah jumped out of her chair. She moved to place the table between them. She touched her lips. She had to. They didn't even feel the same.

Not only that, but her heart raced in her chest. Her blood beat in her ears.

He appeared as startled as herself. His broad shoulders turned to her. Their eyes met. She saw the question there. Understood it. He, too, had been caught off guard.

Who would have thought the two of *them* would respond so strongly to each other?

And she had responded. Even now, her naked body beneath her nightdress wished nothing more than to climb into his lap to see if a second kiss would be as tasty.

"*Out,*" Sarah heard herself say, the sound almost guttural. "Out of my house."

The duke didn't move. He acted as if he was still caught in the spell of that kiss, but Sarah now had her bearings. She marched to the door and threw it open. "*Out.*"

At last, he came to his senses. He snatched up his hat from the table and walked toward her.

Sarah had an urge to step back; however, pride

would not let her. She steeled herself against him, uncertain what she'd do if he gave her another kiss. She pressed her lips tight to deny him, and herself.

He stopped in front of her. Sarah was tall for a woman but Baynton lorded over her.

A tight muscle worked in his jaw.

"Go . . . please," she whispered. "Now."

At her plea, Baynton took a step out, and then stopped. "If you ever need me—"

"I won't."

"But if you do, send for me."

She wouldn't. He'd already gotten too close to her.

"Thank you for your call, Your Grace."

He hesitated as if to argue, but then squared his shoulders. He gave a curt, short bow, and went out the door. Sarah closed it as quickly as she could and turned the key in the lock. She heard his boots going down the stairs.

Then, all was silence. That deep silence that didn't ever bode well.

That silence that spoke of loneliness.

Slowly, she put her back against the door and sank to the floor. He'd left the lantern. The light seemed a piece of him, filling the air around her.

Another man might come storming back, demanding she listen to him, bullying her. But not Baynton. He was too proud. She understood. She also had pride.

Her eyes fell on the manuscripts she had carried with her every time she'd moved in her life. Her work. The very embodiment of herself . . . but that kiss . . .

Baynton's kiss had been simple, naïve even, and innocent in its longing, its passion. It had reminded her of whom she had been.

"Don't believe," she warned herself. "Don't allow yourself wishful thinking."

Still, that kiss would haunt her.

Chapter Six

Sarah woke up with a start the next morning, disturbed to find herself hunched over on the floor by the door.

Every muscle in her back and legs ached. Not all of those pains were from her sleeping position. A good number of them were from the exertion of her Siren performance and her barefoot charge across London.

Memories of the night before came swirling back. She looked at the lantern, proof that she had not imagined the meeting with Baynton. The wick was almost burned down. Sarah hopped up and gingerly moved to the table to blow it out and save what was left of the oil in the lamp.

She sat in the nearest chair. The chairs were still facing each other. She could picture Baynton's broad-shouldered form as he had been last night.

The thought brought a shooting pain of tension to her temple. She pushed the mess of her hair away and massaged her head with one hand. From somewhere in the building, a baby squalled and from another corner, some male made big, hacking sounds.

Last night had been her opportunity to take the easy life.

"And you didn't," she reminded herself. "You would not."

She could hear her mother shaking her head, tsking.

"I'm doing this *my* way," she informed her mother's ghost, and decided she'd best be on with it. She was fairly certain from the sounds of activity passing through the building's thin walls that the morning was well advanced. The *Naughty Review* company members would have started gathering at the theater for their pay. One should never wait too long after a performance to be paid. After Geoff and Charles were finished with that task, they would be ready to talk to Sarah about her play. She planned to make it a productive meeting.

Bathing was always a challenge in her lowered circumstances. Water was collected from a pump further up Bolden Street. Sarah made the trek every day. First, because she believed in daily bathing and second, because she wished to appear her best for her meeting. The latter would be a challenge. She was certain she had huge circles under her eyes and placed the blame for her lack of decent sleep right where it belonged—on Baynton.

Throwing one of her serviceable dresses over her night clothes, she pulled on her shoes and, after giving her hair a brush, went to fetch water. She was back within the quarter of the hour and set about making herself presentable.

Sarah broke her fast with water, what was left of the bread, and a small piece of the dry cheese she'd been saving. She then dressed with care, choosing her forest-green walking dress because the color highlighted her hair. It was also the best dress she owned. She twisted her hair high on her head, pulling long curls to frame her face.

Today was going to be a damp day in London. She'd noted the low, gray clouds. She prayed she would make it to the theater before the rain fell.

She had only one hat and she took very good care of it. The material was a bronze silk trimmed in blue-and-green striped ribbons. Charlene had helped her choose the ribbon and Sarah liked the combination of colors, which was good since she could not afford new. Once her play was a success, then she would spend a whole afternoon picking out nothing but hats and ribbons and shoes. She could not wait to wear shoes with decent heels or stockings that had not been darned a dozen times.

She would also purchase cream for her face. Peering into the piece of mirror she used for her reflection, she was not happy with the lines beginning to show around her eyes. She was thankful her lashes were dark. So many with her coloring had light lashes.

Decked out in her best, she was finally ready to go. She set her hat at a smart angle, put on gloves, threw a cloak over her shoulder in case the rain started while she walked to the theater and then picked up *The Fitful Widow* from the stack of papers by her bandboxes. She believed it her best work.

The play was loose pages. She carefully placed them into a leather folder. She'd already started copying the pages for the different parts to give to the actors but she was out of paper and fearfully low on ink. She must talk about this with Geoff and Charles.

She'd also need to talk to them about a loan. She had waved aside payment for playing the Siren in order to have them agree to staging *Widow*. However, her rent was late and she had no desire to be tossed out of her current quarters, no matter how shabby.

There was also the inkling of a thought in the back of her mind that Geoff and Charles might let her serve as the play's manager. Certainly, she had plans to be backstage and even on stage if need be. She believed she would make the perfect "Widow," the female lead in the play.

But she definitely wished to be the manager. This story had been living in her mind for a good five years and no one knew it better. Or cared more. At last, she would find her place in what had often seemed to her an uncaring world.

The walk to the Bishop's Hill was a good stretch of the leg. A bit of mist was in the air. She kept her cloak over the pages of her play and made her way.

As she came within sight of the theater, she was surprised to see a number of the last night's company still milling around outside. They were obviously not pleased. Several stared at her as she approached. Few would know her. She'd worked hard to keep the identity of the Siren a secret.

William Millroy the tenor did know who she was and he came toward her. "If you are here to be paid, you might as well keep walking," he informed her in his lovely brogue. "They've skipped on us."

Sarah came to a halt. "They what—? Who?"

"Skipped. Run off. See the boards over the door. The landlord came by an hour ago and put them up. The buggers left him high and dry as well."

"Are you talking about Geoff and Charles?" Sarah had to ask. "They made a fortune last night."

"Yes, and apparently they took it with them," an actress Sarah knew as Irene agreed. "When they didn't show by noon, one of the lads went around to their quarters. The place is packed up. The neighbors said they heard them leaving in the night. They have flown."

"*No,*" Sarah denied. She had difficulty wrapping her mind around what she was being told. "I've known them for years. They would not do such a thing."

"Well, they have," Irene countered.

"Bloody bastards," the man who had played the shepherd in last night's performance said. He took off walking. One of the actresses, the one with very curly black hair trailed after him.

"Where are you going? What should we do?" she called after him.

"Find a pub," he answered, turning to walk backward but not slowing his step. "Coming with?"

She looked to the others.

"I'm due at the Covent," one said.

"I'll come," replied another. The two women

took after the shepherd. William Millroy started moving in that direction as well.

In minutes, most of the company dispersed to go their own ways. Sarah stood as if planted to the ground. She did not want to leave.

Irene was still there. "I've known Geoff and Charles since they first came to town," Sarah said to her. "I would not have thought it possible for them to do this. They were going to use the money from last night to keep their theater open."

"That is what they told us. Now, we know the truth. You knew they were deeply in debt?"

"They had expensive tastes, but they always paid their actors."

"And apparently no one else. I've been here since half past nine and we aren't the only ones upset. Their tailor, their butcher, everyone has been here with a hand out."

"I just can't believe this of them." Sarah shook her head. "They promised to stage my play."

"Your play? Ah, now I know who you are."

"You do?" Sarah replied cautiously.

"You are the one Colman relied on over at the Haymarket."

Sarah nodded mutely, too stunned by the turn of events to speak and thankful Irene didn't call her out as the Siren.

"He misses you. Everyone knows that," Irene

said. At Sarah's continued silence, she offered, "He would probably take you back."

"At what cost?" Sarah wondered sadly.

"I don't know," Irene said.

"He'd gloat. He'd tell me I needed him."

"Aye, he would. But, listen," Irene said, taking a step closer to Sarah. "You might need him. *You* have a more pressing problem on your hands."

"More pressing than Geoff and Charles playing me for a fool?" Sarah could have scoffed at the idea.

"Yes," Irene answered and knelt down to pick up a handbill on the ground. There were a number of them blowing around. "Read this."

Reluctantly, Sarah looked at the paper and then felt her stomach drop in horror. "Ten pounds for information leading to the actress known as the Siren?" she read aloud. "Contact Lord Rovington." There was an address to submit information. She looked at Irene. "What is this? A price on the Siren's head?"

"Do you know Rovington?"

"I've heard stories."

"If they are bad ones, then believe them. He is a bastard through and through. Likes actresses, he does. He's ruined many a girl without a moment's remorse. Thinks himself some grand lover. He is not a gentleman. Worse, few want his leavings and perhaps with good cause."

Sarah frowned, uncertain of what Irene meant and yet, there was no doubt it meant ill for her.

Irene tapped the handbill. "They say he's placed wagers all over the city that he will bed the Siren. He was the one whom you kneed last night."

At Sarah's start of alarm, Irene said, "Yes, I knew it was you. I remembered you from your performance years ago. I was in the first show as well. However, thanks to Rovington pulling off your wig, anyone around the theater, including that crowd that was just here now, knows who you are. Your hair color is unforgettable."

"This is ridiculous," Sarah said, holding up the handbill. "I do not know this man."

"You don't have to. I told you, Rovington is a dog. If it moves, he pokes it and he has decided to poke you. You'd best beware. Millroy was telling us that since last night's scene, the wagers have gone up."

"Millroy knew about this?"

"All the men did. Rovington is a braggart and half of that audience was there to have a look at you and see if he'd win."

"Why, that is *immoral*."

Irene laughed at Sarah's outrage. "'Tis, isn't it? You know the fancy bucks, they think they own the world and we are just here for their pleasure." Her tone had turned bitter.

Sarah understood. She looked down at the handbill. "Ten pounds."

"It is good wages," Irene said. "Especially after one has been rooked from what should have been an excellent payday."

A person like her fellow actors in the *Naughty Review*.

"Perhaps some of those lads have gone for a pint, but you'd best be careful, Sarah. They might also be going to pay a call on his lordship."

"I hear your warning," Sarah answered, "but in truth, I can't worry about Rovington. Who I want is Geoff and Charles and I shall find them."

"If I were them, I'd be flying to the Continent," Irene countered. "Can you imagine how much money we took in last night? They could live for years on it. They lived for years off the first review we did."

"This is not right," Sarah said.

Irene gave a fatalistic shrug. "What can we do? Life is not fair. There are those who take and a host of us who are taken."

"But they are playing with *me*," Sarah answered. And her dreams. Her hopes. Her ambitions.

The play she so carefully held in her arms felt heavier than a cord of wood. Her blood boiled with anger.

She could well imagine Geoff and Charles

laughing at how gullible she'd been, how utterly, to their larcenous minds, clueless.

But they had underestimated Sarah Pettijohn.

Chances were that if the two crooks were not in London, then they might still be in England. She'd chase them to the ends of the earth, if possible. And while perhaps *she* couldn't hunt them down, she knew someone who could.

If you ever need me, send for me.

The duke's words echoed in her mind. Did she dare . . . ?

Did she have any other choice? This was survival. Geoff and Charles were attempting to crumple her dreams. She would not let them.

"Are you all right?" Irene asked. "You have the most fierce expression on your face."

"Fierce? Yes, that is right. I'll do anything to find Geoff and Charles. I will find them."

"And how are you going to do that?" the other actress asked.

"I'm going to call on the Duke of Baynton."

Irene laughed and then stopped as she saw Sarah was serious. "Do you really know Baynton?"

Sarah nodded. "And I know how to convince him to help me." Baynton wanted her. Well, then, here was her price: she wanted Geoff and Charles brought to justice. Sarah set off walking. She'd not reached the end of the street before the skies opened and it began to rain.

She kept walking.

Gavin had left Sarah Pettijohn's room feeling as if someone had stirred up his insides with a red-hot poker. He was surprised he could walk away from her with any sense of dignity. He moved as if the world around him had slowed.

His horse waited where he had tied it. He glanced at the whorehouse across the way and found himself hoping that one of those randy bucks who had gone in earlier would come out now and challenge him. He'd like nothing better right now than a good mill.

The thought flitted across his mind that any reasonable person would tell him to cross the road and climb the steps into that house. His was a problem easy to solve, as both of his brothers—and Mrs. Pettijohn—had pointed out to him, but he wanted *her*. Mrs. Pettijohn . . . *Sarah*, because after a man kissed a woman the way he had her, didn't he have the right to address her by her given name?

God, he burned for her, and she had rejected him. *Him*, the man that supposedly every blasted woman in London wanted.

Save for two others. He could almost hear her voice dryly reminding him of the truth.

And perhaps that is why he was so taken with her. She told him the truth. She'd done that during the escapade with Lady Charlene and she certainly had spoken her truth a moment ago.

Gavin mounted. Ares picked up on his mood and danced, testy. With a kick, Gavin sent him on, but his mind was not on his riding. No, he was reliving the scene between himself and Sarah.

Was there ever a more independent minded woman? She'd rather starve than accept his largesse.

Well, it wasn't truly largesse. Sitting there with her wearing that ugly, heavy nightdress that covered her from her neck to her toes, he'd desired nothing more than to gather her in his arms and roger her with all the pent-up passion of his being.

He couldn't imagine another male in London who didn't want the same thing.

Although he was probably the only male who felt confounded by her refusal—and he didn't understand why.

When his long-standing betrothal ended because Elin had chosen another, Gavin had let her go. When Lady Charlene had eloped, Gavin had been insulted, but he had let her go. These women meant more to him than Sarah Pettijohn. They were of his class and he had been planning to marry them.

He just wanted Sarah in his bed. One good night, that is all he wished.

And then there was that kiss.

It had not seemed to have any impact on her, but for him . . . well, he could have fallen on his knees before her—something he would never do. Dukes did not beg. That was one of the first rules his father had taught him.

Still, he'd been tempted to plead for another kiss.

Gavin rode through the park on his way home, giving Ares his head. The sun was just starting to come up. London was stirring. There were other riders at this hour but not many.

It wasn't until he'd traveled around the park that he remembered he had left the lantern in Sarah's room. So be it.

He returned Ares to the stables.

His valet Michael was waiting for him when he reached his bedroom. Talbert, his secretary, always left a list of what appointments and meetings Gavin had for the day so that Michael would know what the duke should wear. Today was to be a busy one but Gavin waved away the elegant jacket his valet had prepared. He knew he would not be worth a farthing until he worked Sarah Pettijohn out of his system.

"Send word round to Jackson." He referred to the renowned Gentleman Jackson who owned the boxing saloon Gavin favored. Since whenever Gavin went there to practice the sport, someone was always vying for his attention to ask a favor or push a pet project, Jackson often sent one of his best pupils to Menheim to give the duke privacy and a challenge. "Tell him to send over someone good. As soon as possible. If I don't pound something I shall explode."

If this declaration sparked alarm in Michael, he was too well trained to show it. "Yes, Your Grace. May I then suggest a simple shirt and breeches with the green jacket?"

Gavin waved his assent. The valet set out the clothes and left to relay Gavin's message for someone to deliver to Jackson's rooms.

While he was gone, Gavin took the liberty of shaving himself and didn't like what he saw in the mirror. He looked as if he was a man possessed. "Take hold of yourself," he warned his image and decided that breakfast, a few rounds of good physical exertion, and he would be himself again.

Down in the breakfast room, he came upon his mother. Marcella, the Dowager Duchess of Baynton, was a lovely woman with silver hair and a regal bearing. Gavin had great respect for her. Over the years since his father's death, she had become his most trusted advisor.

She smiled her welcome. "Good morning, my son. Did you sleep well?"

"Absolutely," Gavin murmured. He wasn't about to confide his difficulties in his mother.

"Good, and I'm happy to see you this morning. Saves me from hunting you down later."

Gavin helped himself to the breakfast dishes on the sideboard. He was pleased to see Cook had included his favorite, beefsteak. "What is it you wish?" he asked.

"I believe Imogen and I have found a wife for you." She referred to his great-aunt Dame Imogen. Imogen was a stickler for bloodlines and had become quite involved in his search for a suitable bride.

He choked back a groan. "How nice."

"This young woman *is* nice," his mother said, leaning across the table toward him as he sat down. "I didn't want to say anything until Imogen had a chance to meet and approve her. You know Imogen feels responsible for what happened with Lady Charlene. She had vouched for the girl and had thought her better mannered."

Gavin shrugged as he cut his beef. "There was nothing wrong. She is making Jack a good wife."

"But it is *your* wife we worry over. My son, you must marry and soon. You are in the prime of your life, the right age for a family."

He nodded. She wasn't saying anything she

hadn't told him a hundred times before. Mothers could be that way. "So who have you found?"

"Her name is Miss Leonie Charnock."

"Charnock? Sir William Charnock?"

"Yes, she is his daughter, his only child. He married Elizabeth Snavely—you remember the Snavelys. Like the Charnocks, they have close ties to India."

"The Nabobs." He referred to those officers of the East India Company, many who had earned great wealth through their services.

"Exactly. Miss Charnock's great-grandfather was Job Charnock, one of the first of the Nabobs."

Gavin set aside his knife and fork, his appetite disappearing. He knew he must marry, but right now, with his heart battered, he didn't appreciate the conversation—

His heart battered.

The direction of his thoughts startled him.

What bloody nonsense. He realized he was becoming ridiculously dramatic and acting like Rovington. His *heart* was not the portion of his anatomy upset over Sarah Pettijohn. It couldn't be. He didn't know her that well. In truth, given her high-handed ways, he was better off *not* knowing her that well.

It was another part of his anatomy that was severely disappointed by her rejection.

"I'd like for you to meet her, Baynton," his mother was saying, after waxing on about Leonie's looks, her breeding, and her manners. "I believe the two of you would be an excellent match."

"Arrange an introduction then," Gavin said.

"I have . . . for this evening."

"*This* evening? Does this mean you and Imogen have already decided the matter and are merely manipulating me?" he asked his mother, only half in jest.

"No, we are prodding you. I don't want you to waste any more time licking your wounds. I want you to have children and know the peace your brothers have found."

"I am at peace," he murmured, nodding to a footman to pour him coffee.

His mother waited until the small service was done and then dismissed the servants attending the breakfast room with, "Leave us now." When the duchess spoke, the servants obeyed.

Once alone, the dowager said, "Are you happy? Remember, I know you well, my son. You are no monk. Although, some are beginning to wonder."

Tension tightened his shoulders. "Do you, Mother?"

"I told you, I know you well."

"You would have made a skilled politician," he answered.

"The territory of men or else I *would* have tried

my hand at it. So, will you meet Miss Charnock this evening?"

Gavin realized when he had been outmaneuvered. "Tell Talbert to arrange my schedule."

"I have," his mother informed him. "We will leave this evening at half past eight for dinner with the Charnocks."

"Have you even informed Michael what I am to wear?"

His mother did not flinch from the mild rebuke. "Do you wish me to?"

Gavin waved away the suggestion, aware that his life was moving on . . . while a part of him moped over Sarah—and, in truth, he was not one to sulk. He liked action. He rarely allowed a setback to disturb him—and yet, her rejection had hit him hard, and it shouldn't have. She was just not that important.

Or so he told himself.

"If you will excuse me?" He rose from the table, gave his mother a perfunctory kiss on the cheek and retired to his study and away from her too astute observation. Henry, his butler, passed on the word that Jackson would be sending over a man in two hours' time.

Good.

Gavin tried to read through the treatises he would need for the Bank of England later that day, but

snippets of his conversation with Sarah kept intrud-
ing. At one point, he was so caught up in his errant
thoughts, he'd snapped his wooden pen in half and
that was as Talbert, his secretary, was giving him
pertinent information about Wellington's latest plea
for supplies and money for his troops.

"I know, Your Grace," Talbert said in commis-
eration. "The Commons sent the bill to the Chairman of the Committees to review. He does not
seem to be moving quickly on the matter. The
prime minister asks if you can use your influence
with him?"

Gavin nodded. He had meant to talk to Rovington yesterday about the Money Bill but there
had not been a good opportunity. Here was
another example where Rov was proving to be a
disappointment. Thankfully, Gavin was certain
Rov did not know he had been in the hack that had
stolen Sarah away or else nothing would be done
in the government's favor. "I'll bring him round."

"I shall pass the word to the prime minister's
secretary."

A sound at the door interrupted them. A footman informed him that Jackson's man had arrived.

"Enough of this," Gavin said, pushing away
from his desk. "Draft the letters I've requested and
send a note to Rovington inviting him to dinner
or lunch, whatever. You know the wording."

"Yes, Your Grace, I do," Talbert announced, happily efficient.

"And now, I do not want any interruptions for the next hour," Gavin said, knowing Talbert would pass on his instructions to Henry.

He went downstairs to the ballroom and was pleased to see Jackson had sent Thomas, a boxer five years Gavin's junior and one not afraid to give him a fight.

"Good morning, Your Grace," Thomas said, bowing and pulling a forelock as he did. He was a country lad, big, brawny, and well matched for Gavin. "Ready to give it a go?"

"Past ready," Gavin said, meaning the words.

Both men removed boots, socks, and shirts and Thomas wrapped strips of rough cotton around Gavin's hands as he had his own. These would soften any blows and protect the knuckles.

"Are you up for a practice or a mill?" Thomas asked in his broad Scottish brogue.

"A mill."

"Very well then, Your Grace." They took up a stance in the middle of the ballroom and set about their business in earnest.

Soon the two men were coated in sweat with the only sounds between them the grunts of physical exertion and the noise of bare skin hitting bare skin. Gavin was pleased. Thomas was a shrewd and clever fighter and Gavin couldn't think about Sarah or he'd have his head knocked off his body.

That didn't stop a stray thought or two, but considering how deeply he'd been mooning over her rejection for most of the morning, this was a welcome relief. Slowly, he was exorcising her from his mind. He was regaining his sanity. *Who was Sarah Pettijohn when there were other women in the world?*

The question spun through Gavin's mind as round and round the ballroom the two men went, each managing his fair share of good hits—

A commotion at the door caught his attention.

Gavin put his hand up in time to stop Thomas's next blow. The younger man straightened, now aware that they were being interrupted as well.

There was a struggle going on between two footmen, Henry the butler, and a furious figure in a wet wool cloak.

And then the figure stomped on one of the footmen's shoes. The man yowled his pain and the figure, a *woman*, slipped under his arms and ran into the ballroom, her wet shoes squishing with each step. She came to a sliding halt when she realized she was before the duke.

"Your Grace," Sarah demanded in typical Mrs. Pettijohn style, her voice one of authority. And then, as if realizing how bold she sounded, she sank into a deep curtsy that took her all the way to the floor with a subservience he would never have credited her. "I *must* talk to you," she said. "I beg an audience."

Last night, she had been any man's lustful vision; today, she had the look of an angry kitten caught in the pouring rain. Her bonnet may have once been stylish and smart but now appeared a damp rag on top of her head. Strands of her hair were plastered to her skin. Her cloak was dripping a puddle on Menheim's always immaculate floor.

And then, Gavin had the strangest sense that she was staring at his bare toes. They actually tingled in reaction. He knew he was right when she lifted startled green eyes and then openly gawked in surprise at his naked chest. Apparently she had been in such a rush to see him, she hadn't taken in his state of undress.

Red heat flooded her face, and Gavin smiled. He'd had the same reaction last night when he'd seen her on the stage.

He had to say it. He couldn't help himself. "I am not naked," he chided softly, echoing her prideful words to him last night.

Without missing a beat, she answered in a humbled voice, "But you *practically* are."

"Only in the nonsense going on between your *female* ears, not anything you can see with your eyes."

Chapter Seven

Only in the nonsense going on between your female ears.

Sarah was embarrassed that she'd ogled the duke like a dairy maid. However, who knew he had such a remarkable form? Why, he was as muscled as a laborer and it was *not* a bad thing.

Having been around the wardrobe rooms of many a theater, she knew men came in all shapes and sizes. Her own husband had been a broad-shouldered man but his chest was no comparison to the Duke of Baynton's. Nor had he had the hard abdomen. *Most* men did not have that.

The truth was she'd lost her temper when the butler had refused to carry her request for an audience to the duke, especially once she heard Baynton's voice from somewhere in the house. And once lost, her temper knew no boundaries.

She'd shoved her way past the surprised butler and made a mad dash in the direction of the duke's voice.

Of course, she hadn't stopped to truly listen to what he was saying or else she would have realized, as she did now, that he hadn't been speaking but grunting, huffing, and snorting in that way men did when they took part in that strangest of all sports, boxing.

Was there ever a more ridiculous pastime? Men deliberately hitting each other?

She would never have considered Baynton a pugilist—until she saw him with his shirt off.

However, it was the sight of his bare toes when she'd curtsied that had startled her into awareness.

Baynton had wonderfully made feet. Masculine feet, with long well-formed toes—and if his chest and feet were so finely made . . . would not the rest of him be as well?

Her mind immediately recalled the feeling of his very obvious desire for her against her thigh last night in the hack.

Furthermore, she wanted a favor from him and knew he would expect in return what all men wanted. It might not be that great a sacrifice to make him happy . . .

Beneath her wet cloak, she tightened her hold on the play.

The butler had started apologizing for letting her slip by the footman but the duke interrupted him. "Never mind, Henry. I am well aware that Mrs. Pettijohn does as she wishes. Besides, my order to not be disturbed did not include her."

On those words, warm heat once again graced her cheeks. Sarah studied a point on the floor, aware of what every man in the room must think of her.

"I am sorry, Your Grace, I did not know."

"How could you? Who thought she would come calling?" She knew the mild gibe was for her. "Have a tray with refreshments sent in. Make certain Cook includes some of those sandwiches I like."

At the mention of food, Sarah's stomach rumbled noisily. She knew everyone heard it.

"You'd best hurry the tray," the duke advised dryly.

"Yes, Your Grace. Michael, see that it is done," the butler said to a footman.

Still staring at the floor, Sarah listened to the footsteps leave the room.

"Thomas, I believe we are finished for the day."

The man the duke had been fighting bowed. "Yes, Your Grace. Let me know when you wish another go."

"I will. Perhaps you would like to stop by the

kitchen. I'm sure you have worked up an appetite as well. Henry, take him there."

"Yes, Your Grace."

More footsteps.

And then, they were alone.

"You may stop pretending you are not here, Mrs. Pettijohn."

That brought a reaction out of her. "I wasn't pretending. I was *hoping* to disappear." She glanced up at him. He was still shirtless and seemed completely at ease with his nakedness and her disturbed peace of mind. "Would you please put on your shirt, Your Grace? And your boots," she ordered fussily. "Put your boots on as well."

He actually laughed, the sound abrupt. "You are becoming bossy."

"I'm learning no good comes of giving the Duke of Baynton too much rein."

Again, there was a sharp bark of laughter, but he reached for his shirt and pulled it over his head. She pretended to study the pattern in the floor as he crossed to the sitting area where his boots were. She'd gawked at him enough for one day.

She could imagine him gathering his socks and slipping them over his well-made feet. He confirmed her fevered imaginings by stomping his foot on the ground as he settled it in his boot.

Sarah allowed herself to peek as he yanked on the other and followed the whole ritual.

Seeing he had her attention, he said, "I usually have a valet for this."

"It is good of you to know how to dress yourself."

He laughed again, this time as if he had expected her tart rejoinder. He crossed to her and offered his hand. "Arise, fair maid."

Sarah wasn't certain what to make of the gallantry, but she released the hold of one arm on her play to accept his hand.

"Let me take your cloak," he said, coming around behind her.

"I'm fine," she said. He stood close and she found that it was difficult to wipe the image of his body beneath the shirt from her mind.

"If you keep dripping on Menheim's floors, the housekeeper will have a fit."

He was right. Sarah was soaked through.

She reached up and untied the string of her cloak. She was surprisingly nervous. The anger that had propelled her to storm past his servants had dissipated at discovering him so . . . human.

Sarah felt the weight of his hands as he removed her cloak. He did not linger at the task, for which she was grateful. He was not the lecherous sort.

He shook out her cloak and draped it over a wooden-backed chair. She hugged her manuscript for courage and faced him. "I need your help, Your Grace. I've been robbed and I must use all the resources available to you to capture the culprits."

"The resources available *to me*? Well, of course," he answered, opening his hands as if to show he had no tricks. "And you were robbed? I'm not surprised. The neighborhood where you live invites robbery."

"This isn't about my neighborhood." She moved to him, hating the sound of her wet soles on the floor. "Geoff and Charles, the ones who staged the *Naughty Review,* they have run away with the money from last night. They haven't paid any of the actors or any of their debtors and they are cheating me."

"Please, have a seat, Mrs. Pettijohn."

She didn't want to sit. She wanted to convince him to help her; however, niceties had to be observed. She plopped herself down on the closest chair in the sitting arrangement where he had placed her cloak.

The duke took the chair adjacent to hers. "How are they cheating you?" He was at ease in his element.

"They promised to stage my play. That was how they were going to pay me. Otherwise, I would never have played the part. Even years ago, I hadn't wanted to play the part."

That information seemed to surprise him. "Why did you do it then?"

Sarah hated explaining herself to anyone, but if the duke could help her, she owed him the truth. "The first time I played the Siren was to earn the money to support Char. You are familiar with her uncle Davies?"

He shrugged. "Barely."

"He is not the sort one leaves alone with a young girl. The man is vile. I would have done anything to rescue her from him, including dancing 'practically' naked. Of course, who knew the Siren would be such a success? We made so much money that night that Geoff and Charles could afford to establish their own theater. Unfortunately, they are not good money managers. They were in danger of losing Bishop's Hill. They told me they were going to put on another *Naughty Review* and asked me to play the Siren again. At first, I said no."

"Even though you obviously needed money?"

"I know you will not believe this, but even actresses have standards."

He held up a hand as if to ward off her temper. "I did not mean insult."

"It was implied."

"No, it wasn't. It is acknowledging a truth, Mrs. Pettijohn. Your circumstances have lowered.

You lost the house on Mulberry Street and anyone with eyes could see that you are living hand to mouth. Especially in that neighborhood."

"The neighborhood is not that desperate."

His expression said he begged to differ.

And Sarah had to, in all honesty, admit, "You may be correct."

A lift of his eyebrow told her he *knew* he was correct and she couldn't help pulling a face in return.

"Anyway," she continued, "Geoff and Charles offered me the one thing I want most in the world— they would stage one of my plays if I would help them. So I agreed. But now I've learned, they had no intention of honoring that commitment to me or any of the other actors. They bilked the whole company out of what we deserved."

"Are you certain they left?" he asked.

"One of the actors went by their quarters. They are gone. This was planned. What I need for you to do is stop them from leaving the country. Make them come back and give us our money."

"And put on your play?"

She shifted her weight, the manuscript in her arms as heavy as a baby. "That would be the ideal."

And yet what likelihood would there be that if the duke found Geoff and Charles, *if* they still had the money to pay the actors, *if* they were willing to stay in London that they would honor their promise to her?

She ran the side of her thumb across the leather folder holding *Widow*. Her throat closed. Tears threatened but she held them back. This was not the time for dissolving into tears. Now was the time to fight.

"It is about justice," she insisted. She met his eye. "Everyone knows the Duke of Baynton does what is honorable and right. You can't let Geoff and Charles run out on their commitment to people, especially to those who can least afford it. The tenor last night? Millroy? He has six children. Most of the dancers have a child or two. One, Liza, cares for a father who lost his sight at Talavera as well as an aging grandmother. I only have myself to consider but others have serious responsibilities."

She stopped, uncertain if she could move him. He listened, but did he understand?

"Why should you care?" she said, thinking aloud. "I mean the chances of finding Geoff and Charles are nearly impossible. By now, they may have fled to the Continent, but it isn't right to take the dreams of others, to make promises, and then use people in such a callous manner. It is the worst sort of thievery and not what we are about in this country. It isn't right," she repeated bitterly.

"It isn't," he agreed. But instead of giving her the support she had come here to request, his attention went to the door and Sarah turned to see two maids enter the ballroom carrying huge trays. "Ah, here is Cook's sandwiches. Lena, place them over here." Another maid held a tray with a pot of tea and a bottle of sherry. They set the trays on side tables next to the seating of chairs.

Only then, did Sarah start to take in her surroundings. She'd been so agitated when she'd arrived, she'd not had a sense of herself let alone the audacity of tracking down Baynton in his house.

If his presence couldn't humble her, the house did.

They were in a ballroom large enough to hold eight score of people. The walls were of cream and gilt; the draperies seemed to be spun of gold.

The very comfortable chair she'd dropped herself down on was of a rich robin's-egg blue velvet. Ornately carved tables were by each chair so that a guest would not have to sit holding a cup or a glass. The floor was of wood parquet; however, the section where the chairs were arranged was covered by an Indian carpet of the deepest pile.

Sarah would have screamed if she'd owned this rug and someone wore their wet shoes on it. She also became aware of the ruined hat on her head. Self-consciously, she removed it, feeling a bit humiliated. She placed it on top of her cloak and retook her seat.

The table beside the settee where Baynton sat was larger than the others. This is where he had directed the maids to place the trays. He now prepared to pour the tea himself . . . for her.

Sarah rested her hands upon the leather folder in her lap and was glad that she had at least worn gloves.

The duke said, "Lena, send Mr. Talbert to me."

"Yes, Your Grace." Both maids left the room.

Baynton added a generous amount of sherry to one of the cups. "This is for you, Mrs. Pettijohn."

"I'm not truly thirsty—"

"*Drink.*"

She drank, and found it quite good.

He handed her a plate loaded with sandwiches. "Now eat."

"Yes, Your Grace," she answered, mimicking the maid's subservience.

"Don't play that game, Mrs. Pettijohn. Humility is not your strong suit."

"As it is yours?" she had to pertly wonder.

A reluctant smile tugged his lips. "Far from it."

She nodded her agreement but did take a bite of sandwich. It was a heavenly delight of roasted chicken, cheese, and chutney between two slices of gloriously fresh bread.

Sarah couldn't remember the last time she'd had anything so delicious. She wanted to stuff the whole sandwich in her mouth and then gobble down more. The tea and sherry was the perfect thing to wash it all down.

So it was that when Mr. Talbert entered the room, she was holding a sherry-laced teacup in one hand, a sandwich in the other, and her mouth was full. In her damp clothing and hair ruined by rain, she imagined she offered a colorful picture, one that such an officious looking man would fail to appreciate.

She was right. He acted decidedly put out by her presence. "Yes, Your Grace?" he asked, pointedly ignoring her.

"This is Mrs. Pettijohn," the duke said. "Lady Charlene's aunt."

"Ah," Mr. Talbert said. Without turning to Sarah, he gave her a short bow. Not a complete one, half of one. Perhaps more of a quarter of one actually. A quarter of a bow.

"Send for Perkins," the duke said. "I have something I wish him to do. Have him here as quickly as possible."

"Yes, Your Grace." Mr. Talbert bowed deeply to the duke as if to contrast the respect he had for his employer against his feelings toward Sarah's presence, and then left the room.

The duke started to put a sandwich on his own plate but then, seeing Sarah had almost eaten all of hers, tossed it on her dish before reaching for another for himself.

Sarah swallowed. "Who is Mr. Perkins?"

"A man I use when I need something done. If anyone can find this Geoff and Charles, it will be him."

"Even if they have left the country?"

"Perhaps. Perkins is resourceful."

"I like resourceful." Sarah took another bite of sandwich. She knew she was gobbling but she couldn't help herself. She had been actually starving. In fact, she needed to stop eating or else she might make herself ill.

"While we are waiting for him, tell me about Geoff and Charles. Do they have last names?"

"Geoffrey Simmons and, oh, I can never remember Charles's. It is Italian." She considered a moment. "Salerno. Charles Salerno."

"And hair color?"

"Geoff is blond but Charles is dark-haired, as one would expect from a Mediterranean. He is the shorter of the two. Geoff is at least a head taller."

"Does this Salerno have family in Italy? Would they flee there?"

"I don't know," Sarah answered. Egged on by the generous drop of sherry in her tea, another concern came to her. "We should discuss the cost of Mr. Perkins's services," she said, trying to be matter-of-fact. "And about your offer this morning."

The duke stood abruptly.

His sudden movement startled her. She looked askance but he moved away as if restless.

"I believe your expectations of me must be discussed before we go further," she pressed. Her heart hammered against her chest. There was only one way she could reimburse him for his help.

She'd always believed herself above prostitution and yet, what else did she have to bargain with if not her body?

"This is not a good conversation for the moment," he said.

He sounded as if he was the uncomfortable one. "Why not?"

He placed his hands behind his back like a schoolmaster. "Do you see where we are? A man doesn't discuss something like this under his own roof."

"You brought it up under *my* roof this morning," Sarah countered.

"We were alone. The walls have ears here."

"I believe the walls of my room are far thinner than Menheim's walls."

"That isn't what I'm saying—"

"I know what you are saying," she interrupted. "I just don't agree with it. I will not be treated like a pariah." Like her mother had been and every other woman she'd known who had accepted *carte blanche* . . . as if there was something unsavory about *them*—and not the men who paid for their services.

Oh no, Sarah would never accept those terms.

However, before either could speak, a man's voice called out from the direction of the front hall with great goodwill, "Don't bother announcing me, Henry. You know Baynton and I don't stand on ceremony. Do we, Your Grace?"

Sarah did not recognize the voice, but the duke did. He stepped in front of her to greet this new visitor—the man she had kneed the night before. "We do when I don't wish to be disturbed, Rovington."

Rovington?

He hadn't noticed her yet. His attention was on the duke. She endeavored to make herself as small as she could behind the back of her chair, hoping to escape being seen.

"I'll have you know I am closing in on my quarry," Lord Rovington bragged as if the duke hadn't spoken.

"Quarry?" the duke said.

"Yes, the Siren. I have her in my sights—!"

His voice came to an abrupt halt as his gaze fell upon Sarah.

He recognized her immediately.

She stood, facing her enemy.

Lord Rovington grinned as if Sarah was a beef-steak and he had a knife and fork in his hands. "This is *her*. You found her for me. You are the best of friends, Baynton."

He would have moved toward Sarah with an eagerness that was off-putting, except the duke blocked his path. "Wait, Rov. She's not for you."

"Of course she is for me," he countered, indulgently, his beady gaze on Sarah. "I've spent a fortune already this day hunting for her. She's mine."

"No, she's *mine*. She is under *my* protection."

Rovington whirled on him. "What are you saying?"

"I'm saying she is my woman."

Sarah did not know what to make of all of this. In another time and place, she would have been offended by Baynton's proprietorial air. She'd always been her own woman, thank you very much.

But she was no fool.

What sort of man hunts down a woman with the intent of bedding her to win wagers? Not one she wished to know.

Lord Rovington cocked his head to one side. Perhaps another man would bow to Baynton's claim. He was not of that mind. "You can't have her. Not yet. I'll give her to you when I'm done."

The duke shook his head as if he didn't believe what he'd heard. "She is not a horse to be passed around, Rov."

"She's an actress."

That statement sent Sarah's temper soaring. She started forward, ready to give the arrogant Rovington the sharp side of her tongue, but the duke held out a hand, warning her to be still. "She's mine," he repeated calmly.

His lordship shook his head. "I am not offering offense to you, Your Grace. We have known each other for a very long time. I count you among my closest friends and I'm certain you would say the same?"

"Aye, Rov, I value your friendship."

"Then why let this bit of muslin come between us? I need her, Baynton. I staked a claim to her."

"Go conquer some other woman."

"I don't have *wagers* on other women. Can't you

understand, Baynton? The betting is high. I could be cleaned out. Ruined."

"From losing one wager?" Baynton challenged. "Rov, you were done up before this. You have been spending money you don't have for a good year and more."

Lord Rovington did not like that statement. His scowl deepened. "I've had a run of bad luck but it is not anything I can't overcome. In fact, I *will* recoup my losses—if you let me have that woman. Everything will be fine then."

"What of your marriage, Rov? Do you believe your wife wants you to do this?"

"She would if she knew what is at stake. Give the Siren to me, Your Grace . . . and I shall be forever in your debt. For example, we have the vote today on the Pensions Duties Act. You need my vote, remember? My influence? And I know Liverpool is anxious for the Money Bill to be out of the Commons?"

"I will not pander flesh to earn your support," Baynton answered, heat coming into his voice.

"And you would throw over our years of friendship for a bitch?"

Baynton's hand shot out. He grabbed Lord Rovington by his neck cloth and lifted him from the floor until he stood on his toes. "She is under *my* protection," the duke reiterated with an anger that was almost frightening to behold. "She is *mine*."

Lord Rovington's face started to turn colors. Sarah put her hand on Baynton's arm. "Your Grace, you are choking him. Please, let him go."

The duke released his hold and Lord Rovington almost collapsed. He reached for his throat and then rounded on Sarah as if he would strike out at her. The duke put a protective arm around her waist and pulled her to him and out of harm's way.

Lord Rovington caught himself in time from the rudest sort of violence, but he was not done.

"I will have satisfaction, Your Grace."

Satisfaction?

The word lingered in the air, confusing Sarah.

But the duke understood. He answered calmly, "Name your seconds."

"A duel?" Sarah said, trying to make sense of what was happening. "You can't fight a duel over me. I will not let you."

Both men ignored her.

Chapter Eight

Gavin had never fought a duel. He thought them senseless.

However, standing in his ballroom, facing Rovington, he recognized that perhaps the long course of their friendship had always been leading to this moment.

Rov was a brat, plain and simple.

He enjoyed manipulating others to give himself more consequence and hadn't hesitated to use the Duke of Baynton's name or their friendship if it could open a door, or lead to the powerful position of Chairman of Committees. It was actually Gavin who did the work, who read the bills, who made decisions. Rov was to have been merely a figurehead, but his overweening sense of confidence led him to believe he was more important than he actually was. The faults in his nature were beginning to hold sway. A man receiving thirty-two thousand pounds annually from the position should be set for life—instead he gambled on ridiculous, shameful wagers like "bedding a woman."

And Gavin would not let such a man have the better of him, no matter what their history.

At Gavin's calm acceptance of the challenge, Rov frowned as if he had not expected it being taken up. Then again, why should he have? Gavin usually favored diplomacy over force.

For a moment, Rov seemed to stand in indecision.

Withdraw the challenge, Gavin silently ordered. *Don't be a fool.*

And then Sarah spoke, reminding them both of her presence. "Did you not hear me?" she said with growing alarm. "You will not duel over me. Oh no. No, no, *no*."

The moment to bow out gracefully passed.

Rov would not recall the challenge with a witness present, especially a woman. It was not in his nature.

"I shall have my seconds contact you before the day is out, Your Grace," he said as if they had never known each other in their lives. He made a formal bow and left the ballroom, his booted heels clicking on the parquet floor with his departure—and with him may have gone Gavin's assurances to the prime minister that Rov would move the Military Money Bill expediently out of the Commons. *Damn.*

Gavin had no doubt Rov had the power to delay the bill and would out of spite. And what of the vote today? The Pensions Duties Act? Gavin had needed Rov's vote—

A hand waved in front of Gavin's face. "*Hel-lo?* Hello?" Sarah said.

He blinked, annoyed, and looked down at her. She'd positioned herself right in front of him, her expression reminding him of nothing less than an angry chipmunk.

"Have you taken leave of your senses?" she said. "You can't duel over me."

"Apparently I can." He walked over to the tray, poured a good splash of sherry into a teacup and drank it down.

"You don't have to defend me," she informed him. "I can take care of myself."

"This *isn't* about you."

Her brows rose. "*Oh.*"

There was a wealth of meaning in that one word.

He'd heard men complain before how their wives could, just with the tone of their voice, convey a litany of opinions. He'd not understood how that could be until this moment when Sarah

Pettijohn decided to school him, and he did not like her disdain. Perhaps she needed to be schooled back.

"It was either accept his challenge or let you go with him," he informed her, his mind working on the problem of Rov's vote. Perhaps he could sway another man's vote in his favor—

"I would never have gone with him," she answered nobly.

Distracted, Gavin said, "He wouldn't need your approval, Mrs. Pettijohn. In order to win the wagers he has made, all he has to do is bed you, one way or the other. By force if necessary."

"He wouldn't dare."

"After you kneed him on stage last night, I believe Rov would do that and maybe more to salvage his reputation." That statement felt good. She did bear a responsibility, albeit an unwitting one, in this new chain of unfortunate events.

"Including shoot you?" she flashed back.

"Or run a sword through me," he agreed.

He wished the sherry was whisky. Sherry would never have the same mind-steadying qualities as whisky. However, that didn't prevent him from pouring another as his mind worked over this devilish twist to the many promises he'd made—

"I'm *done*," she announced, interrupting his

thoughts. "I'm sorry I came here." She moved toward the chair where he'd placed her cloak. She set down her precious play so that she could throw the wet garment over her shoulders. "Please, forget my request for your help," she declared dramatically. "It is no longer of importance."

Her ruined hat fell to the floor. She picked it up, shook it out, started to put it on her head, realized how comical that would appear and tucked it in a pocket of her cloak. She picked up her play. "Thank you for your time, Your Grace. I shall see myself out." She began walking toward the door.

Gavin raised his voice. "Do you truly believe that if you just leave you will stop a duel?"

Sarah stopped, faced him. "If I had never come here, it would not have happened."

"How little you know of men, Mrs. Pettijohn. Considering Rov's irresponsible behavior, sooner or later it must have happened. He isn't one to listen to reason."

"But I wouldn't be involved."

"Not with the duel. However, Rov would have found you and then who knows what he would do? Certainly he would boast about it. Also consider your noble cause. What of your friends who have been robbed of their wages by this Tom and Clarence."

"Geoff and Charles," she corrected. "Why are you arguing this?" She moved back to confront him. "They are not worth your life, Your Grace. None of them are."

"You touch me, Mrs. Pettijohn. You are worried that I might be killed. There has been a time or two in our short acquaintance when I feared you would be the one to wield the sword."

"There are times when I *do* think of doing you bodily harm, Your Grace, such as right now. How can you possibly imagine I would wish you harm? I could pull out your arrogant tongue for even voicing the thought."

Gavin pretended to frown, enjoying the moment. "If you think about taking out my tongue, then that *is* wishing me harm." He had her on this one.

She started as if confused by his logic and then made a frustrated sound. "You know what I meant. I wasn't being literal."

He had to tease. "I'm not entirely certain I do—" His voice broke off into a grunt as she kicked him in his booted shin.

Sarah was incensed that Baynton could mock her worry over him. Had he no sense? Men *died* dueling.

Of course, kicking a duke was not the most mature action but there were moments when he annoyed her beyond all reason. Such as when he believed his impervious will was the only one that mattered.

Worse, kicking a man wearing boots, especially such a brawny man as the duke when one was wearing well-worn kid slippers, did not protect the toes.

The pain that shot through Sarah's foot almost caused her to drop the *Widow*.

She hobbled several steps, waiting for the sharp pain to subside to a dull ache.

And, no, she was not pleased when he said with mild amusement, "Mrs. Pettijohn, have you hurt yourself?"

"No, I just jump around like this because I wish to dance."

"That is a relief," he said. "I would not want you to have broken a toe because you wished to 'harm' me."

For one sizzling second, Sarah had the image of taking the *Widow* and pounding him around the ears with it.

Instead, she managed to match his overpolite tone and say, "I now understand why there are people who would adore to run you through."

His laughter this time was full-bodied, unrestrained, and rich. However, before he could respond, someone cleared their voice from the door to announce his presence. Sarah turned to see Talbert accompanied by another, exceedingly nondescript man. He had brown hair and wore brown clothes. He was the sort one would not notice immediately.

"Ah, there you are, Perkins," the duke said in greeting. "Please come in and meet Mrs. Pettijohn."

"Your Grace," Mr. Talbert said, "I need to remind you that we must leave for the Pensions vote shortly. I'm certain you wish to change. Michael is upstairs and I have your town coach outside."

"Yes, yes, I must go, but a moment with Perkins." The duke waved Mr. Talbert to leave them. He motioned Mr. Perkins forward. "We have a task for you."

"*We* do not. Not any longer—" Sarah started to remind him, but he held up a hand to cut her off.

"*We* do," he informed Perkins who bowed to the duke, a sign he was going to do anything Baynton ordered. "We need you to find two men who ran off with the money from a theater last night. The Bishop's Hill Theater. What are their names?" He turned to Sarah.

"Are you going to duel with Lord Rovington?" If he could be stubborn, she could be stubborner.

To her joy, a look of annoyance twisted his noble lips. "Of course I am."

"Then I don't know which two men you are

asking about." And with those coolly spoken words, Sarah walked out of the room with great righteousness and a good amount of pride.

She doubted if anyone had ever defied him before. However, as the two of them had discussed, she had *principles*.

"Mrs. Pettijohn, come back here," he said, his voice reasonable. She kept moving.

"*Sarah*."

At her given name, she faltered a bit. How strange to hear him speak it. How familiar—and yet she recovered her stride, her toes still tender, and kept walking.

In the front hall, the butler and the two footmen who had tried to accost her earlier lingered by the door. Behind her, Mr. Talbert, who had been waiting in the hall outside the ballroom, reminded His Grace that he needed to dress for "the vote." She easily pictured the officious looking secretary blocking the duke from coming after her, that is, *if* he was of such a mind to chase her down. She nodded to the surprised servants, opened the door and let herself out.

Rain was pouring from the sky.

She pulled the hood of her cloak over her head and started walking toward home. Beneath the folds of wool she protected *Widow*. Her plays were all she had of value. She would see them staged. She would.

And Baynton would call off the duel. He may be overconfident and ducal, but he was sensible. She'd seen that in the way he'd let Charlene marry the man she loved. He would come around.

She would be wiser to worry about herself. Her rent needed to be paid. She might have to humble herself and return to Colman. What had seemed impossible months ago—working for him after he'd reneged on his promise to stage one of her plays— now seemed to make sense as the water oozed though her shoes and beat down upon her head.

Sarah had not traveled far when she heard a coach approaching from behind. Since she was now on a main thoroughfare, she did not think much upon it. She was too busy trying to protect her play and to stop her teeth from chattering. There was something about the damp that could give a person a chill no matter the warmth of the day.

The coach pulled past her and then stopped. The door opened, blocking her path.

"Mrs. Pettijohn, climb in the coach," the Duke of Baynton ordered.

She frowned at him. He was snugly inside with the disapproving Mr. Talbert.

"I'd rather walk," she answered and would have gone on, except he unfolded his tall frame from the coach, reached for her before she could take another step, and unceremoniously tossed her in the coach.

"Onward, Ambrose, to the address I gave you."

"Yes, Your Grace," was the reply a beat before Baynton folded himself back into the coach beside Sarah.

This was no hired hack. The seats were of luxurious velvet. The air seemed to be scented with sandalwood and Sarah was nigh on overjoyed to be out of the rain, even if her wet garments were not good for the seat—but she wasn't about to concede defeat. A woman must never give in when she was in the right.

"Stop this coach immediately," she ordered.

"I will do no such thing," Baynton answered. "It's raining."

"Yes, I noticed," Sarah answered with a toss of her wet hair.

He muttered something about stubborn women. Mr. Talbert gave a sly grin of agreement and Sarah wished she could kick the duke's shins again, except her toes still hurt from her last attempt.

So, since he'd given the driver the address to her rented room, the least she could do was rest a moment. She had no doubt there would be another argument between the two of them in the near future, but for right now, she needed a bit of peace.

She noticed that Baynton had managed to be suitably dressed and was impressed he could change so quickly. His neck cloth was impeccably knotted and he now wore a canary-yellow waistcoat beneath a jacket of fine marine-blue worsted. A bolt of material of that quality cost a pretty penny and made her feel all the shabbier.

Of course, what she truly coveted was the oiled canvas coat he wore over his jacket. No rain could penetrate it. Meanwhile, she felt soaked to the skin and she feared her best dress was ruined.

"I gave Perkins what little information I could remember about those theater men," he said. "I remembered the name Salerno. He'll be able to do something with it. He is a master."

Sarah refused to respond, although it would be a good thing to see Geoff and Charles caught before they could spend everyone's money. As for herself . . . the *Widow* weighed heavy in her lap. The pages had got a bit damp. When she returned home, she'd spread them out on the floor to let them dry. Because of the leather folder, she was certain the ink had not run and counted herself fortunate.

"Your Grace," Mr. Talbert said, "do you wish to review the list of votes in our favor before arriving at Westminster?"

"Later, after we have seen Mrs. Pettijohn safe. Although one would never be safe in such a neighborhood."

"Says those who don't live there." The words just flowed out of Sarah's mouth. She couldn't stop them. Baynton was a hard man to ignore, especially when he was baiting her.

In truth, secretly, she was beginning to admire him. He was everything a nobleman should be— tall, strong, trustworthy, and blessed by God with good looks. And that chest. She considered that chest a blessing.

If she ever did take a protector—which she would never do—she would want someone like him. She was actually going to be a bit sorry when their association ended. There was an energy around him that made her feel present and alive, something she hadn't felt since Charlene left.

And safe. She did feel safe with him.

Sarah glanced over at him. He watched her, his sharp blue eyes filled with concern.

The most natural thing in the world would be to slip her hand around his arm to reassure him she was fine, maybe to cozy up to him and his body heat and the scent of the shaving soap he favored. If she closed her eyes, she could swear she was so aware of him in this moment that she could hear the beat of his heart.

No good would come from that sort of thinking.

The lessons she'd learned from Roland had been hard ones. Her emotions had proven traitorous. Nor was she her mother and doomed to trusting one man after another. No, she guarded her trust . . .

The coach turned down her street. Because of the rain, few were out and about to watch her arrive with such style. The Duke of Baynton even had windows of real glass in his coach. Sarah looked outside and noticed masses of wet paper all over the street.

Paper—the lifeblood of her profession. She didn't know why it was littering the street, but she could collect it, dry it, use it.

"This is where I live, Your Grace."

She didn't need to remind him. He had already reached up to knock on the roof, a signal for the driver to stop, and it was a good thing because she was shocked to spy her bandboxes out in front of the building where she lived.

And the papers? They were her precious plays, scattered by the wind and the rain, the ink on them all but vanished.

"Wait and I'll help you out—" he started, but Sarah had already turned the handle and was climbing out almost before the coach stopped, leaving *Widow* on the seat.

Her bandboxes were open and what was left of her clothes was a sodden mess. They'd been rifled through and the very best items taken. The Siren costume had been trampled into the muddy street.

But what brought her to tears were her plays. What had not blown away still lay next to what was left of her possessions. Sarah fell to her knees in horror at the damage. She gathered the pages to her chest. Her work. All her work was ruined.

Hot tears mixed with the rain down her cheeks.

She sensed him before she heard him speak. He stood beside her. "Mrs. Pettijohn, Sarah, please, come back to the coach," the duke said gently.

"The landlord has tossed me out," Sarah said, stating the obvious as if she could not believe it. "I was late by only a month. I've been later in other places . . ." Places where she'd been put out, such as her precious home on Mulberry Street.

And then her confusion turned to anger. She was overcome with rage.

"That building is a *complete* hovel. Even the rats have rats," she shot out as if she could wound the building with words. Or as if the landlord cared what she thought.

He didn't. He was a miserly character who lived in the country and sent some gruesome figure named Parsons around to collect the rents.

Sarah struggled to her feet. The duke's hand came to her elbow to help steady her. "If I had money, do you know what I'd do?" she informed him. "I'd buy this place, burn it down and build a new one without rats and where there aren't holes in the walls or mildew forming dark stains in the corners. And I wouldn't let anyone rent from me who drank gin."

But she couldn't buy it. She couldn't even pay the paltry rent.

Nor did anyone care what she thought. No one had *ever* cared. "Why is life so *bloody* hard?"

In answer, the skies seemed to open up above them, pouring down upon her, muffling her cry.

Rain sluiced off of the duke's hat. "Come."

One word.

Her life was spread out on the street around her, and he was asking her to leave.

Then again, the path of her life had always been carrying her to this moment. Her mother had told her more than once that there was only one calling for women like them. She'd laughed at Sarah's belief that she could be something more than what her mother was.

And now Sarah conceded defeat. She didn't

have the heart to fight any longer. The hopes, the dreams, the hours she'd spent believing in herself . . . she'd never had a chance.

Sarah let go of the wet papers. They fell to her feet. She let the duke guide her to the coach's open door. The *Widow* in its leather folder still sat on the seat where she'd left it. Sarah reached for it, ready to toss it out and let it join her other plays. Her other follies.

Baynton took it from her, held it away from her. "Let us go."

With a prod, he encouraged her into the coach. She was vaguely aware that she was a muddied mess and Mr. Talbert stared at her as if she was mad, and perhaps she was. Yes, this is what madness would feel like. She ignored him. He didn't matter in her life. Nothing mattered.

Baynton closed the door and came around to the other side of the coach. Sarah tried not to pay attention. Instead, she huddled down in her wet clothes, closed her eyes and wished she could vanish from this life. Then all her problems would be solved.

The coach started moving. She didn't ask where. She didn't care. She was busy trying to disappear. Mr. Talbert sat across from her, his attention on the folders on his lap as if he, too, wished she would be gone. She ignored Baynton.

When the coach stopped, she didn't move. The duke and Mr. Talbert climbed out and she assumed they were at Westminster for the "vote."

She sat alone. She thought about opening the coach door and just leaving, but that called for more energy than she currently possessed and so she stayed where she was.

The door opened on her side. Baynton offered his hand. Sarah took it. Since she had no will of her own, why not use his?

He led her forward and she was fine, until she recognized the façade of the Clarendon Hotel. It was an elegant establishment, one that catered to the wealthy.

She had no illusion about what was happening. Baynton was moving her here. Her! Wet, bedraggled, muddy. People who would see them come in together and would surely think the handsome, dashing Duke of Baynton could find a better mistress. They probably would believe her some witch from the swamp.

The idea made her laugh but the sound came out as a sob.

He shepherded her up the stairs and down a long hall. A hotel porter followed them, stepping in front of the duke to put the key in a door and open it.

"This way," Baynton said and with a gentle hand at her elbow escorted her in.

Sarah shuffled forward into a set of rooms fit for royalty. There was a sitting room with elegant chairs for the comfort of the occupants. A desk was in front of one of the room's many windows and there was a table and chairs.

She did not need any help going to the bedroom. She was exhausted. Completely done in. She barely registered the soft blues and creams of the furnishings. The room was dark and she preferred it that way.

So, here she was.

In the place she'd vowed she'd never go—she was a kept woman.

She remembered Baynton's request, that he was a virgin. Well, that was about to change—and she found she didn't care what he did to her. Her plays were destroyed. She was an empty shell.

And that was enough, wasn't it? Isn't the shell all men really wanted from her anyway? All they'd ever wanted. Even Roland, her bastard of a husband.

Should she warn Baynton how much she detested sex? No, let him find out.

Sarah yanked at the ribbons of her cloak and

let it fall to the ground. She stumbled directly to the bed and threw herself upon the coverlet, shoes and all.

The mattress was stuffed with cotton. She'd never felt one so soft. And the pillow was of feathers, lovely, lovely down.

Sarah buried her face in the pillow and tried to ignore the duke's presence, and succeeded as she shut her eyes and fell into oblivion.

Chapter Nine

$\mathcal{S}$arah didn't dream.

Her sleep was that deep. She hadn't been truly conscious of closing her eyes and even now did not wish to open them. She drew a deep breath, inhaling the scent of clean bedclothes. They carried the mix of lavender and soap. Heaven.

She remembered falling upon the bed, so tired she'd lost the will to fight.

Now, caught in the hazy state between sleep and waking, her thoughts went to her last happiest memory. It was when she'd lived on Mulberry Street, when Charlene had lived with her.

Charlene. She'd loved her niece as fiercely as if she had been her own child. In truth, she would be the only child Sarah ever had. She'd never hold a baby in her arms . . . especially at the ripe age of four-and-thirty.

And now Charlene was living her own life, building her own family so very far away from Sarah, because that is what one did with people they loved—they let them live their own life.

Sarah was ready to drift back into sleep when she sensed movement. She wasn't alone in the room. Someone quietly closed a door.

Complete recollection returned. Sarah opened her eyes.

She was in the room at the Clarendon. She knew without opening the bedroom drapes that it was late evening. She'd slept for several hours and she could sleep for several more.

A lamp burned low on the table next to the bed, its yellow light highlighting the whiteness of the sheets and the graceful carving on the bedposts. The door between the bedroom and sitting room was closed.

This is where the Duke of Baynton had brought her. She'd been evicted and her plays were gone. All of them. Everything that had mattered in her life had been treated as if it was of no consequence.

Realizing with a touch of horror she'd been sleeping with her mouth open, Sarah closed it and pushed herself up. Her hair was a shambles and her dress, her best dress, was hopelessly wrinkled. She still wore her wet shoes.

Sarah put her legs over the side of the bed and

that is when she noticed the hip tub full of steaming water in the corner of the room. She rose and crossed to it. Someone had set a table close at hand and there was a stack of clean linen towels and soap. Finely milled soap. She picked it up and smelled it. The scent was floral, not heavy with rose or lavender but a soft mixture.

She stood a moment, listening. She could hear no sound from the sitting room beyond the closed door—and yet she knew *he* was there.

Baynton was waiting for her, and she knew why. She knew what he wanted.

Her gaze fell upon a glass of claret wine by the lamp. How thoughtful of him. He should have left the bottle.

She walked around the bed to the table and lifted the glass. The wine had a bite to it. She was not fond of the taste, but considering her new circumstances, anything to dull the senses was appreciated.

As was the bath.

Looking over to the washbasin beneath the room's mirror, she found tooth powder and a brush for her hair. He had thought of everything.

Running a hand through her curls, she realized that very few of the pins she'd used that morning were left. Draining the last of the wine in the glass, she set it aside and picked the remaining pins from her hair, placing them carefully next to the brush. She undressed.

It had been months since Sarah had enjoyed a hot bath, and back then, she'd had to heat the water herself and prepare the tub. No easy task.

She allowed herself to luxuriate in the water's warmth a moment before lathering up the soap on a cloth. She washed as if she could remove the uncertainty and frustration from her very soul. There was a pail with water for rinsing so she washed her hair and rinsed it well.

Not even Cleopatra could have ever enjoyed a bath the way she did this one. She could almost allow herself to forget her circumstances—until a knock sounded in the sitting room on the outside door.

She heard the door open and the low rumble of male voices. She could not make out the words, but she smelled food. Sarah's belly rumbled in anticipation.

The sitting room door closed. She listened closely, expecting Baynton to interrupt her haven.

He didn't. And he was so quiet, she couldn't tell what he was doing.

Finally, it was curiosity more than hunger that brought her out of the bath.

She dried herself off and for a moment considered putting the green dress back on. After all, it was currently the only piece of clothing she owned.

And then she decided she'd not sully her body, all warm and smelling like a field meadow with the abused dress. Besides, if her memory of her mother's many lovers served her correctly, mistresses rarely required clothes.

She pulled the top sheet from the bed and wrapped it around her, fashioning it into a gown without sleeves. Her hair was beginning to dry, its heavy weight curling below her shoulders. Studying herself in the glass, she knew there was nothing she could do about the apprehension in her eyes.

Think of the time when you loved Roland, she ordered herself. *Not as it grew to be, but back in the beginning when he'd been kind and you were innocent.*

Of course, the Duke of Baynton was a far cry from her late husband who had taught her to hate the marriage bed. To hate what a man could do to a woman.

She didn't believe Baynton would be brutal . . . but he would expect her to submit, something she'd promised herself she would never do again.

Her mother, once, after a beating by the hand of one of her lovers, had informed Sarah that all men could be cruel. Sarah had not wanted to believe her, until Roland had proved her mother's words prophetic.

Sarah placed both hands again her abdomen, there, where a baby had once grown inside her. A child she'd never stopped mourning even though she'd never held her in her arms.

"You believed your life was destroyed then," Sarah softly reminded her reflection. "You survived."

It was a good reminder. She would always survive. Look what she had managed to live through already.

That didn't still the tremble in her lips or ease the tension in eyes that threatened to swallow her face. Her cheekbones were very pronounced. She'd lost weight over the past several months. Perhaps she had become too thin?

But she had not lost her spirit, her will.

She would give Baynton what he wanted, but she would dictate the terms. Her body would not be sold cheap.

Sarah moved to the door and opened it.

The sitting room was ablaze with the sort of light provided by one who never worries about the cost of candles. There was no fire in the hearth but the room exuded a cheeriness Sarah was far from feeling.

On a table was a tray with several covered serving dishes. The aroma of roasted meats and fresh baked bread almost brought her to her knees.

She forced her attention away from those tantalizing dishes to face the man in the room, and then her mouth almost dropped open in shock.

The duke sat in a chair at the desk. He was reading from a stack of papers. He had removed his jacket and loosened the knot on his neck cloth. A man at home with himself.

But it was lenses connected with gold wire perched on his quite noble nose that startled her. She had come to think of him as larger than life, perpetually vital, flawless. Vain even . . . until she saw the glasses. They gave his face character and a touch of humanity.

For his part, Baynton appeared equally stunned.

His gaze took in every nuance of her appearance, the draping folds of the bed sheet, her curves, her hair, and then he lowered his eyes as if looking for her toes.

Sarah found her voice first. "Wondering what else about me is naked?" she asked. She sounded bold, in control.

"I believe I know," he answered, a new huskiness to his voice.

However, instead of pursuing the matter, he took off the lenses and tapped what he was reading with one of the wire temples. "This is very good."

Only then did Sarah see that he was reading her play. *The Fitful Widow* lay open in its leather folder across the desk.

Her heart gave a wild leap. In her fit of despair, she'd thought that she had tossed it out in the rain with the others. He must have saved her from herself. She had *not* lost everything. This play, the one written from her heart, still existed—and with it, her dreams.

And then a jolt of anger shot through her, a sense of violation. "I don't remember giving you permission to read my work."

He dropped his glasses and raised his hand as if to gently ward her off. "I meant no insult. I was curious and there isn't anything else to read in the room."

She glanced around as if confirming his words but truly to take a moment to calm herself and to regain her perspective. She was overreacting.

"I don't normally read plays," he confessed, marking his place in her play and closing the folder. "Or attend the theater."

"Yes, I know. 'Only the occasional Shakespeare.'" That had been what he'd told her during their chase to stop Charlene from eloping.

He nodded, conceding her point. "I know that

my opinion means little to you, but I have been entertained. Well done, Mrs. Pettijohn."

Her attitude toward his reading her work changed.

"Have you reached the part where they duel over her hand?" she wondered.

"No, I am at the section where he is in the wardrobe while the Duke of Bumble—whom I assume is the villain of the piece—"

"He is the clown."

"Exactly. He comes across as a bit of a knobby know-it-all."

As she'd written him to be.

And she'd put that part in the play after she'd returned from Scotland. She'd been so thoroughly annoyed with the Duke of Baynton, she'd had to use him as a character.

Had he recognized himself?

His level gaze told her nothing.

She wondered what he'd thought of the description of Bumble as being unusually handsome? She'd not meant to write those words but they had flowed from her pen, and now, short of her rewriting the page, were very much a part of the story.

"He has a tendency to want everything his way," Sarah informed him. "The duke in the play, that is."

He changed the subject.

"I didn't know what you liked to eat so I took the liberty of ordering the best the kitchen offered." He stood, crossed to the table, and lifted the covers of the dish nearest her. "This is hare. They do it very well here. And this," he said, lifting the other cover, "is God's gift to England, roast beef. The chef is French. I once tried to hire him but he prefers his kitchen here."

The food smelled enticing. "Your choice," he invited. "I'm happy with either. Oh, and there is wine, or cider, if you prefer."

Nobly, Sarah did not want to accept his food until they had discussed the terms of what was going to happen between them, except her brain could not muster the thoughts necessary to form any demands until she'd eaten. "The hare is fine." Sarah sat at the table, picked up a fork and tried not to dive into her plate headfirst.

Baynton appeared hungry as well. He did the gallant thing and poured her a glass of cider and then he did justice to his beef. As for herself, Sarah finished her plate and, if she'd been alone, would probably have licked up every last bit of sauce.

Food was a great restorative.

Pushing her plate to the side, she folded her hands in her lap to appear as composed as one could wearing a simple sheet for a dress and said, "I wish you to know my terms."

He reacted as if she'd fired a warning shot. He sat back, a hand resting on the table. "Very well."

Sarah eyed her play on the desk. For once, she would not let herself be sold cheap.

"You offered a house," she said.

"I did."

"And to help me find Geoff and Charles."

"Perkins is looking even as we sit here."

"I would have the company paid."

He tilted his head. "The company?"

"The actors and the workers who helped with the *Review*. Many of them are in worse circumstances than I am." She gave him a glance, wondering what he thought.

His expression was considering, as if he took her measure . . . and she felt uncomfortable. It was not her way to demand.

"I'm certain," he said at last, "that a generous benefactor can be found for them if we are unable to retrieve what they are owed from Geoff and Charles."

Sarah was surprised to realize she'd been holding her breath. She released it, nodded. "Thank you."

"Is that all?" he asked.

"No." She forced herself to meet his eye. "My mother started as an actress. She was quite good, or at least everyone assured me she was. But the theater is fickle and eventually, she received smaller and smaller roles until she said she felt like she ceased to exist."

He was listening and Sarah shifted her gaze away from his intense study. The ability to give his full concentration to one person was one of his gifts, she noticed. It could be a bit overwhelming.

She continued. "Her first keeper was Lord Twyndale, my father, although he would never deign to recognize me as his child. Men are of two minds—some are generous to all of their children, even their bastards. And there are those who pretend their by-blows do not exist." She couldn't prevent a rueful smile. There had been a time when her father's rejection had been a crushing blow. Now, it was of just passing import in her life.

"After Twyndale turned her loose, Mother had a succession of lovers until her death. Some were kind; some were not. Some I hid from." Did he understand what she was saying?

"My half-sister Julia—she was Charlene's mother and a child born on the right side of the blanket—took me in when I was thirteen. She gave me an education of sorts but she had her hands full with Dearne. The man lived to gamble."

"I had heard that of him."

"He was so self-destructive." She shook her

head. "However, Julia taught me that a woman could have honor. She was always strong and graceful, no matter what happened in her life and I vowed to be like her. I did not want to earn my living on my back the way my mother had."

Baynton shifted in his chair.

"Does my plain speaking make you uncomfortable, Your Grace? Good," she said, not letting him answer. "I want you to know what becoming your mistress will cost me. We are talking about my soul, Your Grace. About everything I wanted to believe of myself."

A concerned line formed between his brows, but he said nothing.

Sarah forged on. "So here is the heart of the matter. I wish to stage my play. I would have your support." With a benefactor as wealthy as the Duke of Baynton, she would see the *Widow* done right. "That is the cost of my being your woman."

He looked over to the play spread out on the desk. "Would you have me purchase a theater?"

That was a shocking suggestion. He could buy a theater? "You needn't purchase it. One could be let."

He considered her statement and then said, "In turn for my meeting your requirements, what are you offering me?"

Sarah blinked. She had thought it was obvious. He'd asked her to go to bed with him, a simple transaction that happened all over London at any given moment.

Or was this tactic to make her reconsider her worth? The Duke of Baynton had to be a shrewd negotiator. He could not be so successful if he wasn't.

She stood and walked around the table to him.

He watched her approach, moving his chair so he faced her like a king accepting homage. Such a scene this would be upon the stage and Sarah knew the moment was at hand to play her part for all she was worth.

She was not ashamed of her body. As an actress, her body was a tool she used to create a character. However, it was one thing to appear almost naked as the Siren, and something completely different to stand before him as herself. Sarah Pettijohn, actress, seamstress, struggling playwright, loving aunt, and now mistress to one of the most powerful men in London.

She opened the sheet and let it fall down around her feet.

Chapter Ten

For a long moment, she refused to breathe, to think, or to feel. She forced herself to meet his gaze, refusing to give in to the shame inside her.

Baynton sat as if frozen. His eyes had gone bright and hungry. They took in every curve, every hair of her person.

And then he stood. Almost reverently, he walked to her and took her by both arms. He kissed her.

His earlier kiss had been timid compared to this one. He was not shy about holding her. Her breasts flattened against the material of his waistcoat. He was aroused and strong and pressed against the center of her being.

It was as if he wished to devour her.

All Sarah could do against the onslaught of his desire was try to keep herself calm, to not panic.

What role are you playing, Sarah? Bathsheba before David? Cleopatra before Antony? Judy before Punch?

Oh, yes, she was the consummate actress.

She tried to focus on the kiss and not the worries. A mistress should be willing to be kissed. She struggled to relax but her mind was too busy. She knew where this was going, could anticipate the pain already.

Don't cry, she warned herself. *Many women found pleasure in this. Think of anything other than what is happening. Think of a life where you never have to submit again.*

Let him use her.

Her play was worth whatever it took, even her pride.

He must have sensed her reticence. He kissed harder as if willing a response from her.

This morning, she had submitted. He had surprised her with his kiss. It had actually been more than pleasant, but this was different. Baynton wanted more than a kiss. He would want it all and then he would learn how miserable she was at pleasing a man. Roland had always claimed that she was little more than a board in bed.

Then again, what was it to her if Baynton was not happy? He wanted to bed the Siren. The Siren was not Sarah. The Siren was a creation of many fantasies.

She also believed that what the duke wanted, whether he would admit it or not, was to best his friend Rovington, to enjoy feeling superior in that peculiar way men had about one another.

All she had to do was hush her frantic mind and be still. After all, the act of joining never took long. It was messy and abrupt, but over quickly.

The duke would do as he wished and then she would be free. She just needed to be patient.

Baynton lifted her up in his arms.

She recalled how he'd looked this morning without his shirt. He had the chest of a man un-afraid to use his body.

He carried her into the bedroom and laid her on the bed. He began to undress himself, his fingers fumbling with the buttons in his urgency.

A few minutes more.

She closed her eyes. He was fully aroused and perhaps it was better if she didn't watch. Her breathing had gone shallow. She inhaled fully, letting the air fill her lungs, holding it, and then released it. She tried not to think of the past, of the sweatiness, the searing pain, the tearing—the loss of her child . . .

Push those thoughts away. Her fingers closed around handfuls of the coverlet. She could do this. To live the life she longed to live, to have a chance to see her work staged, she could do this.

A boot hit the floor, then another. She heard the slide of clothing against skin.

The mattress gave as he placed his weight upon it.

The spiciness of his shaving soap mingled with the scent of masculine need—and then he stretched out beside her.

His hand cupped her breast. Her nipple tightened, responding to the warmth of his touch.

"You are so beautiful," he whispered. His voice had deepened, and instinctively, between her legs, she felt a need. Her mind might be shrieking to be wary, but a part of her responded, and that frightened her all the more. No good came of losing control.

No good came of stalling the inevitable.

Without opening her eyes, she spread her legs. Cold air brushed the most delicate folds of her body.

She expected him to pounce on her then. She knew he was ready. She anticipated the weight of his body, the intrusion.

And yet, he did nothing.

In fact, his hand on her breast had not moved. She'd been so overwrought, it had taken her a moment to realize how still he'd become.

She kept her eyes closed. She knew what was coming. He would be disappointed. Roland had always had sharp words when they reached this stage. Angry barbs that he hurled before he pounded himself into her, claiming her dry and haggard.

"Sarah?"

Baynton did not sound angry. He sounded confused.

Be quick. Be done quick, she wanted to whisper . . .

"You're trembling."

She didn't answer. She kept her eyes closed.

His hand caressed her breast again. She waited for him to do more, the tension almost beyond what she could bear—and the mattress dipped as he rolled off the bed.

Sarah opened her eyes, surprised.

He was pulling on his breeches. She frowned, not understanding. She reached for the coverlet to hide her nakedness before sitting up. "What is the matter?"

She knew the answer. She feared it. He found her disappointing.

Baynton reached for his shirt and pulled it over his head. She could see he was still aroused and probably uncomfortable. Roland had always told her that being hard and unfulfilled was a very painful state for a man.

He turned to her, ready to say something and

yet he did not speak. Those all-too-seeing eyes assessed her. She held the coverlet to her breasts. She shook her hair back out of the way.

Baynton sat on the edge of the bed, and she tensed.

He leaned toward her, and she stiffened.

"It isn't me, is it?" he said, his voice low as if he was reasoning more with himself than expecting an answer from her.

"*What* isn't you?" She threw the words out as if they were a challenge.

"The way you are right now. You are afraid." His expression wasn't one of repulsion or anger. Instead, he appeared concerned—and she couldn't stand it.

"*Do this.* Have me," she ordered, anger making her voice harsh, ugly . . . as ugly as she felt inside. She threw herself back on the bed. She tossed aside the coverlet and focused on the ceiling so that she wouldn't have to look at him. "*Do it.*"

"You act as if I will hurt you. Why, Sarah?" He spoke with empathy, and she hated him for it.

She rolled away from him and stood, the bed between them. Heedless of her nakedness, her fury all-consuming, she ground out, "Now I know why you are still a virgin. If this is the way you are around women, is it any wonder the deed hasn't been done?"

And then she braced herself.

Roland's temper had been quick. He'd not liked her tongue and there had been many a time she should have bitten it.

But Baynton didn't rise to her goading. Instead he answered, "Or perhaps I want something more from you than just doing 'the deed.'"

More?

The word vibrated in the air between them. He reached down and calmly started putting on his socks and his boots and she could have damned him.

Instead, she said, "There isn't any 'more.'"

"Aye, you may be right." He stood, pressing his heel into his boot. "But if there is, Sarah, then that is what I want. I certainly don't want rape."

He acted at ease and without rancor . . . but that could not be possible. Men did not like being thwarted.

"Don't resent me later because this was not done," she warned him. "I will not have you hold it against me. I offered myself."

"That you did. Duly noted." He picked up his vest coat as he walked to the door. "Be ready on the morrow. Talbert will take you around to look at theaters. Then there is the matter of a house.

I don't know if you will have time to search for both." He paused at the door, looked back at her. *All* of her. "And we'll need to buy clothes. I didn't realize mistresses were such devilishly tricky creatures. I shall see you tomorrow evening for dinner."

He walked out the door.

Sarah stood a moment, puzzled by his quiet acceptance of her. He wasn't angry.

Then what was he?

She suddenly felt exposed, naked in a way she'd never experienced before. She picked up the coverlet, held it in front of her. "What of our bargain?" she called out, moving toward the door.

The duke was in the sitting room, shrugging on his jacket. "What of it?"

"Do we have one? You asked me for something specific." He reached for his spectacles and placed them in an inside pocket. He tossed his neck cloth around his neck and began to absently retie it. "Don't you want me? Isn't that what all of this is about?"

"Do I want you?" he repeated softly with a hint of self-mockery. He approached her, stopping when the toes of his boots met her bare feet. He leaned forward, his lips brushing against the delicate place where her neck joined her shoulder. He held them there as if drinking in her warmth, her presence, her scent. She felt his breath release against her skin before he straightened.

Looking into her eyes, he admitted, "I want you very much. But not this way."

He stepped back. "I want to know you, Sarah. To understand you." He turned to the door.

"We shall do this," he promised pointing back toward the bedroom as he made his way across the sitting room. "It is the bargain between us. However, when I come to you, Sarah, it will be because *you* want me as much as I desire you." He reached for his hat and coat off the rack by the door.

"Then you shall never have me," she assured him.

If he heard, he did not reply. Instead, he opened the door and left.

He was gone.

Sarah stared at the closed door, her feelings in a jumble. *I want to know you, Sarah. To understand you.*

He asked for trust. She had none to give. Ever.

She moved to the sitting room. His presence lingered in the air around her. He was that powerful and she—well, she was nothing. If she were to vanish, to shrivel up and disappear, no one would know that she had even existed . . . and then her eyes fell upon the leather folder holding the only play she'd written that still existed. *Her* work.

Talbert will take you to look at theaters.

Men had made so many promises to her over the years. The most laughable had been her marriage vows because when she'd been physically broken, that is when Roland had abandoned her completely.

But you want to believe, a small voice inside said.

That was true. In her plays, she wrote about love, about honesty and goodness between men and women, and about all the amazing things she prayed must exist someplace in the world and not just upon a stage in a theater. She wished to believe, but wishes were not truths.

Sarah walked over to the table, ran her hand across the leather folder as if the words inside could give her strength, and they did. They were her soul.

Whatever else befell her, she must try to see her work staged. She'd borne too much to give up now.

Then you shall never have me.

God, he was a fool.

Pride, his temper . . . and shame stopped Gavin at the top of the stairs in the hotel hall.

She had him in knots. Primal need begged him to go back, to crawl to her if necessary, to take what he wanted from her.

What did it matter that she offered herself to

him with all the charm of a bored whore? He could imagine himself fumbling his way with her, laboring over her while she stared at the ceiling and wished she was anywhere else but under him.

Aye, he could have claimed the pound of flesh his money had purchased, could have had his rite of passage—but he would have been disgusted with himself.

Someone was coming up the stairs. Gavin set his hat on his head, pulling the brim low over his eyes as he made his way down. It was hard to walk, to be sane. His body ached for her.

It had taken every measure of his vaunted self-control to not ravage her. But if he had slaked his lust on her, she would hate him forever.

And he didn't want that from Sarah.

The realization was a bit of a shock. He should not have such strong feelings for her. No good could come of it because there could be no future between them.

She was an actress and he was a duke expected to marry a woman of good family, breeding, and fortune. Why, Sarah was as old as he was. How could he be so attracted to her?

Perhaps her lure was the bit of a mystery about her. She'd put forth a brave face but it had been a false emotion. Her body on the bed had been as taut as the rope on a windlass. The proud spirit he'd always associated with her had vanished and in its place had been fear.

He hadn't liked seeing her that way. She had been expecting ill treatment. She'd steeled herself for it. Worse, she'd retreated inside herself. He could have been any man. She hadn't cared.

Gavin stepped out onto the street, drawing deeply of the city's night air.

The doorman asked if he wished to have a ride signaled for him. He shook his head. He needed the walk. Menheim was less than a mile from the Clarendon.

As he made his way, he could almost hear Rovington laugh at him. If Rov had been in his place, he would have won his bet right or not.

Rovington's name reminded him that he still had details to settle about the duel.

So he was happily surprised when he returned home to find his youngest brother Ben sitting on the steps in the front hall, a glass of Gavin's whisky in his hand.

Gavin handed his coat and his hat to the night footman. "Are you a mind reader that you knew I needed to see you?" he asked Ben.

"You missed the Pensions vote today, brother," Ben replied.

The vote. How could Gavin have forgotten the vote? And yet, once he saw how upset Sarah had been when she'd discovered her plays ruined, he had not been able to leave her. He'd had to stay to be certain she was all right when she woke.

Of course, Talbert had urged him to leave, but Gavin had sent him back to Menheim, promising he would make it to Westminster in time for the vote. In truth, those votes always took hours. There were delays or negotiations. He *had* meant to be there for it . . . and then he'd started reading Sarah's play and had lost track of time.

"It slipped my mind." He moved toward the front reception room where there was always a good supply of his whisky.

"Well, that is a wonder of wonders," Ben said, following him. "My brother is human. Liverpool will expect an answer, of course, one better than, 'I forgot.'"

"You will think of one. And how is Elin?" Ben's wife was expecting their first child.

"Sleepy," Ben answered. "She has become a true snug in bed. I should also warn you that Mother is greatly offended with you. She had arranged an introduction this evening with you and a suitable young woman?"

Gavin groaned his remorse. Before leaving the room at the Clarendon, Talbert had also reminded him not to forget the engagement for the evening.

"I'll apologize in the morning and do what I

must for the young lady." What a wrinkle. Gavin knew his mother would, rightly, have more than a few tart words for him. He poured whisky into a glass.

"And," Ben continued cheerfully, but with that hint of mischief that warned Gavin he'd better listen well, "you have set tongues wagging all over London. I heard your name in the halls of Whitehall today and on the street on my way home. I am also certain you have been the topic of conversation at every dinner party this evening and every soiree."

"Because I missed the vote?"

"No, because you have taken a mistress."

Gavin put down his drink.

"From what I hear," Ben continued, "she isn't just any woman. She is the one every man in London wants—including Rovington. Is it true he issued a challenge?"

"Aye. May I count on you to be my second?"

"Proudly."

"Be prepared. Rov is out for blood. His pride is on the line. He'd wagered a fortune that he would bed her, a fortune he can't pay if he loses."

"That is what I've heard. Bad business. He was very vocal about you before the vote today. He claims you betrayed him."

"I put him in his place."

"Meanwhile, the men who had bet against him had their hands out. He is in a devil of a fix. He also made a point of letting me know that the prime minister will be waiting a good long while for his Money Bill to come out of the Commons."

"The bastard. It is one thing to have an argument with me to but to keep that money from our generals is a different matter."

"Exactly. Liverpool is not happy."

"I can't imagine so."

"He asked me to give you a message."

"And that is?" Gavin asked, expecting it to be a rebuke for Rov's threats.

"He told me to tell you to 'put a hole in the man.'"

"I will," Gavin answered grimly. "I will."

Chapter Eleven

$\mathcal{S}$arah surprised herself by going back to bed and sleeping long and hard in spite of the earlier nap.

This time, her sleep was filled with dreams. She dreamed of her mother and summer days when Sarah had been sent into the garden to play.

"Don't come into the house until I call for you," her mother said in her dreams, words Sarah had come to understand meant she was to disappear, to pretend not to exist. Her mother's gentlemen were far more important to her than a daughter.

"Give us a few moments, my little love."

"Leave us be while you play with your doll, precious."

"Do not interrupt Mother when she is with her friend."

"Do not knock on my door—"

The sound of someone knocking on the door woke Sarah. They had apparently been doing so for some time because a male voice—Mr. Talbert's—said impatiently, "Mrs. Pettijohn? Mrs. *Pettijohn*."

Sarah stretched, blinking and trying to regain her bearings. The sunlight in the sitting room told her it was early morning. She was still naked and wrapped up in the coverlet.

The knock at the door was turning into pounding. "Mrs. Pettijohn, we have many tasks today and I have a dressmaker with me."

Dressmaker? Sarah unwrapped herself from the bedclothes and stood. Her ruined forest-green dress was where she'd placed it over a chair. Yes, a dressmaker was in great demand.

"One moment," she managed to squawk out, her voice hoarse. She pulled on the dress then quickly polished her teeth, splashed cold water from the basin on her face, and gave her hair a brush. The hip tub and bath things were still in the corner. She skirted around them and went out into the sitting room.

Once he'd heard her voice, Talbert had stopped his incessant knocking. However, that didn't stop him from letting his impatience be known with a snort of derision when she opened the door.

Sarah could have slammed it in his face except for the crowd of women behind him. They carried bolts of fabric, beautiful materials in colored muslins and radiant silks.

Talbert indicated with a snap of his fingers for the women to follow him into the room. The woman who entered first was obviously the leader of the dressmakers. Her burgundy gown was an understatement in refined grace. She wore a charming straw hat trimmed in silk ribbon and one jaunty ostrich feather. Her dark hair was streaked with the silver of age and yet the amusement in her eye over Talbert's high-handedness gave her youth.

With a professional's glance, she seemed capable of measuring Sarah's person. She noted the bare feet, the wrinkled dress, the unruly hair. It took all of Sarah's considerable will to not run to hide in the bedroom.

"This is Mrs. Hillsman," Talbert threw out as if the name should mean nothing to Sarah—but it did.

"Mrs. *Hillsman*?" Sarah had to stop from sinking to her knees in admiration. In a city overrun with fashionable dressmakers and seamstresses, Mrs. Hillsman was the finest of them all. Only the very crème of London Society were her clients. Her dresses were in such demand that the papers made mention when a gentlewoman wore one to an event.

And the idea that Sarah was standing there looking like a wild-haired harridan in front of the esteemed Mrs. Hillsman horrified her. Dear Lord, she still had sleep in her eyes.

Fortunately, Talbert was on hand to keep Sarah firmly in reality. He opened the ledger he carried, tapped something on the page with his finger and then snapped the book shut.

With a haughty flare of his nostrils, he said to the dressmaker, "You will provide Mrs. Pettijohn with a full wardrobe. Please keep in mind her station in life. She is dressing for His Grace and *not* her own preferences." He gave Sarah a tight smile as he said the last. He then added, "You do understand what is expected, Mrs. Hillsman? I'm certain you have dealt with these sorts of circumstances before."

"I do indeed, Mr. Talbert." She spoke with the authority of a woman who understood her business and her place in the world. She also considered Talbert a minion.

Sarah was jealous of her quiet confidence.

"*Mrs. Pettijohn,*" Talbert barked as if Sarah needed scolding, "I will return to take you to look at—" he opened his book and reread it again to confirm "—theaters and possible residences at half past one. We have a full afternoon before us. Do not keep me waiting in the hall the way you did this morning."

With that, he closed his ledger, performed a most

excellent about-face, and marched out of the room, a soldier for the Duke of Baynton. Lest anyone believe he was enjoying his new duties of shepherding Sarah, he slammed the door behind him.

And Sarah wanted to go after him and rail at him for such dismissive treatment. She confronted the esteemed dressmaker and her staff who had witnessed his patronizing behavior. They were certainly forming the worst sort of impression of her. "How dare he behave as if I'm a pest? This is not my idea. I've been locked in here by the Duke of Baynton. He left me without a key and no way to fend for myself."

"No key?" Mrs. Hillsman questioned. "Like this one?" She walked to the desk and picked up a key that had been beside Sarah's play. "In fact, the door was not locked. Mr. Talbert assumed it was, but I did not hear a key turn in the lock when you opened it."

A hot flush made Sarah shift uncomfortably. Baynton had left the key for her. "I did not realize."

"And if you are a prisoner, this is a lovely prison," Mrs. Hillsman observed, taking off her gloves and giving the room the same scrutiny she had used on Sarah's person. Seeing her assistants still held their wares, she said, "Put those down and have all these taken away." She indicated the serving dishes from last night's meal on the table.

"This stack of papers as well." She referred to the *Widow*.

Sarah swooped in and picked up the play. "I shall see to this." She carried it in to the bedroom.

Meanwhile, Mrs. Hillsman was giving orders to her assistant carrying the dinner tray into the hall. "Have a tray sent up of breakfast dishes. You know what I like. And a pot of good strong black tea. A hot one, mind you. Test it yourself to see that it is right."

"Yes, ma'am," the assistant said.

Sarah stood in the bedroom door, taking in the busyness of the room. While the assistant left with the empty dishes, two others were moving the furniture toward the wall, clearing an open space. Another placed a huge leather portfolio on the table and then began setting out scissors, pins, and chalk from a basket. Mrs. Hillsman took off her smart bonnet and set it carefully on the table next to her gloves.

"Thank you for ordering breakfast," Sarah said. "I would not have known what to do, not here."

Mrs. Hillsman opened the portfolio. It was filled with dress drawings. She began flipping through the pages. "There is a floor steward at the top of the steps. You need only stick your head out the door and tell him what you need. He knows who is paying your account. He will do anything to please you, as will I."

"Oh," Sarah said, mortified that she was not more worldly. If Mrs. Hillsman had not told her about the steward, she might have starved in the room. She crossed to look over the dressmaker's shoulder. The gowns on each page were of the very height of fashion.

Mrs. Hillsman set aside one particularly lovely day dress and assessed Sarah a moment before studying the fabrics her assistants had spread out on the furniture. Offhandedly, she said, "I usually don't make these calls myself."

"What kind of calls do you refer to?" Sarah asked.

"The mistress ones." A well-manicured hand on the drawing, Mrs. Hillsman faced her. "I came because I had to meet the woman who has caught the interest of the Duke of Baynton. Many have angled for him but you are his first mistress to my knowledge."

Sarah could confirm her conjecture, but chose to be silent. She had enough respect for Baynton to not reveal his secrets.

At her silence, Mrs. Hillsman nodded her approval. "There are many who will ask me about you. They will ply me for information."

"And what shall you tell them?"

"That it is not my place to blabber," Mrs. Hillsman answered.

"Yet, you are personally curious as to why he chose me?"

"A woman always is," the dressmaker said. "It is our nature. Later today, when my special clientele come calling in my shop, I shall artfully drop hints that I have met you. My custom will increase threefold this week from those looking for an excuse to hear me describe the woman who inspired a duel between two important nobles."

The duel. How could Sarah have forgotten? "I had no hand in its making. In fact, if it is in my power to dissuade the duke and Lord Rovington to forget the challenge, I will do so."

"Even better," Mrs. Hillsman said, her voice taking on a bright tone. "If you succeed then I shall have met the woman who caused two honorable men to dishonor themselves."

"There is no honor in dueling."

"How little you know of men, Mrs. Pettijohn, and yet you have captured Baynton. There are times I wonder if God knows what He is doing?"

Before Sarah could manage a suitable retort, a sound at the door warned them that the assistant had returned with two hotel stewards carrying breakfast trays. "Good, here is something to start off our morning. Mrs. Pettijohn, tea? You will need all your strength for what we have planned for you."

And she was right.

As an actress, Sarah was accustomed to good dressmaking and the measurements needed. She'd also worked with the wardrobe mistresses enough to understand garment construction and to be a judge of quality materials.

The fabrics Mrs. Hillsman had brought were the best and very suitable for Sarah's coloring. Apparently, the duke himself had sent instructions to Mrs. Hillsman. He'd described Sarah's hair as "the red of the richest garnets." Therefore, Mrs. Hillsman had chosen the greens and blues that Sarah herself favored, as well as ivory muslins. White never suited her coloring.

There were also laces and ribbons to choose and within the first hour, Mrs. Hillsman sent her assistant with an order for the shoemaker and milliner to join them and to bring whatever they had available because it was needed *today*. Another assistant was sent off to purchase stockings, gloves, and small clothes. Another was dispatched to Mrs. Hillsman's shop for a dress that was almost finished for another client that the dressmaker believed would be better suited for Sarah.

"You truly have nothing," Mrs. Hillsman happily complained. "We shall be working day and night to finish your wardrobe so that you have something to wear." Sarah did not want to think how much all of this was costing Baynton. At the same time, it was a pleasure to choose without worry about cost.

By noon, Sarah felt as if she had been dragged behind a cart. However, the woman who stared at her reflection in the glass was a far cry from the one who had woken naked that morning.

The dress that had been waylaid for Sarah's use was a fine muslin dyed bishop's blue and covered with tiny lavender flowers. It sported cap sleeves and a low neckline. One of the assistants had styled Sarah's hair, pinning it high on her head and letting a few curls fall free around her face.

"He won't be able to stop looking at your chest," Mrs. Hillsman predicted, primping the lace edging around Sarah's bodice a bit, "although few men need such a lovely display to stare." She frowned and murmured, "The dress does cry for a necklace, but I shall leave that to you to earn, my dear. When the duke is ready to buy you jewelry, contact me. I know an excellent jeweler who will pay us both a commission."

"A commission?" Sarah repeated, surprised.

"Of course." Mrs. Hillsman shook her head. "You really are very green at this, and you'd best wise up. I like you, Sarah. Now that we know each other a touch better, I can confess I had assumed you would be much younger and all dewy fresh. One of those girls that hasn't a wrinkle on her skin."

"There was a time I didn't," Sarah said. "However, if the duke wishes someone flawless, he has chosen the wrong woman."

Mrs. Hillsman laughed. "Perhaps he is looking for something else. Perhaps he is that rare man who values character."

"I don't know if *that* is a compliment or not," Sarah answered.

"It is, Mrs. Pettijohn. Never doubt for a moment, it is." The dressmaker held out her hand, an offer of friendship.

Sarah took it. "Thank you. I *don't* know what I'm doing."

"All you must do is please him—and in that dress, half your work is done. Any other time you need advice, you may call on me. You have a good head on your shoulders. You shall do well."

"What do you mean?"

"You have some sense. There aren't many ways for women like us to make our own way in the world. Most of the young things waste opportunity."

"You have had a protector?"

"How do you think I gained my shop?" Mrs. Hillsman answered.

"My mother was not so fortunate. Or wise."

Sarah found it suddenly hard to look at her reflection. She turned away. "She died poor and alone. All of her lovers abandoned her. I swore I'd never be like her."

"You aren't," Mrs. Hillsman said sagely. "You are a survivor, as am I. Those others, they lose sight of what is important. Eventually, they lose faith."

"And what *is* important?" Sarah wondered. Right now, her once ordered world seemed a jumbled mess.

Mrs. Hillsman didn't even take a moment's reflection. "Security. It is all any of us need."

But not me, Sarah wanted to say. *I have big dreams.* And yet she held her tongue. After all, perhaps the older woman was right and Sarah had been chasing the wrong thing such as her need to see her talent validated.

An assistant came to the door with a shawl in colors that reminded Sarah of a peacock's tail. "Yes, Eloise, that is what I wanted." Mrs. Hillsman motioned the girl forward, took the shawl and draped it over Sarah's shoulders. "With the straw hat we purchased, you are ready for Mr. Talbert. Don't let him bully you. He is afraid you will have more power than he has, and you will."

With that confident prediction, Mrs. Hillsman called, "Come, everyone. It is time to leave. We shall send the dresses as we finish them, Mrs. Pettijohn. Wear them with joy."

In moments, Mrs. Hillsman and her entourage picked up every bolt, pin, and other accouterment of their art and left, just as Mr. Talbert arrived, followed by a footman in the Baynton colors carrying an ebony wooden box with brass fittings in his arms.

The secretary entered the sitting room his usual officious self, but then pulled up sharply at the sight of Sarah.

For a long moment, he appeared speechless.

"Hello, Mr. Talbert," she said, pulling on the short white gloves purchased for the dress.

"Yes, hello," he managed and then took another stare as if he still couldn't quite believe his eyes.

"Are you ready?" Sarah asked, rather enjoying herself.

"There is a vehicle waiting downstairs. However, first, His Grace asked me to see this delivered to you." He nodded for the footman to put the chest on the table. "He picked it out himself and bid me to tell you that he wished he could give it to you in person. Unfortunately, there are some difficulties over a vote he missed yesterday—" he said this as if she was in some way responsible "—and he is currently in a meeting with the prime minister."

Sarah took off a glove to run a hand over the smooth wood. "What is it?"

"I don't know. Perhaps you should open in it," the secretary said with a hint of a snit.

She lifted the handle and was delighted to discover that the box was a traveling secretary complete with an inkpot, pens, and a stack of paper. She touched the paper, overwhelmed by the gift.

"His Grace said for me to set up an account at Fieldings, the stationer on Pall Mall." Talbert placed a card on the table beside the box. "Any time you wish to order more supplies, you may do so."

"This is too generous," Sarah murmured.

"His Grace is a generous man," Talbert said. "Now, if you are done staring at the box, we need be on our way. I have a schedule."

"Of course, let us go." Sarah picked up the key from the table and locked the door as they left. She had a puzzling moment when she stopped at the top of the stairs to ask the floor steward to remove the dishes and the cold bath from her room. She didn't know if she should also hand him her key or not.

"He has a key to all the locks," Mr. Talbert said, rightly guessing her dilemma.

She gave both men a smile to hide her discomfort over her naivetiés and went downstairs.

Sarah had been so disheartened when she first arrived at the Clarendon, she did not remember very much of Baynton's leading her across the reception area. She now appreciated her lovely clothes that allowed her to hold her head high as she made her way to the front door and out onto the white stone step.

She remembered Mrs. Hillsman's words about all the gossip over Baynton's mistress. She wondered if there were those who stared. She tried not to pay attention but moved with unhurried grace to the ducal coach waiting for her.

Apparently, Mr. Talbert was aware of the fuss. "That was easier than I anticipated," he said once they were in the coach. He knocked on the ceiling to signal the driver to go.

"Where are we going?"

Mr. Talbert referred to his ever present ledger book. "His Grace suggested a place called the Bishop's Hill Theater. He understood that it might be available for lease."

Geoff and Charles's old place would be the perfect stage for *Widow*. Had the duke known that? She doubted he had. Instead, he would have surmised the landlord would be happy to have a paying lease, and he was.

He bowed and scraped before Sarah and Mr. Talbert to a point that was almost embarrassing.

"What do you think?" Mr. Talbert asked Sarah as they stood on the stage still in need of a cleaning after the *Naughty Review*.

She was pleasantly surprised that she had a voice in the matter. She was tempted to ask to look at other theaters just to see how *much* of a voice she possessed, but dared not tempt fate.

"This is fine," she managed.

"Good," Mr. Talbert answered. To the theater owner he said, "I shall contact you in the morning at eleven to discuss the details."

"Yes, sir. Very good, sir. Please, offer my congratulations to His Grace. If he wishes to change the theater name, he may."

Mr. Talbert dismissed him with a wave of his hand that was more ducal than any gesture Sarah had seen Baynton make. They returned to the coach.

"That was easy," Sarah said, settling back on the coach's velvet cushions. "Having money does make all the difference."

She'd spoken her thoughts aloud and had not considered how they could be interpreted. Mr. Talbert's frown warned her—not well.

Sitting up, she was ready to clarify her thoughtlessness, but the secretary spoke first, holding her off with his raised palm.

"Please, Mrs. Pettijohn, no excuses. I understand what the rules are. You are not the first mistress I have been expected to escort around for an employer." He said this as if he would just as soon toss her into the Thames.

And Sarah had the unsettling sense that this man had a grievance—not against her—but certainly against Baynton. He was not happy with his employer.

"Let me inform you," Mr. Talbert continued, "that these arrangements between a woman and her benefactor always end. You may believe you own the enviable position, but you do not."

"Are you warning me, sir?" If so, Sarah could tell him a thing or two, having watched her mother and her lovers over the years . . . but there was something else here. A discontent that she sensed had nothing to do with her.

"Why should I do that?" he said, his face suddenly a mask. "However, I shall ask you not to lead him to his ruin."

"I have no desire to do such a thing," Sarah answered soberly.

"Aye, but I don't trust what is between the two of you," Mr. Talbert said. "I grew concerned in the way he used his own coat to protect you in the rain yesterday when we learned your landlord had turned you out. He also missed several important engagements for you. He's never done that before to my knowledge. He is an important man, Mrs. Pettijohn. England needs him and the political world is fraught with intrigue. He has enemies."

"I'm not one of them."

Talbert gave her a tight smile. "Whether you are or you are not, I'll not stand by and idly watch you toy with the honest emotions of this great man. After all, I know your kind."

"You do not know me at all sir," she said. "And you have no basis other than your own prejudice to believe ill of me."

"My prejudice? Heavens, woman, he's fighting a duel over you. Have you stopped to think of the cost if he is killed?"

Sarah sat back in the seat, both incensed and justifiably upset by his accusation because she did feel guilty. "I had nothing to do with their argument."

"Says the Siren," he replied softly, his disdain in every word.

"The Siren is not *me*, the person," Sarah shot back. "I did not ask His Grace to miss his appointments. Is it not your responsibility to see that he maintains his schedule?"

"And he usually listens to me. Or he did . . . before you appeared."

"Oh dear," Sarah replied mockingly. After years in the theater, she'd worked with spite before. She understood this game. Talbert had no cause to hold a grudge against her, but she sensed there was more to the matter. Perhaps he'd been disgruntled for some time? If that were the case, he would certainly be annoyed at the attention the duke lavished on her.

The coach began to slow to a halt. They pulled up in front of a charming house off of Knightsbridge, a neighborhood where she would never have imagined she could have lived.

"This is the first house I have chosen for you to see," Mr. Talbert started, his manner formal, distant, but then he changed abruptly. He asked, "Are you sincere in your desire to help His Grace? To prevent the duel? I warn you, Lord Rovington has already killed two men dueling."

"And what of the duke?"

"He has never faced the fire or sword of another. He is a novice."

"Dear Lord," Sarah whispered. The implications of what could happen were horrific. "I did not ask to be a part of their argument," she said. "I have done nothing and wish only for them to set this argument aside." She thought of the man who had refused to basely use her last night, who had been so generous to her this day. "Please believe me, this is not what I want."

"Speaking to you now, I believe you." He paused a moment as if considering and then said, "Perhaps there is something you and I may both do together to save His Grace."

"What would that be?"

Again, he seemed to deliberate, and then pulled from his jacket a small vial. "This is a sleeping draught. It will not hurt whoever drinks it but they will slumber deeply."

"You wish to give this to the duke?"

Mr. Talbert lowered his voice to say, "I believe *you* should give it to him."

Shocked at the suggestion, Sarah said, "Why?"

"Because he is taken with you. If he oversleeps in your arms, he'll assume the fault was his. I have word that the duel will be on the morrow. At dawn. If you give this to him before you take him to your bed, he will not wake for a good twelve or more hours."

"But he will miss the duel. What will happen?"

"He'll live. Lord Rovington will be declared the winner because his opponent failed to show. Meanwhile, I will spread the word that His Grace didn't show because he was so lost in making love to you—and all will be well because each man will have what he wants."

The plan was simple enough to make sense.

"Isn't it a matter of honor that the duke appear?"

Sarah asked. "Will there be repercussions harmful to His Grace?"

"What good is honor when one is dead? Of course," he continued, sitting back, "if you have no desire to see him safe, well, I must consider another way to administer the draught or let him die—"

"I will help," Sarah said. She could not have Baynton's death on her conscience. Mr. Talbert's plan was sound. She held out her hand.

With an approving smile, the secretary said, "I must apologize, Mrs. Pettijohn. I was wrong about your character." He gave her the vial. She tucked it in the small pocket of her jacket.

"How shall I see that he drinks it?" she wondered.

"I'm assured it has little taste. He always enjoys a bit of whisky before bed. I had been thinking to find a way to pour this into his glass."

She nodded mutely. The plan seemed simple. It would also stave off the inevitable bedding . . . and that was good. She was not ready yet. She didn't know if she would ever be ready.

Mr. Talbert opened the door and climbed out. His tone was warm as he said, "Come, Mrs. Pettijohn, I believe you will like this house." He invited her to climb out of the coach.

She accepted Mr. Talbert's hand as she alighted.

She did like the house though she barely registered anything she saw. Her thoughts were on the vial in her possession.

Whether Baynton was a great man or not, last night he had showed restraint beyond any she would have expected from a man. Today, he coupled it with kindness.

And, their differences between them aside, she found herself willing to do whatever she must to keep him whole and healthy. Even trickery.

Chapter Twelve

Gavin expected to spend a few unpleasant moments with the prime minister. He was certain Liverpool had choice words about the vote the day before.

But upon greeting Gavin in chambers and their taking their chairs, the prime minister surprised the duke by saying, "I understand that you are *enjoying* yourself." He winked his meaning . . . but Gavin wasn't certain he understood.

His mind was on the vote. Was this Liverpool's sly way of letting Gavin know he was disappointed?

"Sir?"

"The Siren." Liverpool looked around his office as if he feared someone lurked who might overhear him. "She's yours, right?"

Of all the topics Gavin had expected to discuss with the prime minister this morning, Sarah was not one of them. And the term *she's yours* was a delicate one.

But Liverpool needed no answer. He'd been speaking rhetorically. He'd already formed his own conclusions about Gavin's relationship with Sarah. "I wish I could have attended her performance but then I did not think it completely proper for the prime minister to be seen in that crowd. Or possibly safe. I'd not have those heads of cabbages and mushy tomatoes usually reserved for disliked performers thrown at my head."

"It was a rowdy crowd," Gavin assured him.

And since the assassination of the former prime minister, Perceval, at the hands of an angry citizen last May, caution was warranted.

"I would have liked to have seen her knee Rovington," Liverpool responded wistfully.

"That was a good moment," Gavin had to agree.

"So . . ." The prime minister leaned across his desk. "Is she *all* everyone claims?"

Gavin's first response was anger. *What* did they claim her to be?

Of course, he knew. He'd thought the same . . . and the image of her trembling in the bed with fear the night before rose in his mind. The memory had haunted his dreams. Dogged his steps all morning.

He didn't answer the prime minister. Throttling a head of state was bad form.

Instead, he did the ducal thing and changed the subject. "You wish to speak to me about the vote? I regret it did not go the way we anticipated."

Liverpool sat up. "I've been led to understand Rovington had a hand in the matter. We needed the Act passed."

"I shall see it is revisited."

"Thank you, Your Grace. And about the military money bill in the Commons. Rovington is making noise especially with the members who do not support our policies. Does the fool have no fear?"

"Apparently not."

"We need that bill to go forward. We have two battle fronts and we cannot fight without those monies."

"Commons will pass the bill."

"You put Rovington in power, Your Grace," Liverpool said. "I expect you to do what you must to keep him in check. Did your brother give you my suggestion?"

"To put a hole in him?"

Liverpool did not answer. He knew there was no need.

Gavin spoke. "It was my mistake to recommend him for Chairman of the Committees. I sought to help a friend and earnestly believed he would do a good job for all of us. Apparently there were parts of his character I did not know."

"There are no friends in politics, not when power is involved," Liverpool answered.

How many times had his father said the same thing? He'd drilled it into Gavin. *There is no place for friendship in your life. Not if you would be a great duke. Your power is predicated by the expectations of others.*

And Gavin had allowed Rov to slip past his guard. He'd let friendship blind him to Rov's faults. Now, betrayal was the price he paid. Just as his father had predicted.

He thought of Rov's wife Jane and her worries about her husband's mounting debts. The least Gavin could do was speak to her before everything came crashing down around her. Because it would. Her husband's excesses would ruin her as well.

"I expect you to do what is right, Your Grace," Liverpool continued. "These matters always resolve themselves when you are at hand."

To wield the stick, Gavin could add silently. He understood exactly what the prime minister meant and for the first time in his life, he experienced a flash of resentment.

It was startling. He usually thrived on these

challenges. They were a demonstration of his power. His father had groomed him to control such situations—and he never once questioned his purpose, until this moment.

As quickly as he could manage, Gavin took his leave and hustled himself out in the hall. Finding a window corner where he could take a private moment, he examined his reaction to Liverpool's instructions.

Gavin knew his position in life. He facilitated the smooth order of his political party. He'd made an error of judgment with Rov. It happens.

But why did a part of him bristle at the prime minister's assumption that Gavin must take care of the matter? Isn't that what Gavin had always done?

Gavin wasn't even certain what he was questioning except something inside of him was rebelling and he had no idea why.

It was almost as if he were mimicking the thoughts of the Widow Peregrine, a character in Sarah's play that he had read yesterday—and that was a ludicrous suggestion. Her play was a flight of fancy. He was living real life.

Granted, while reading the play, he had understood how Peregrine would grow tired of always being the moral person, the upright one. He had enjoyed her mutiny against the powers-that-be in the imaginary parish of Lofton. He'd silently cheered when she'd given the gossips their come-uppance and had been pleased when the obvious hero of the piece, Jonathan Goodwell, had recognized Peregrine's sterling qualities, admired her pluck, and had dropped to his knees in front of her and declared his undying love.

He had found *The Fitful Widow* vastly superior to Shakespeare's comedies, which he thought unbelievable and tedious. After one was read, the others were very much the same and lacked the brilliant wording of the tragedies.

In contrast, Sarah's play had entertained him, and yet, there was a kernel of human honesty in the characters. Why else would he have related this situation to what he'd read? Indeed, Sarah's play may have jolted his personal complacency and made him think a bit beyond his usual sensibilities—and that meant she had talent, even if she wasn't a male.

Offering to stage her play had been an easy matter after he'd read *The Fitful Widow*.

But widows were not dukes and he'd best not let anyone else know the comparisons he was drawing. He had meetings scheduled for the day and he should be about them.

And so he set off to undo the damage Rov was hell-bent on stirring with his childish actions. He and Gavin were already fighting a duel. That should have been enough for one man, but not Rov. He appeared bent on wreaking as much havoc as possible for no other reason than his own vanity. Gavin had truly misjudged his former friend.

As he went about his duties, he discovered Ben had been right in claiming tongues were wagging about his new mistress. Everywhere he went, he received winks and nudges and more than a few sly, jealous innuendoes from his peers. Bedding the Siren had burnished his reputation, which was puzzling to Gavin. He'd never once judged a man by the woman he poked.

Apparently he was in the minority.

And it wasn't just the men who commented. Feminine interest had also been stirred.

He discovered this when he attended the afternoon garden party to meet Miss Charnock.

Over breakfast, his mother had given him quite a set down. She had informed him she'd made excuses the night before, citing his importance to the nation. "However, I have rearranged an introduction for this afternoon at the Countess Fizzwill's garden party. I expect you to be there."

The only answer to such a declaration was, "Yes, Mother."

And he was there. The introduction went smoothly.

The Charnock heiress was an uncommonly

beautiful woman of what Gavin guessed to be two-and-twenty. She reminded him of a tigress with her abundance of tawny hair and dark, almond shaped eyes. There was a rumor that she had Indian blood. However, Gavin knew her family lines were impeccable because she'd already received the approval of his great-aunt Imogen. She was all a duchess should be—young, which meant she was fertile, very attractive, and well connected. That she was an heiress was an additional advantage. The title could never have enough money.

Gavin also met her father and mother, both beaming their approval of him and behaving as if they would plaster themselves to his side.

To his relief, when he suggested he and Miss Charnock stroll around the countess's gardens, they did not follow.

Gavin opened the conversation with some talk of the weather.

Miss Charnock's responses were unremarkable in their politeness. She mentioned she was fond of roses and Gavin made a mental note to have Talbert send roses to her.

However, once they reached the haven of a rose arbor and were out of earshot of eavesdroppers,

Miss Charnock shocked him with a different side of her character.

The veneer of bored society miss dropped away. She whirled on him. "Is it true that you have claimed a woman known as the Siren for your mistress?"

"I'm not certain this is polite conversation," he answered, glancing around to see if anyone could have overheard her.

"I'm not polite," she informed him. "Not when I have questions."

"And here I was thinking you performed 'polite' rather well."

She blinked at his mild rebuke and then laughed as if delighted. "You are vastly more interesting than what I'd heard."

Now she had Gavin's attention. "And what have you heard?"

Her nose wrinkled as if in distaste. She reached for one of the lush blooms on the arbor and pulled a velvety petal, rubbing it between her fingers before deigning to say, "That you are all that is right and proper."

"You don't say that as a compliment."

"It isn't," she answered. "Who wants to be leg-shackled to a paragon?"

"Or an unconventional young woman," he added, although her honesty was revealing. *A paragon?* Is that what people thought of him—and not in a complimentary way?

She laughed. "We are all unconventional if we allow ourselves to be. So tell me about this woman. Is it true she danced naked?"

Gavin could well imagine Sarah's response to that statement. "Not naked," he said dutifully. "However, it was a stunning performance."

"I would so love the freedom of being an actress."

Thinking of Sarah's hardships, he answered, "It is far from free."

"But it must be better than being a wife."

"You don't believe being a wife would be fulfilling?" Her statement had surprised him because here was the second reference this day to a thread of dialogue in Sarah's play—the value of being a wife—and it sparked his curiosity.

"Would you?" she pertly countered.

"I would think being a duchess would be a very good thing."

"I think that now you have taken for a mistress the woman everyone is talking about, you might be right."

"And why is that?"

She leaned into him so that her young breasts were almost offered up for his pleasure. "Because," she said, drawing out the word, "if a woman with that sort of experience finds you fascinating, I can only wonder what you have to teach the rest of us?"

If only she knew.

Gavin laughed. He couldn't help himself. The minx was bold as brass. Sarah was outspoken, yes, but she had a bit of class to her directness. "I should take you back to your parents." He offered his arm.

She placed hers behind her back, refusing him. "You aren't going to try and kiss me?" she asked.

"Is that why you brought me to the rose arbor?"

Miss Charnock made an impatient sound. "I didn't take you anywhere. You are the one who requested a stroll. But now that we are here, Your Grace—" she said, taking a step closer to him "—perhaps we should take advantage of the moment. I would like your kiss. I would like it very much."

She leaned toward him and Gavin instinctively leaned back. He had no desire to kiss her. It was Sarah's lips he craved.

And yet, Miss Charnock could well be his duchess.

"We need to return to your parents."

She made a small moue of disappointment but took his arm. "Does this mean you shall not call upon me?"

"Would you wish me to?"

"I pray that you will, Your Grace. In fact, my father has urged me to consider you many a time, and I, well, let us say, I *now* find you exciting."

Nor was she the only woman who now found Gavin "exciting." *All* the women at Countess Fizzwill's event seemed to know. There was flirting in every flick of the fan and batting of the lash. Gavin had never experienced such favor before.

He knew women were attracted to him for the title as well as his wealth. He held no pretenses about himself. However, now they apparently saw him as a lover, and he received a completely different reception.

Here was the secret behind his brothers' successes with women, the reason that ladies, even gentlewomen, favored the rake and the scoundrel. It had to do with the mystery of sex.

No one seemed to favor what was upright and moral. *They want adventure and expected the men in their safe little lives to provide it.*

The line was a direct quote from Sarah's play.

He might need to read that play again—

A woman bumped against him. At first, he thought it was an accident until she slipped a note into his hand. Excusing himself from the conversation, he stepped off to the side and read it. What the lady was proposing shocked him. When he looked around for her, he discovered her with the female friend she suggested they share—and Gavin quickly broke eye contact.

He knew this sort of licentious behavior existed. He had heard men boast but he'd thought it was exactly that—boasting. A gentleman would not use women in this manner . . . and then he thought of Sarah trembling on the bed. Caring people did not use others.

Soberly, Gavin put the note in his pocket.

He needed to leave. He'd met Miss Charnock. Now, he had a strong desire to see Sarah. Things had not been good between them when he had left and he was anxious to learn how her day had gone. He knew Talbert would see to matters, but Gavin wished to spend time with her.

His mother was discussing an upcoming outing with the countess when Gavin came to her side and made his apologies about leaving. His mother walked with him a moment. "What do you think of Miss Charnock?"

"She is all that you said," Gavin replied. "And a bit more," he had to add.

If his mother heard the amusement in his voice, she made no mention. Instead, she said, "You will call on her?"

Gavin knew that calling on Miss Charnock would be tantamount to making a declaration. It didn't matter. He was tired of the wife search. "I will call on her. You and Imogen have done well." He kissed her on the cheek but she caught his hand.

"I want you to be happy, my son."

"I am," he assured her.

"But not like you will be once you have a wife. You have put this off too long."

He thought of his shock over the note in his pocket. "So everyone tells me."

"You need children."

"I want children." That was true. He longed for children, more so now that Elin and Ben were having a baby. He often wondered what kind of father he would be.

"Will you be home for dinner?"

He thought of Sarah. "I doubt it."

She nodded as if he'd confirmed what she thought. "Have a good evening then." She released his hand.

"You as well, Mother." He happily left.

He stopped by Menheim to see if Talbert had anything for him or if there was word from Perkins in his search for the theater owners. His secretary was not in and there was no message from Perkins; however, Ben awaited him.

"I'm glad I caught you," he said. "Rovington wishes to meet in the morning."

Gavin was surprised by how calm he was about the matter. He'd heard men talk of nerves, but he didn't feel any, not yet. Perhaps they would come as the hour drew near. All he'd truly thought about today was Sarah.

"What time?" Gavin asked.

"Preferably at dawn. He knows how much you hate rising at an early hour."

And Rov would use it to his advantage. "Will it be someplace close?" Gavin asked, annoyed.

"Meadow Field."

"On the other side of the river and a bloody hour away."

"We can counter—"

"No, we won't. I want to be done with this business. Swords or pistols?"

"Pistols."

"Good." Gavin was a crack shot. He was a good swordsman as well, but he'd never injured a man and if a duel was going to be fought, then let it be quick. "Thank you. Give my best to Elin."

"I will." Ben left to deliver the terms to Rov's second and within the hour Gavin was at the Clarendon and climbing the stairs. It was half past five of a very trying day.

But he found his step quickening the closer he came to Sarah. He was curious how her day had gone. Had she been pleased with his gift? He was sorry he could not have given it to her in person and he was anxious for her reaction.

He also wondered how he should approach her after last night. He wanted her. He had only to think of her to grow hard . . . and yet, he sensed more lay between them than pure physical release—

Gavin's thoughts broke off as he reached the floor for Sarah's room and saw Rov's wife Jane sitting on the chair reserved for the floor steward.

He slowed his climb to a halt, keeping a stairs' distance between them. When she stood, they were on eye level.

She was of Gavin's age with clear skin and blond hair. Years ago, she'd been an heiress and the catch of her debut season. Rov had quickly claimed her and Gavin could admit he had been somewhat jealous. Jane was a fine woman. She had the qualities to make a man an excellent wife, a better one than Rov deserved.

Her expression was composed as if they had just happened upon one another on the street. "Hello, Your Grace."

"My lady. Where is the floor steward?"

"I sent him away. I need a moment to talk to you where others can't see us."

The last time she'd begged a private moment with him, he'd made the disastrous decision to push Rov for Chairman of the Committees. She'd told him that her husband's compulsion to gamble was ruining them and he'd felt pity for her plight.

And now, he was scheduled to duel with his boyhood friend, the man who was her husband.

Wary, he said, "What do you wish to discuss, Jane?"

"The *truth*," she declared. "I've come here to let you know *I return* your feelings."

"Return my feelings?"

"*Yes*, I do. I've yearned for you for years. And now, I can't believe you are going to free me from my husband so that we can be together—"

And before he knew what was what, she threw her arms around him and covered his mouth with hers—just as a hallway door opened, the door to Sarah's room.

Chapter Thirteen

For a wild second, Gavin teetered for balance, his arms full of Jane.

He leaned forward and tried to set her on the floor, but she wouldn't work her legs and he had to pick her back up again. Nor had her kiss ended. Her lips were literally sucking his as if she'd never let him go. It took effort for him to pull himself away, and his first act was to look to the door, not knowing what to expect—and being thoroughly surprised.

Yes, Sarah stood there but not the trembling woman he had left last night.

No, this woman could easily pass for a peeress of the Realm, an exceptionally lovely one. The fashionable dress hugged the curves of her figure. It emphasized her narrow waist and more than ample chest and made him believe his money to the dressmaker had been well spent.

The curls escaping from her hairstyle reminded him of how her glorious hair had appeared fanned out around her on the bed. His mind immediately pictured her naked. He even knew the color of her nipples, a thought that sent a jolt of desire right to his core.

Now, he was the one who felt like trembling— except he had his arms full of Rovington's wife.

"I heard a noise and I thought I should investigate—" Sarah started and then stopped, holding up her hand as if to ward off anything else she might have said. Her lips struggled to contain her laughter and he realized how comical he must look holding Jane who had buried her head in his neck and was nibbling on his neck cloth.

Making a great show of composing herself, Sarah said, "When you are done, Your Grace, I'll be waiting inside."

He opened his mouth to call her back but Jane plastered her hands against the side of his face and went for his mouth again.

The door closed, and so did his gentleness toward Jane.

"Stop this," he told her, keeping his voice low. "We need to maintain some semblance of good order."

Jane apparently didn't agree. She rubbed her

breasts against his chest and tightened her hold around his neck.

Gentleness would not work. Who could have imagined the diminutive Jane could be so strong-willed?

Placing both hands at her waist, Gavin physically pushed her off of him and plunked her down in the chair. She started to rise again, but a firm *"sit"* kept her in place.

Her antics had pushed Gavin's hat off his head. He picked it up from the floor and gave it a brush with one hand. He looked to Jane. "What took hold of you?"

"You did," she said and made to stand again but he directed her back in her chair with his pointer finger.

"Certainly you knew I had strong feelings for you," she said.

"I did not, my lady."

"You *must*," she insisted. "Why else would you have gone out of your way to help me all these years?"

"Kindness," Gavin assured her.

She shook her head, her lips twisting into a knowing smile. "Or so you say, but I know better."

He knelt so he could look her in the eye, ready to protect himself if she leaped at him again. "Jane, we have known each other for a long time."

She nodded. "I've *admired* you for a long time."

"You are married to another man, one whom I had considered a friend."

"I thought it excellent the way you held yourself back around me."

Perhaps she truly was mad? "What have I done to make you believe I was paying you advances?"

Her face broke into a beatific smile. "You listened to me. No one else hears a word I say, especially Rovington. When I came to you worried about our debts, you rescued me by seeing him named to a position with a very handsome stipend. You wanted to take care of me."

"Out of friendship," he reiterated.

"For *me*," she concluded. "Of course, Rovington has been quite capable of gambling that away just as he did my inheritance. But then, in your wisdom, you understood the only way you could truly protect me is if you shot my husband. Challenging him—"

"*Wait.*" Gavin shook his head. "He challenged me."

"Yes, over *that* woman. The one in the room. I've thought hard about your motives. I've come to realize that you are keeping her away from Rovington to help me save face. It has been humiliating the way my husband has been carrying on about having seen her years ago and placing all those wagers. He has acted as if he a lovesick cow herder."

She leaned toward him, causing him to lean away from her, but she didn't seem to mind. Instead, she practically hummed her happiness as she said, "I know the Siren isn't really your mistress."

Gavin became cautious. "Why do you believe that?"

"Because I follow you whenever I can."

This was shocking news, especially since he had not noticed.

"I have been ever since I understood your plan," she said proudly. "Once I understood how far you would go to help me, I could not stay away. I think about you day and night."

"Jane, you should not follow me. You should not be here now. What will your husband say?" Perhaps there was more behind Rov's challenge than Gavin had originally thought.

"He doesn't care what I do anymore."

"Of course, he does. You are his wife."

"Do you think he remembers that when he is fiddling with his actresses? You think I don't know he has an itch down there? I'd just as soon he *not* touch me."

Rov enjoyed complaining about his privates. Gavin thought the information far too personal but had always suspected Rov's complaints were another way to boast about his sexual conquests. However, Gavin was shocked Jane knew.

"You mustn't follow me," he repeated.

She answered with a complacent smile.

"I'm serious, Jane. I will not allow it. There will be no friendship between us if you do," he added, thinking this last might be a suitable threat and force her to consider her behavior.

"When you left here last night, you did not appear a man satisfied. Which is completely understandable because from what I've heard about this Siren creature, she is a tawdry thing. She is far from worthy of you—"

"Jane, I have no feelings for you."

Gavin wasn't about to let her carry on against Sarah. The idea she spied on him was uncomfortable but that she would speak against Sarah made him angry.

"You *must*," she countered.

"I *don't*. Now, go home. Return to your husband," he said. "You have misinterpreted my actions. You've twisted them."

The earnest light died in her blue eyes, replaced by the flare of anger. Jane rose to her feet. "You are choosing her over me?" she asked, drawing the words out in disbelief.

"You are another man's wife," Gavin said carefully, distrustful of her tone.

"Is it because she dances *naked*?" Jane asked, her voice rising. "I can be naked as well, if that is what you want."

And to his horror, she tore off the short jacket over her dress and threw it on the floor.

"Jane, be sensible," Gavin commanded. He reached for the jacket but she was busy unlacing the back of her dress. Her gloves made her fingers clumsy. With an angry mew of frustration, she pulled one glove off using her teeth, kicking off her shoes as she did so—

Gavin was not about to let Rovington's wife undress herself in the Clarendon's hallway. His patience for both Rov and his wife had reached the breaking point.

He dropped his hat and came to his feet. Unceremoniously, he swung her up in his arms before she could do more undressing. She blinked in surprise and then cooed her delight, putting her arms around his neck.

He started down the stairs.

This was not the direction she had thought he'd intended. "Why are we going this way? Let's go to your rooms. We will throw the Siren out." She nuzzled his neck, as playful as a cat, and Gavin could have growled his exasperation.

"I knew you loved me," she whispered. "I knew it all along."

They reached the hotel reception. Gavin was so intent on his purpose, he didn't notice anyone as he strode through, Lady Rovington in his arms. Out on the street, a hack was just discharging passengers.

Without missing a beat, Gavin walked by the startled gentlemen and placed Jane inside the vehicle. He was not overdelicate about the matter and she had a bit of a scramble with her skirts and the like to right herself.

"Where are we going, Baynton?" she asked, even as he closed the door firmly in her face. Keeping his shoulder against the door in case Jane tried to escape, he took his money purse from his pocket and poured out a handful of coins.

Jane lifted the window flap and attempted to grab hold of Gavin's face. "If you want a whore," she said, "I'll be your whore. I'll be whatever you want."

"I want you to go home, Jane."

"Then come with me."

He handed the money to the driver. "Take her away from here."

"Aye, sir."

"I love you, Baynton. I can make you happy." Her fingers curled in his hair and he pulled away.

She reached for him. "Don't abandon me," she cried. "Not after all you've done for me."

The woman was mad.

Or was she making a scene for reasons only she and Rov understood? There was that. He would not put it past his conniving friend.

And a scene it was.

The driver snapped his reins and his horse moved smartly forward into the late-day traffic. Jane tried to open the door, hanging out of it and letting all the world know she would do anything for the Duke of Baynton. "I will dance naked," she called as the vehicle turned a corner, almost throwing her forward and forcing her to close the door lest she be hurt.

Gavin let his breath go in relief. She was gone.

He pivoted, ready to see Sarah—and then realized he had an audience.

The Clarendon was a popular and busy hotel. At this hour of the day, travelers mingled with important visitors and those who enjoyed the French chef. Gavin counted no fewer than six members of the House of Lords watching him with mouths agape. Then there was a group of military men who could barely hide their snickers. They gave him nods of encouragement and sly winks commiserating with him over Jane.

More interesting was the expression on feminine faces. The older ones standing beside their husbands were shocked. The younger ones eyed him with open speculation.

Disconcerted by all the attention, Gavin started for the stairs. He had just made a scene. It was completely out of character for him. Of course people would gawk—

A woman's embroidered silk reticule fell right in his path.

"Oh, I'm so sorry. My bag slipped from my hand," a woman said. The speaker was a brown-eyed, fashionably dressed woman Gavin had not met before.

He picked up the bag for her.

"Thank you," she said, her gloved hand closing over his holding the reticule, and added in a breathy tone, "Your Grace." She ran the pad of her thumb over the back of his hand. "I'm Mrs. Vaughan. Olivia Vaughan."

"My pleasure, Mrs. Vaughan." Gavin tried to step out of her way but she tightened her hold.

"You don't recognize my name, do you?"

"I'm afraid I do not, Mrs. Vaughan."

She took a step closer. Her perfume was a cloying, Eastern scent. Mrs. Vaughan lowered her voice. "Many of your friends know me well, Your Grace." She gave a slow smile that told him louder than words what she meant by the word "know."

And Gavin felt dirty.

He took back his hand. "Good day," he said to Mrs. Vaughan and moved to the stairs. He took them two at time, wanting to push Jane's shouts and threats out of his mind and rid himself of the scent of Mrs. Vaughan's perfume . . . and then he came to Sarah's floor.

She was sitting in the floor steward's chair, just as Jane had been. She held his hat in her lap. She was waiting for him.

He came to a halt and all the blood in his body rushed to his loins. She had that impact on him. However, there was another sense as well. He felt as if he was coming home. A peace fell over him.

"Did you hear?" he asked.

The sad smile that came to her lips commiserated with him. "There were few on this floor who didn't."

"Or in the lobby."

Sarah digested this and then announced, "I shall say again, I was *not* naked when I danced."

Her piqued declaration caught him off guard, and then Gavin tilted his head back and laughed. The release felt good. Sarah had a refreshing ability to go directly to the point.

But then his mind immediately turned to calculating the incidental results of this new notoriety. "I wonder how many columns of the morning news will be dedicated to the scene?"

In answer, Sarah stood and held out her hand. "Come."

He placed his hand in hers and let her lead him into her rooms. Inside, the late-afternoon light from the window bathed the room in a serene, golden glow.

"Sit down," Sarah invited and went over to some decanters on a small table and poured him a whisky. "Thank you for the ink and paper. The box is precious."

Gavin sat at the table. "You are welcome."

"Talbert said you picked it out yourself. That means more to me than anything else."

She placed the glass in front of him but he didn't touch it. Instead, he pushed the crystal away with one finger, realizing how much he had been drinking lately.

And it wasn't drink he wanted.

She had taken a chair at the table and he now turned his chair to face her.

"You are beautiful," he said, the words leaving his lips without conscious thought. No politics, no manipulation—nothing but honest, almost raw emotion.

Her eyes widened and a blush rose to her cheeks.

Gavin leaned forward, fascinated. "You act as if you had not expected such words from me."

"We have a short acquaintance," she said, "but it has been one marked by our strong personalities."

"Aye, we have squabbled," he agreed, smiling at the wrinkle in her nose over the word. "If you would only listen to me," he had to add teasingly, "we would argue less."

As he had anticipated, she came back roundly, "When I hear good sense from your lips, I will, Your Grace."

"You may have to wait some time. It has been a damnable day."

"Before the lady on the stairs?"

"Unfortunately."

She glanced at the untouched glass. "Mr. Talbert was insistent I understand your likes and dislikes."

"Was he now?"

"Yes," she said before doing a very passable imitation of his secretary giving orders. "His Grace expects a whisky when he first arrives home and one before he retires."

Gavin eyed the glass. "I am alarmingly predictable."

"Do you wish to talk about your day?"

"I like your dress." He'd like to take it off her body.

She seemed to hear his thoughts. Her head tilted as if evaluating him and he had a sense that if he made one wrong move, she would fly.

And he wanted to know why?

She accepted his change of topic. "I thank you for it, and the many others Mrs. Hillsman is making for me. However, it was not necessary."

"Seeing you like this makes me believe it was absolutely of the greatest importance. Did you find a theater?"

"The one you suggested, Your Grace. The Bishop's Hill that Geoff and Charles abandoned. Mr. Talbert says you have set funds out for me to start hiring actors."

"When will you begin?"

"Perhaps on the morrow, if you agree."

The morrow. He would fight a duel on the morrow. "Of course, I agree. Whatever you wish."

"Thank you."

"And did you find a suitable residence?"

"We looked at one, but I wish to discuss the wages for my actor friends first."

"Oh?"

She folded her hands in her lap, giving the impression of being a prim and very stern, but attractive, governess. "It is too much."

"It is our agreement."

"Still, I expected that you would wait until Geoff and Charles could be brought to justice. Thank you," she said, the words so heartfelt, they humbled him. "It was not your battle."

"Sarah, it was a small matter."

"What is small to you was vitally important to them. I've not witnessed much open kindness in my life. Of course—" Her voice broke off as she questioned the wisdom of saying more.

Gavin could feel her distrust. He didn't want the easy, open conversation between them to end. "Of course?" he prompted.

She shook her head. "Would you care for something to eat?"

"If you wish to know what I care about, it is that you finish your statement. Go ahead, Sarah. Tell me what you were about to say."

She ran her hand along the material of her dress covering her thighs, as if she could pull the garment off of her. "Of course, let us not forget that you want something of me. Something you could have taken last night. I offered."

He could have argued that point. He didn't. He sat back.

"But you didn't, Your Grace," she pointed out.

"But you didn't, *Gavin*," he corrected. "I prefer you to use my given name. After all, we are beyond some formalities, aren't we?"

"It doesn't feel right."

"It won't if you don't become accustomed to it. I would have you say it."

Her stubbornness came out. Instead of granting his small request, she said, "We both know you want something from me, but I'm not certain exactly what it is."

Nor did he know himself.

Yes, he wanted to bed her.

But he also wanted her regard. He wanted her to not be suspicious. He wanted her to care for him . . . because, and he wasn't yet certain, he believed she was of importance to him—

Gavin shot to his feet. This was dangerous thinking. There were lines that he could not cross, and yet, she tempted him. He did want more than sex.

"Let's leave this room," he said.

"And go where?"

Anywhere, he wanted to say, realizing he had no desire to spend the evening here with her waiting for him to pounce. "Tell me, where would you go on a July evening like this?"

"Where would *I* go?" she repeated, confounded by the request.

Gavin took her hand and pulled her from the chair, suddenly ready for fresh air and time with this woman without the damn barriers between them. "Yes," he said, "if you had an evening to go anywhere, *for fun*—where would you go? What would you eat? What would you enjoy?"

"I haven't had the money to enjoy anything but work," she started.

"But if you could go someplace, where would you go?"

"Vauxhall," she said. "On a summer evening like this, I would want to go to Vauxhall."

Gavin had never been to Vauxhall. His father claimed it was where the rabble went. Even when he'd received invitations there, his sire had refused to go, and Gavin had done the same—more out of habit than preference.

And now he realized what a terrible mistake he'd made. No wonder he was seen as a paragon. He'd set himself aside.

"Let us go to Vauxhall," he announced. "Where is your hat?" He reached for his own where she'd set it on the table.

"You are jesting, aren't you?" she said, not moving.

In answer, Gavin walked into the bedroom and saw her hat beside the water basin. He carried it to her.

She still didn't seem certain even as she placed

her hat on her head and tied the ribbons. She picked up the shawl draped over a chair. "You really wish to go to Vauxhall?"

"I can't imagine any place better," he said and offered his arm. There would be no ghosts of his father there. For one evening, he wanted to be like every other man. Who knew? Considering the duel on the morrow, this might be his last night. He wished to enjoy it.

She placed her hand on his arm, staring at him as if she was truly seeing him for the first time.

Perhaps she was.

Gavin didn't understand himself. The duel might be an impetus. Or could it be that he was tired of fetching and carrying for the government? That he wanted a respite from all the formality, that he wanted Sarah Pettijohn?

Having her sitting close to him in the hack he hired for their trip, he could feel the tension easing from her as, instead of discussing their hell-born bargain, she began to anticipate the outing. In that respect alone, he believed going to Vauxhall a stroke of genius.

He had no idea what to expect, but she knew. Instead of letting the vehicle take them over the bridge, she had them delivered to the riverbank.

There, hired boats carried them across the river.

Gavin couldn't remember the last time he had been out on the water. He thought of his country estate and realized it had been years since he'd visited there as well. Or had taken time to indulge himself in something that wasn't an obligation.

The gardens were alive with music, acrobats, jugglers, and revelers—and that was before they made it in the front gates. A large party of people was dressed for a masquerade. The costumes appealed to Sarah's sense of the theatrical and Gavin enjoyed her observations.

Inside, paper lanterns brightened the encroaching darkness. He rented a box and they ate what had to be the worst supper he'd ever had and yet, the most entertaining. For once, he and Sarah were talking to each other as friends.

On a small outdoor stage, an Italian singer was followed by a quartet of musicians. After eating their cold chicken and having a few glasses of iced champagne, Sarah and Gavin walked the paths. They were not alone. There were scores of couples out this night.

Sarah talked easily about her plans for her play. Gavin enjoyed her enthusiasm. That, too, had been something missing from his life.

Night settled upon them. The conversation

was light, teasing, easy. He did not have difficulty expressing exactly what was on his mind with Sarah. She was not one to hold back, either, giving freely of her opinions.

The first time she touched his arm without his encouragement, Gavin almost froze. He did not comment on it and a few minutes later, she tapped his arm, to let him know she didn't think Liverpool was doing all that he could—an opinion Gavin agreed with.

Sarah was a surprisingly astute observer of politics. They even verbally sparred a bit when their opinion differed and then—wonder of all wonders, she said, "I don't know how you manage to listen to them carrying on in the Lords, all saying the same thing over and over again, Gavin. I would go quite mad."

Gavin. He came to a dead stop while she walked on, wrapped up in her topic until she realized he wasn't beside her. She faced him.

He toyed with the idea of letting her know what she'd done, and then decided to let it go, to see if she would speak his name again. He moved to catch up to her and let his hand brush hers before boldly taking hold.

Sarah did not pull away. She looked up at him. "You are quite good at this, you know."

"At what?" he asked innocently.

"Managing your own way. Don't think I don't know what you are doing."

"What am I doing?"

"This." She lifted the hand he held.

"And is it so terrible?"

She looked up at him, her eyes reflecting the lantern light. "I don't want to trust you," she whispered.

"But you do."

Sarah ignored him, saying, "I'm best alone. Can you understand that? I have peace alone."

Thoughts he had once believed, but now he wondered. "I'm being told there can't be any of us alone." He referred to his mother and aunt's plan for his marriage.

"It is different for you. I've tried marriage. It was not good."

"In what way?"

She pulled her hand from his and he let her go. However, he wasn't going to let the topic escape.

His step in line with hers, he said, "Speak to me, Sarah. Tell me. Don't hold another man's sins against me."

Her back stiffened. For a heartbeat of time, he expected her to demand to return to her hotel, but then she said, "I don't believe in love. I won't. Do you understand that? I don't have anything in me to give."

"And yet, you championed your niece's desire to marry for love."

"Did I have a choice? I wanted her to have what was due her because of her class, her lineage. It was the only route open to her. I am proud to say, she did not make a bad marriage."

"I agree. However, I remember you were set on letting her make up her own mind."

"As should be her right."

"And yet you keep a tighter rein on yourself."

She started as if his observation had surprised her.

"I do the same," he admitted.

"We are nothing alike," she assured him.

"Perhaps we are more so than you imagine? We are both fiercely independent and have high ideals and are willing to battle to the wall for what we believe." He didn't wait for her response but concluded, "We are also both afraid of making a wrong decision. And powerless to make the right one."

That was true. Gavin no longer knew what he wanted.

"Come," he said, taking her arm. "The hour grows late. Let us leave." He would have started in the direction of the gate, but Sarah pulled away from him.

"What is it you want?" she demanded. She took a step closer to him, lowering her voice. "Do you want sex? Then why didn't you take it last night? Or when we were back at the hotel? Why go through this?" She motioned to include the gardens.

"What is your complaint?" he countered. "You haven't shown enthusiasm for our agreement."

"Oh," she said, feigning ignorance, "you want me to be enthusiastic as I sell myself? I didn't understand. Here, let me try again, Your Grace." She shook her bosom at him and pursed her lips. "Gavin, I am beside myself. Thank you for keeping me as a pet—"

"That is *not true* and you know it." Heat colored every word.

Her anger evaporated. "I do. You are a decent man and I don't say that lightly. But I don't know what you want. Do you want me to fawn over you? To offer love—?"

"I've not asked for love. Just a bit of grace, Sarah. I feel like one of the jugglers this evening, constantly meeting others' expectations. Even yours. I yearn for a safe place."

It wasn't until he spoke the words, he realized how true they were.

And how had he arrived to this moment in life when he had done everything expected of him and yet felt as if he lived a life that was not his own?

And what had made him think he could find the answer in Sarah?

"Let's leave," he said and began walking to the gate.

Chapter Fourteen

Sarah watched him walk away.

Roland had not been the only one to teach her hard lessons. Men in general were not to be trusted. How many times had she witnessed the faithlessness of men like Geoff and Charles and a host of others who had assured her she had no place in their world?

And yet, Baynton had given her *paper*.

He'd *given* her paper.

However, he did not stop to see if she followed.

For a second, she thought of staying right where she was and letting him go, but then her feet moved in his direction, and she didn't understand why. It had nothing to do with her play or his wanting her in his bed.

It was something deeper than those things. He was the most obnoxious man she knew, and the only one she'd come to respect.

Baynton seemed to know she was coming. His step slowed, giving her the opportunity to catch him. She stopped when she was within a foot of him.

He halted as well.

"My following you doesn't mean I've decided to do whatever you wish," she informed him.

"Oh no, Sarah, I could never imagine that."

His dry comment startled her with its truth. Every step of the way, Baynton had allowed her to meet him as an equal. Here, at last, was a man who was honest with her whether she wanted to hear what he had to say or not. Deception was not part of his character—and that was when she knew they could be lovers.

Lovers.

The word had a delicious feel to it. She hadn't had a lover since Roland. She'd never felt the desire for one until . . . now.

He held out his hand, and she knew she could refuse it. Baynton would let her walk away.

But if she took it, then she was accepting all of what he asked, and it had nothing to do with money or her play or houses. This was about them, about her and him, and about trust.

In that moment, Sarah realized what a great weight her life had become. She wasn't just trying to survive—she was also dragging the burden of all her disappointments and her fears. Then again, her doubts came down to this one certainty: She'd trusted love once before and love had deceived her.

So, why not put her faith in respect and honesty? Perhaps her mother had been right when she'd claimed there was only one way a woman like her could survive.

And, Baynton had given Sarah paper.

Walking past his hand, she reached up and kissed him.

They stood in the shadows, off to the side of the traffic on the footpath, but it didn't matter if anyone was attending them or not. In this moment, the only thing Sarah was aware of was the feeling of his lips against hers, of the slightly rough whiskers of his jaw beneath her hands.

He kissed back, greedily. Demanding. Hungry for her touch.

She started to panic and then told herself this was Gavin. Slowly, she allowed herself to relax and he did as well. The kiss deepened.

What had he said the night before? It wasn't *him* she feared. That's what he'd said . . . and he had been right.

No, what she feared was losing herself again the way she had with Roland. Did Gavin understand how much courage it took for her to be this close to him—?

He broke off the kiss. He bent down. "You're crying again, just like last night. Sarah, what is it?"

She hadn't even been aware of her tears and she could not explain them. She placed her hands up to her face, drying the damaging evidence with her gloves.

The duke took her hand. "Let's leave."

This time, he hired a hack to drive them across the bridge. The driver had no sooner started them on their way when Baynton turned to her and said, "Tell me."

Sarah knew what he wanted. Her story. One she hadn't fully shared with anyone. Once she'd told Charlene but not all of it, not the worst. She'd wanted Charlene to believe in the good of marriage. She'd wanted her niece open to taking her rightful station in life.

"I asked you last night who hurt you," he prodded.

Sarah felt her chest constrict at his words. It became hard to breathe. She started to ease away from him, wanting a boundary of space.

However, Gavin would have none of that. "You must speak."

"I can't."

"Yes, you can," he said quietly.

"I can't breathe."

"You are breathing."

She shook her head as if to deny his words, although he was right. She knew it, she understood, but still she held back.

"Was he your husband?" Gavin asked.

Sarah nodded.

"Not a good one, I imagine."

She shook her head.

"What was his name?"

"Roland. He had been a soldier when I first met him."

"Was he a brute?"

Sarah had to think on that a moment. There had been times when she'd been happy with Roland. When all had been well between them.

This was the problem. She could never paint him completely black—until she remembered him pushing her . . .

"I always wanted to be better than I am." Her damning words came out as barely a whisper, but he heard them.

"Is this what he told you?"

Sarah sat back in the seat. "No, my mother." She fell silent, feeling guilty for she knew not what. It didn't make sense and yet the indictment, especially since she'd lost the house on Mulberry

Street, was a heavy mantle around her. "She hated what she called my 'airs.'"

"Because?"

"It is as I told you last night," she answered, finding it easier to breathe the more she spoke. "She assured me there was only one role for a woman like me in life."

"And so she ordained you to it?"

"But I married instead. She had already died by then but I remember standing in front of the parson and feeling her spirit. I could hear her mocking me." She looked down at her gloves. "I know I sound silly."

"My father mocks me all the time from the grave," Gavin said. "I don't find you silly at all. A disapproving parent is an impossible weight."

"Why would he disapprove of you?"

"He had exacting standards for me and no matter how much I gave or how hard I tried, I always fell short of the mark. He considered my brothers as little more than fortunate spares in case anything happened to me. I was his project and the complete focus of his life. I understand why my brothers wanted to escape him."

"But you never did."

"No, I believed in my responsibilities. He started my training at a very young age. He let me know that I was not on this earth to think of myself."

"And so here you are—alone."

"The Duke of Baynton must always think of others before himself," he replied as if by rote.

"A girl like Sarah can't be anything more than what her mother was or her mother's mother before her," she recited back. "When my mother realized how much I hated having the men she entertained around, how frightened I was, she'd slap me and tell me I'd be wiser to learn a trick or two from her. I'd still hide. I didn't want those men to know I was there."

"That *was* wise."

She nodded. She knew she had been. "But then I married the worst of the lot. Roland was bold and handsome and I fell in love—whatever that means. However, by the time I received word he had died, I was glad to be rid of him. Then again, I also believed I'd failed him."

Those last words poured out of her, spontaneous and unconsidered. The tightness left her chest, but there was the shame. "The cruel trick was, I had no idea what a wife was supposed to do or be and so I was a miserable one to him."

"What did he expect?"

"For me to be there when he wanted to remember he had a wife. And to do whatever he bid."

She was not conscious that she had curled her hand into a fist until he covered it with his own.

Sarah looked at their gloved hands. She tried to unclench the fist, but it held firm . . . then she said, "I have done things of which I am ashamed."

"Such as?" His voice was gentle.

"He whored me out."

There, she'd said it. The thing she'd not spoken of to any other soul. She'd just confided in Baynton, and she wasn't certain why.

"It had been over a card game," she said. "He lost. I was the debt that had to be paid. We didn't have money and I was so afraid he would be locked up that I did it. I *hated* myself, but I did it."

Sarah didn't look at him. She couldn't. "After that, I abhorred him. Every time he touched me, I cringed. Then I learned I was carrying a child." She took a deep breath and released it slowly. She hated remembering that moment when her life had irreversibly changed.

"Roland was not pleased to learn he was to be a father. After all, after that card game, he claimed he was not certain the child was his. I didn't know, either. We argued. We always argued. We were in Clitheroe, a small village with a stone tower. It had been a lovely afternoon and Roland and I were out for a walk. He suggested we climb the tower's stairs. On the way down the steps, he pushed me. I didn't remember what happened but there was a witness. A vicar. I'm certain Roland had acted on impulse or else he would have been more careful about being seen. The fall was bad. I not only lost the baby but I nearly died from the blood loss. The midwife said I could never have children."

Sarah took a deep breath and released it, steadying herself. There was so much she wished to forget and couldn't. "I had always wanted children. I was devastated. I attempted to claim my own life and Roland put me away in an asylum."

She closed her eyes a moment and then confessed, "I've witnessed horrors. A month after he put me in that place, the midwife who had tended me during my accident came to see a patient at the asylum. She recognized me and knew I should not be there. With her help, I was set free."

"What of your husband?"

"He'd abandoned me in the asylum. Nor was I healthy when I left. I almost died there from lack of care. It took me months to regain my strength. The midwife took me in for that period of time. She told me I was better off without him. Of course, she was right but I struggled with the guilt of what I'd done to my child, to my marriage. Several years later, I received word he was dead."

"Good. That saves me from hunting him down and killing him."

Sarah looked at Gavin in surprise. She had not expected him to champion her.

"How long ago was this?" he asked.

"Fourteen years ago."

He was quiet a moment and then said soberly, "Thank you for telling me. You were afraid last night. Now I understand."

"Do you? Has anyone ever taken away your trust, your faith in yourself?"

"And yet you go on."

"What else am I to do? I'm not a coward. Not anymore."

In response, he slid his thumb into her fisted hand. Instinctively, at last, she opened her fingers and he laced their fingers together. It felt good to hold his hand this way.

It felt good to have told her story, and to receive compassion.

The hack pulled up at the hotel. Baynton opened the door, paid the driver and helped Sarah out. They were quiet as they entered the Reception. He retained his hold on her hand.

There were several people milling about but all was quiet. Still, Sarah felt they all stared as she walked with the duke. If he thought the same, he didn't say.

Then again, he was the Duke of Baynton. He was accustomed to people noticing his presence.

They went upstairs and that is when she remembered the vial. Her stomach twisted into a knot.

She now began to question Mr. Talbert's request.

If she gave Gavin the draught, he would not be able to have sex with her. Mr. Talbert's guess that everyone would believe his absence was due to her, would be correct, but for the wrong reasons. Gavin would know the truth. He was wise enough to sense a deception.

Would he be angry? She would be.

And what if she forgot the draught? What if she allowed him to make his own decision for his life? What if she did let him have her?

That thought startled her. She was no longer afraid. Gavin had managed to breach her defenses. This evening had added a new dimension to their relationship. She was beginning to trust.

The duke nodded to the floor steward who took up his candle and led them to their room. He opened the door with his own key and lit several candles in the room.

As light warmed the room, Sarah noticed the glasses from earlier had been moved and the decanter of whisky freshened. Perhaps that was the manner in a hotel such as this, but it made her nervous. She couldn't help but imagine Mr. Talbert watching, managing.

Pour the vial in his glass and he'll not wake until well into tomorrow afternoon. Then we shall have handled the matter with Rovington.

Those had been Mr. Talbert's last instructions to her for the day. He hadn't said who "we" were and she had been so rattled, she hadn't asked.

"Are you all right?" he asked.

"Yes, yes, I'm fine," she said, startled. "Why do you ask?"

"Because you were staring at the decanters as if something troubled you."

Sarah tried to recover gracefully. "I was wondering if you would like something to drink?"

"Would you?" he countered.

"I believe I would," she said and crossed over to the whisky. She wasn't one for strong spirits, but suddenly needed the courage of them. There was a decision to be made. She would either use the draught and put Baynton to sleep or she would not use it. The choice was hers.

Sarah realized she could give them both the draught and then they would both sleep, both be victims.

Removing her shawl and her hat, she managed to take the vial from her pocket without being detected. She poured two glasses. She put a bit of the draught in each. She half expected him to notice her actions but instead, he had walked over to the window . . . because he trusted her.

Picking up the glasses, she started for him. He

turned from the window, faced her, and she could see in his eyes that he still wanted her.

And from someplace deep within her, a place she had believed dead, she felt the stirring of desire.

It caught her with such surprise, she almost tripped and dropped the glasses.

She had lost her fear of being intimate with him. In fact, she believed that Charlene had been a fool to let this man slip away.

A fool.

Sarah turned toward the table and set the glasses down. She met Gavin's eye. "I've been asked to give you a sleeping draught," she said.

That news surprised him. "By whom?"

"Mr. Talbert."

He shook his head. "Talbert? For what reason?"

"So that you would not meet Lord Rovington on the dueling field in the morning."

"He would betray me?"

There was doubt in his voice and too late, Sarah realized it would be her word against that of the secretary, a man who had served Gavin faithfully for who knew how many years.

"He wished to save your life. Mr. Talbert said that if you met Lord Rovington on the morrow, your death would be on my hands. He said that Lord Rovington has killed two men in duels."

"That is true."

"He said you have never dueled before."

"That is also true. I find dueling foolish."

"I do as well," Sarah said stoutly. "Which is a good reason for you not to be there."

"So then, why are you confessing now?"

"Because," she said, her voice uncertain of his response, "if you are killed, I don't know how I shall live with myself."

"Why, Sarah? Then you would be free of me."

"Would I? Do you believe me so callow I would rejoice at your death? At any death? And if I had given you this whisky, I would never forgive myself for playing a part in your disgrace. I am not that sort of woman."

"Did Talbert offer you anything to betray me?"

"Just the promise that this was the best solution. He believes that if you miss the duel everyone will believe it is because you are happy in my bed. Therefore, he thinks any disgrace would be tempered by envy." She shook her head, wondering if she should have been silent. "Why should you believe me? I have no proof of what I say . . . save for the vial—and what does that prove?"

"Sarah, I believe you."

"You shouldn't," she argued. She wouldn't.

To her surprise, he laughed.

"This is not humorous," she returned.

He walked up to her. "I'm not laughing out of humor. I'm laughing because you are so concerned and you needn't be."

"I beg to differ, Your Grace," she answered tartly. "I feel like I am caught in a difficult position."

"And you are, my dear Sarah, and for that I am heartily sorry. I do not know why Talbert would wish to betray me. However, of late, I have noticed he has been less than satisfied with his position on my staff. He is an ambitious man. I must ask myself, who benefits from my disgrace?"

"Not him," she said.

"And not you. However, Rovington could use all of this to his advantage. He knows I will see him removed as the Chairman of the Committees. I put him there and I can take him away. He would do anything to usurp my power."

"So, you are saying that Talbert might be doing Lord Rovington's bidding?"

"And using you. Tell me the conversation when Talbert asked you to drug me." He pulled a chair out for Sarah and then took one for himself.

As she recalled the exchange with Mr. Talbert the best she could, Gavin listened intently. When she was done, he sat for a moment and then said, "Of course, I will stay here for the night," he said. "Let them believe you drugged me."

"But you will meet Rovington in the morning."

"Undoubtedly."

Sarah heard the steel in his voice and she wished she could dissuade him. "Men who use trickery cannot be expected to fight fair."

"Is that Shakespeare?" he asked, teasing her.

"No, it is what I've learned through a life of hard living. You have power. Go to some authority. I will testify what Mr. Talbert asked me to do."

"Talbert is only a small part of this. Rovington is the betrayer. But he has been clever, using people around me as a boundary between the deed and his manipulation. I will not let him escape, not without exacting a price."

"Will you kill him?"

The duke appeared surprised by her question, and then answered, "I don't know."

"Don't let him kill you," she begged, suddenly frightened of the prospect.

"I won't, Sarah." He smiled. "Now, the hour is late. Go to bed. Go on now," he prodded as if she was a child.

"Are you coming?"

"I have a few things to write," he replied and crossed over to the portable desk he'd given her. He pulled out paper and pen.

"Last instructions?"

"It would be wise, although my affairs are

always in order. A few last thoughts. I would also document our discussion this evening."

Sarah wanted to pretend that it wasn't necessary, that the whole situation was something that could be ignored. However, the way Gavin sat down at the desk and started writing told her that it would not be.

She went into the bedroom and undressed, feeling as if she was in a dream. She climbed beneath the sheets naked. She rolled on her side and watched through the door as Baynton wrote.

Would he join her?

What would she do if he did?

She could still taste the heat of the kisses they had shared that evening . . . and she knew that when he joined her, she would give him what he asked. Her stomach hollowed in fear, but it was not as great as it had been. She knew she could be calm. This was their bargain. She not only owed it to Gavin, she wanted to please him. She waited for him to come to her.

However, at some point, she fell asleep.

She woke with a start to see that the only light in the other room was from a candle burned down to the nub and she was alone in the bed.

At first, she believed he had left. She rose from the bed and with silent steps peered into the sitting room. Gavin was sprawled out in the upholstered chair, his booted heels propped up on a chair. He had removed his jacket and waistcoat and untied his neck cloth, but he still looked decidedly uncomfortable.

On the table were three folded sheets of paper. Each said, "Upon my death," and were addressed separately. There was one for Lord Liverpool. Another for his brother Ben. The third was addressed to her—

"You remind me of one of those stories," Baynton's deep voice said, catching her off guard, "that my Nan used to tell of fairies who stole in the night and counted the sins of bad little boys. Except I never imagined fairies being so beautiful."

Sarah's first impulse was to want to hide her nakedness, but then where was the trust? She lowered her arms. "And what did these fairies do to those boys?"

He dropped his heels heavily on the floor and sat up. "They lured them away and stole their souls and they were never heard from again." His keen gaze wandered over her. Her breasts grew full, tightened.

She told herself it was the night air.

She knew it wasn't.

"Come to bed," she said and held out a hand.

Chapter Fifteen

Gavin rose, took her hand, and let her lead him into the bedroom. Sarah walked to the other side of the bed while he undressed.

She slipped between the sheets. His shadow blocked the light in the other room. She closed her eyes, listening to the sounds of his boots being placed on the floor, the rustle of his clothing sliding over his body.

The air was full of him, the spiciness, the masculinity, the person.

He did not join her under the sheet but stretched beside her and pulled the coverlet over him. Her body naturally moved toward him as the mattress accommodated both of their weights, the sheet the only barrier to his body heat.

The duke bunched the pillow up beneath his arm and rested his head.

With eyes shut, Sarah waited for him to move upon her. He didn't.

She opened her eyes. He was watching her. His lips curved into a smile at her notice. He traced her bottom lip with the tip of one finger. The motion tickled.

"Don't you want to complete this matter between us?" she asked, the combination of fear and anticipation making it hard for her to speak.

"Is that what you want?"

"I'm ready," she answered. And she was. She was resolved to see the matter through.

"So lovely," he whispered. His fingers followed the curve of her neck, down to her breasts. His palm covered her and the nipple tightened under the smoothness of the sheet and heat of his touch. "So afraid . . ."

"I'm trying not to be," she said in her defense. "I'm better than I was last night."

"This is true."

"It isn't you."

"I know." He was not looking at her as he spoke, but at the way his thumb now circled that one tightened nipple. The move, even in spite of the sheet, inspired that hitch of anticipation, that stab of need.

His fingers moved the sheet down, exposing her breast.

Sarah started and then willed herself to be still, just as she had in the sitting room. This, too, called for an act of faith in him.

He watched her intently as if he had expected her panic—but she was better. Couldn't he see that? She reached over and placed her hand against the side of his jaw. His whiskers were smoothly rough beneath her touch. She pressed her lips to his.

His body pulled her closer, the sheet still between them.

She let him kiss her just as he had at Vauxhall, and then she surprised herself by stroking him with her tongue, an invitation—a hesitant, yet bold move, and it felt right. Gavin responded and for a moment, they breathed as one.

His hand ran over the curve of her hip and buttock. She warned herself to relax. All would be fine if she would just relax.

He nuzzled his way down her neck. Through the sheet, she could feel the strength of his arousal against her thigh.

And then all conscious thought left her as his lips covered her breast. He sucked gently. His tongue brushed her and a jolt of heat she'd never known before shot straight to her core. She held him, not wanting him to ever stop what he was doing. Her fingers curled in his hair. She moved, her legs suddenly restless.

He found her other breast and gave it the same attention and Sarah heard herself gasp with both surprise and pleasure.

Pleasure. She was completely vulnerable to him . . . and yet, the fear ebbed to be replaced by this certainly sinful desire.

And then his lips were upon hers again.

There was need in his kiss, a driving need.

His hand slid to the juncture of curls at her thigh. She was moist, something she'd never experienced before. His fingers teased her. A sharp, deliciously raw sensation enveloped her. With a will of their own, her legs parted, inviting him to do more.

And he did.

Exploring fingers slid inside her and she thought she would come undone. This felt good. But it wasn't enough. Sarah released her breath with a soft moue. A need was in her, a need only he could relieve.

He lifted himself up over, giving his wondrous touch more freedom. She wrapped her arms around his shoulders, reaching for him, but he held back.

"No, Sarah, this is for you. So that you will never tremble again. Trust me, love. Trust me."

She couldn't have argued. Her whole being was lost in the spell of his touch. He seemed to know her better than she knew herself.

A pressure was building inside her. She turned her face into the warmth of his neck. Her body wanted to be covered by him—and then suddenly, sharp, pure sensation swept through her.

It was as if her being had become as focused as a pinprick of sunlight in the dark before bursting into warm, glorious flame.

All Sarah could do was hold on to Gavin as wave after wave of emotion flowed, relentless and pure, through her.

She couldn't speak. Words were not adequate. It has all been so simple and yet satisfying, delightfully so.

He held her as if he understood. "Sarah." He whispered her name as if it was a benediction. As if *she* mattered.

His hand found hers. He placed it upon him. He was long and hard and if he was feeling half of what had driven her, she could not imagine going without release. He guided her in what he wanted. It did not take much. He acted as if he'd been as caught up in the same storm, as if in pleasing her, he pleased himself? An astounding thought.

He gasped aloud with his own release. She felt the essence of him against her skin. He'd needed her. He was far more robust a man than Roland could ever have been, and yet, for her, he'd held himself back.

His body fell against hers after his release. The rushing beat of blood pumping through her veins matched the beat of his own. He gathered her in the haven of his arms, pressed a kiss to her hair, to her forehead, to her temple. "Ah, Sarah, you break my heart."

She didn't answer. She'd been robbed of speech. For a long moment, she let herself be at peace, her head on his shoulder, savoring the aftermath.

Ever so slowly, consciousness returned. He pulled the coverlet over both of them. She stared into his eyes. "Why just for me? Why did you deny yourself?"

"I don't want you afraid. Not of me, Sarah. Never of me—and yet, I had to do something or I would explode."

All her life she'd witnessed men taking what they wanted without thought to anyone's needs but their own.

And now Gavin had proven to her, that not all men were selfish, that there was *more*. She wrapped her arms around his neck and burst into tears.

He held her, whispering words she could not hear and yet understood. He didn't just want her body; he wanted her trust. He may even want her soul, and in this moment, Sarah could have given it to him. She was so tired of being afraid, of being alone, of being forgotten.

She hugged her arms around his torso, her legs intertwined with his, the sheet still between them.

Didn't he know she was flawed, imperfect?

In time, he'd realize the mistake he'd made in choosing her. But for right now, he held her.

For right now, she would be at peace.

In this manner, she fell asleep.

At last, Gavin now knew her taste, her scent. He understood men, but women were a mystery.

He had pleased her. She had tried his self-control. It had taken all his will to not bury himself deep in her. Even now, the animal instinct to mate was upon him. Then again, it had been since he'd seen the flash of her bare legs upon the stage.

Or did it go back further?

The first time he'd met her, she'd been masquerading as Lady Charlene's maid . . . and he'd noticed her green eyes, the glint of intelligence in them—so unfitting a maid—and the dark sweep of her lashes.

Now he knew more about her. He had learned her fears. She could not afford to trust easily. *Neither could he.*

The thought startled him.

He'd always believed his motives were clear. He prided himself on his honesty and yet he saw bits of himself in Sarah's doubts.

His father had been the first to betray him with his stern, often brutal expectations for his son while squandering the family fortune with insane schemes and investments. Gavin had been shocked when he'd realized he had inherited an estate in disarray.

It had taken years and iron discipline to replenish the coffers. It had also taken luck, a quality Gavin hated because he had no control over it.

And then there was the politics, the negotiating and bargaining and arguing against men's base natures.

He'd been everything he'd been trained to become. He wielded power, made decisions, delivered what needed to be done, and he never had a moment's peace. He'd never been content . . . until now.

Sarah's breathing was gentle and relaxed. She slept deeply as if she knew he'd not let harm come to her. He brushed her hair with his lips. Such a vibrant color, one that matched her spirit. *His* Sarah.

Would she thank him on the morrow? Or return to her prickly self?

He didn't know. What he did understand is that for this moment, all was right.

And, if upon meeting Rov, this was Gavin's last night on earth, then it was a good one.

With that thought, he surprised himself by falling into his own tranquil sleep.

He woke well before dawn, alert and relaxed. Sarah was still in his arms. He, of course, was hard as an iron pike. He'd give everything he owned to ignore the duel, to kiss her awake, to be inside her—

Gavin cut short his wistful lust and carefully eased out from beneath her sleeping form. He poured water into the basin and slapped his face with it, thankful that it was cold enough to bring him to his senses. He began dressing—

She sat up in bed, the sheet dropping to her waist. Her thick hair was in charming disarray. She pushed it aside and then, heedless of her own lovely nakedness, stood.

Gavin suddenly found it hard to button his breeches.

"Sarah, go back to sleep."

"I'm going with you," she answered. She frowned groggily as she reached for her dress.

Shirtless, Gavin took her by the arms, preventing her from dressing. "You will stay here. This way I know you are safe."

She stared at his chest a moment. Her breasts had hardened into two tight points and he remembered the feeling of them in his mouth. His grip tightened on her arms as he struggled with the knowledge he must push her away and ignore the desire to toss her onto the bed and have his way with her. The perfume of her body, still warm from sleep, was intoxicating.

Sarah pulled away from him and drew her dress over her head. "I'm going." She efficiently braided her unruly hair and then began lacing the back of her dress.

Gavin watched her a moment and then decided he didn't mind having her with him. He finished dressing himself. By the time he'd pulled on his boots, she had used tooth powder and washed her face and was ready to go. She had twisted her braid into a graceful knot at her neck and was tying the ribbon to her hat.

After hearing her tell of the plot to give him the sleeping draught, he had written a note to his brother to meet him at the hotel and given it to the hall steward to deliver. Therefore, as they stepped out the Clarendon's front door, Ben waited. He had driven a smart phaeton with his tiger, a lad named David, on the step behind the seat. "Good morning, brother," Ben called.

"You are a cheery man this morning," Gavin said.

"I always feel good when I believe a rascal is going to receive what he deserves."

"Are you talking about Rov or myself?"

"I'll let you guess." Ben's interested gaze wandered over to Sarah.

Gavin said, "This is Mrs. Pettijohn. She is accompanying us. Sarah, this is my brother Ben. Do not believe anything he tells you unless he is talking about his lovely wife."

"Mrs. Pettijohn," Ben said with a slight bow. His voice held no warmth.

If Sarah took offense, Gavin couldn't tell. She gave a small curtsy. "Lord Ben."

"Up you go," Gavin said, helping Sarah maneuver the step onto the phaeton's open and narrow seat.

"I wasn't expecting there to be three of us," Ben complained.

"Sarah insists on going." Gavin climbed up to sit beside her. Sarah was squeezed between two good men. "Let's be off and I'll tell you what has happened."

"More intrigue?" Ben said, setting his team forward.

"Talbert," Gavin said. "He gave Sarah a sleeping draught to administer to me last night."

"There is a story here," Ben said. "Did you catch her? Is that why she is with us?" He spoke as if Sarah was not there.

"She told me about the draught," Gavin answered. "She realized I needed to meet Rov."

For her part, she looked straight ahead, her hands folded in her lap. She had that ability to appear serene even though Gavin knew she wasn't. And he did know. He was becoming quite adept at divining what was on her mind.

He wondered if she was learning the same about himself?

"And you are certain it was a sleeping draught? Why not poison?" Ben wondered.

Sarah whipped her wide gaze around to him in shock. Ben shrugged. "It would be one way of removing my brother permanently. And perhaps myself, because since I'm his heir, everyone would immediately blame me."

"But to what purpose?" Sarah asked. "I could see wanting to disgrace the duke by having him not show for the duel, but why murder?"

"I don't know," Ben said easily. "However, poison is a woman's weapon."

"So you think Talbert meant to implicate Sarah?" Gavin asked.

"Perhaps to throw the trail off of him. Rumors are flying through London, you know. Many claim Mrs. Pettijohn is either a harlot who has bewitched the very important Duke of Baynton, or a French spy who has bewitched the very important Duke of Baynton."

Sarah bristled with anger. Gavin put his arm around her. "Steady," he warned.

"How can I be steady when I now have such a desire to murder someone?" she demanded.

"Not me, I hope."

"Not yet," she countered.

That elicited a chuckle from Ben. "You may have met your female match, brother."

Gavin laughed. If only Ben knew.

"Do you have some of the draught Talbert gave you?" Ben asked.

"It is in the room," Gavin said, "next to the whisky. Sarah poured it into two glasses and they are still untouched and on the table. We can take them to a chemist."

"Why did you not follow through with the plan?" Ben asked Sarah. "And why two glasses?"

"I had thought to drink the draught myself," she said. "It seemed only fair."

"Or sporting?" Ben questioned. "Well, if it was

poison, then you speaking the truth may have saved two lives."

"I'm certain whatever was plotted, Rov is behind it," Gavin said. "We'll know by the way he behaves when I make my appearance."

"Why would he stoop so low?" Ben asked.

"He doesn't want to lose his position as Chairman of the Committees and he knows I will take it from him. He always had a hot head but I had believed he had sense." Gavin was quiet a moment and then said, "Damn, but Talbert was a good secretary."

They drove over the river. Just as the sun was beginning to appear on the horizon, they pulled into a large expanse of meadow. On the far side was a sheltering oak. Four men stood there. One of their horses whinnied a greeting to Ben's team, alerting the men of their approach.

Sarah recognized Lord Rovington's figure as he stepped away from the others.

Lord Ben drove his team to the oak and then set the brake. His tiger jumped down to see to the horses and the brothers climbed down. "You are best staying here with the vehicle," Gavin told Sarah.

She looked to Lord Rovington. He had watched them with a grim expression. If he had been surprised to see them appear, she could not tell but she was glad his plans to disgrace the duke had been thwarted.

Gavin and his brother approached the men. She could hear the introductions. Lord Rovington and the duke sounded cordial. One of the men was Lord Rovington's second and the other was a physician. Another gentleman was present as a spectator and was a friend of his lordship's. Sarah thought he had the look of a moneylender.

Lord Ben spoke to the second. "The duke has agreed to a count of five and then fire."

"Who shall count?" the second asked.

"Since my brother is the one challenged, I shall," Lord Ben said in a voice that would have frozen any dissent.

The second looked to Lord Rovington who stood a bit away from the group, his back toward the duke, his manner aloof. Now, in early morning light, even Sarah could see the strain on his lordship's face. He appeared a man overburdened—but not one surprised at his opponent's appearance. It made her wonder if Talbert had acted alone and if so, why? Certainly the secretary knew this would be the end of his career. None of it made sense, especially after Talbert's impassioned defense of Baynton yesterday to her.

Or had he been preparing for her to be blamed? Much in keeping with the rumors Lord Ben claimed swirled around her?

The seconds moved to a level spot on the meadow. Lord Ben and the other second marched off paces. The duke removed his jacket and neck cloth, carrying them over to her. As he approached, Sarah could see past him to Lord Rovington. She'd rarely seen such undisguised jealousy on a man's face. Perhaps as the duke thought, Rovington was angling for power but in this moment, intuition warned her that she was somehow involved. Without any encouragement on her part, without even two words to her, Lord Rovington had in some way branded her as his.

And now the duke wasn't just fighting for his honor, but hers as well.

Gavin had not shaved that morning and there was the faintest hint of stubble along his lean jaw. She took the jacket and neck cloth from him. Their gloved hands brushed each other and, in that moment, she could recall the feeling of having his hands upon her body.

He gave her a small smile, his manner obviously preoccupied with the task before him—and yet he was calm. She looked over to Lord Rovington. One of his seconds said something to him and he snapped back an answer she could not hear.

She reached forward, placing her hand on his shoulder. The duke had pulled his glove on his right hand and tested squeezing his fingers as if he would wear the glove in the duel. He looked up at her, expectantly.

Sarah had meant to mention that she believed Lord Rovington was tense, but words vanished from her mind as she looked into his blue eyes. Without conscious thought, she leaned down and kissed him.

This kiss was without the heat of their previous ones but it did not lack passion. Their lips now melded together easily. There was no resistance.

She broke the kiss. "Don't lose," she whispered.

He grinned, the expression almost rakish. "I don't intend upon it."

"That is good. We have unfinished business." And she meant those words. She now didn't know why she had ever opposed him. The truth be told, she thought Gavin was a wonderful man. Yes, they were often of differing opinions but he listened to her. He let her be herself.

If he lived through this duel, Sarah vowed she would honor her part of the agreement and it would not be a chore. He'd shown her a side of herself she had not known existed. How much better would their coupling be if she gave as freely of herself as he had—?

"We are ready to start when you are, brother," Lord Ben said. "We've marked off the distance. See if you approve."

Sarah had been so intent on the duke, she hadn't heard Lord Ben approach. Neither, apparently, had the duke because he pulled his gaze reluctantly away from her.

Both Sarah and Baynton looked to where Lord Rovington's second and one of the witnesses stood at about ten paces from each other. It seemed a very short span to Sarah. How could anyone miss? And she wanted Lord Rovington to miss.

Panic threatened to engulf her. In the span of minutes, Baynton had become important to her. She didn't know how she would react if he was injured . . . or killed.

"It is fine," Gavin said. He pulled the glove off.

The tiger opened a gun case and offered it to the brothers. "Is it mine?" the duke asked.

"I picked it up last night," Lord Ben answered.

"Not from Talbert, I hope?"

"Talbert was long gone when I came by. I took this from the gun cabinet and inspected it myself."

Baynton looked over the weapon and then nodded. "This is the one I wanted."

"Come with me," his brother answered. "We'll present it to Rov for his approval. You also need to see his weapon and then Harris and I will load them." Harris evidently was the name of Lord Rovington's second.

"Very well," Gavin said. He gave Sarah one last reassuring smile and then both he and his brother walked away from her.

She rolled her arms in his jacket and pressed them against her stomach to ward off a sense of impending tragedy. Dueling was a ridiculous way to solve an argument, especially for the challenge Lord Rovington had issued. She wasn't about to go with the man if he defeated the duke.

At the same time, she was proud that Baynton had accepted the challenge. That he was not going to let Lord Rovington run roughshod over him. That he was defending her.

She'd never had a champion before and if he died because of it, well, she could not think on it. She must not.

Lord Rovington and Gavin shook hands in the center of the field. It was obvious the two men no longer considered each other friends.

Their seconds inspected the weapons and then loaded them. They examined them again and handed them to the duelists, who once again looked them over. They moved as if in ritual.

Sarah wondered if Gavin wished he had his gloves on. Lord Rovington was wearing them.

His lordship said something to his second, who

spoke to Lord Ben. Lord Ben walked over to her. He spoke to his tiger. "David, Rovington wants the phaeton moved over about four yards toward the center."

"Yes, sir." The tiger climbed up on the seat to move the vehicle.

"Why does he want this?" Sarah asked Lord Ben.

"He is being fastidious." He started to go but she called him back.

"Wait." He turned, lifted his brows expectantly. "Please tell me the duke is a good shot," she said.

For the first time since she'd been in his company, Lord Ben gave her a smile, one reminiscent of his brother's. "You needn't worry. He can break the stem of a wineglass at fifteen paces. He will be fine. If I had thought there would be a problem, I would have driven my coach in case my brother was injured."

She nodded, not sharing his confidence but relieved to know that the duke was no stranger to a pistol.

Lord Ben moved to the center of the field to stand beside the physician. "Does the position of the vehicle meet your approval, my lord?"

Rovington nodded.

Stepping forward, Lord Ben said, "I shall count to five and then say the word *fire*. No one discharges his weapon until that moment. Are we understood?"

Both Lord Rovington and the duke nodded that they understood. Gavin was all business now. His complete attention was on his opponent. Sarah swung her gaze over to Rovington, wanting to see him as the duke did. She watched him intently.

Both men took a stance. The pistols in their hands were pointed to the ground.

"Are you ready, Lord Rovington?" Lord Ben asked.

Rovington nodded, but Sarah did not think he looked confident. Indeed, he had gone quite pale.

"Your Grace?" He turned to his brother.

Gavin nodded.

"Very well," Lord Ben said. "All ready!" He waited a beat and then began the count. "One . . . two . . ."

He had not reached three when Sarah noted a slight movement on Lord Rovington's part. Instinctively, her trained actor's eye, honed in the art of anticipating the actions of others upon a stage, knew he was going to fire before the count.

"*Gavin,*" she shouted in warning, a split beat before Lord Rovington's shot cracked through the air.

Chapter Sixteen

Sarah's shout saved Gavin's life. The warning in her voice had broken his concentration and he'd given a start, the slightest of movement but a telling one.

Rov had aimed for the heart. Gavin would have been mortally wounded.

Instead, because he'd turned toward Sarah, the ball went through his shirt into the fleshy part of his left arm. Gavin felt the burn of it as it traveled out the other side.

There was a beat of shocked silence from the sidelines, and then Ben shouted, *"Murder."*

The charge was quickly agreed upon by Rov's second and the witnesses with disapproving faces. Sarah scrambled from her perch on the phaeton and was ready to charge out onto the field. Ben caught her and pulled her back.

"Wait," he ordered. "It is His Grace's turn for the shot."

Gavin tipped his pistol at her. "I'm fine," he assured her.

She looked as if she didn't believe him. Why should she? Like all flesh wounds, the one on his arm was starting to bleed profusely, staining the white sleeve of his shirt and making the matter appear more dire than it actually was.

Gavin turned his attention to Rovington who appeared ready to swoon. The next shot was Gavin's and both men knew it. Rovington was nothing more than a simple target should Gavin choose to see him that way—and he did.

This man he had once considered his closest friend had not only set about undoing politically all that Gavin had accomplished, he had just attempted to murder him and had probably been behind a plot to disgrace him. There was no honor in Rovington.

And yet, putting a ball in Rov, no matter the momentary satisfaction, would create sympathy for him from certain quarters. Gavin would not allow that to happen.

He pointed his pistol off to the side toward the ground, and fired. The gesture was a symbol of disdain.

Across from him, at the crack of his shot, Rovington collapsed to the earth as if struck or perhaps as if relieved he still lived.

"Both men stay your mark," Ben announced. He set Sarah aside with the admonishment to wait while the physician walked to Gavin. Ben and Rov's second walked over to Rovington who had risen to his feet.

"Not a scratch on him," Rov's second declared, something all the witnesses knew, and then Ben and the second came back to Gavin.

"What a cowardly worm," Ben said, letting his voice carry.

"I am ashamed," the second agreed, equally loud. He bowed to Gavin. "Your Grace, I pray you will pardon my role in this disaster."

"May you choose your friends more wisely in the future," Gavin suggested.

"I shall."

There was the sound of hooves and they all turned to see Rovington riding away. "If he believes he can escape the story of this morning's work, he is wrong," his second said with disgust. "I shall personally see that it is all over town. The man has no courage."

Gavin was pleased. The muscle of his arm burned where the shot had gone through but he would heal.

Rovington, on the other hand, would not recover. His reputation would be in tatters. He must resign as Chairman of the Committees by nightfall and Gavin would send him a letter to that effect. After all, who would follow Rov's advice or directions now?

The physician had Gavin remove his shirt and inspected the wound to see that it was clean and no fibers from the fabric were caught in it. He then bound the wound tightly and the bleeding began to slow.

Sarah stood away from the men by the phaeton. She was pale and quiet.

Gavin put on his shirt and crossed over to her. She didn't greet him, but watched his approach with solemn green eyes.

He reached for his jacket. Ben's tiger helped him pull it on, taking care with the injured arm. Not fooling with the neck cloth, Gavin motioned with his head for the tiger to give them a moment's privacy.

Sarah looked at him then. Tears brimmed in her green eyes. "You could have been killed. He is a terrible man."

"Aye, he is," Gavin said. "I owe you a great debt. If you had not called my name, I would not have moved and his bullet might have found its mark."

"I never wish to witness another duel as long as I live," she replied fervently.

"I pray to never be in another one."

"Lord Rovington is *not* a gentleman and there should be a way to announce that fact to everyone in the world. He should be *shunned*." The tears had evaporated and color returned to her cheeks. She was magnificent when her temper was up, especially in his defense.

"He will be," Gavin assured her, and then he asked the question that teased him. "How did you know he was going to fire before the count?"

"I saw the tension in his shoulder. Intuitively I understood he was not going to honor the count. He was too quiet before, too withdrawn." She shook her head. "My training in the theater is to anticipate what another actor will do. One learns to read the slightest hint of movement in their bodies."

"Your training has saved my life. Come, let us leave."

"What of your arm?"

"The physician has handled it."

"But do you need laudanum? Something for the pain?"

"Right now, what I need more than anything is you."

That was true. How close he had come to being mortally wounded was sinking in along with a giddy gratitude that he was alive. His opponent had been defeated. He need never worry about betrayal from Rov again.

And along with that elation was a strong desire to finish what they had started the night before.

Sarah knew what he was thinking. To his everlasting joy, she reached for his hand. "Yes," she said, one simple word that said everything.

He helped her up into the phaeton. Ben was still discussing the duel with the witnesses. Gavin placed his hat on his head and picked up the reins. Sarah placed her hand upon his thigh, holding on to the seat with her other. He drove by the group of men and stopped. "I'll return your vehicle later." He nodded for the tiger to hop aboard.

"How shall I return home?" Ben protested.

"You are resourceful, brother. You shall think of a way." And with that, Gavin snapped the reins and set the team forward, Ben's laugh of agreement following them.

The hour was still early but London's streets were active. Gavin concentrated on his driving and the heat of Sarah's hand on his thigh. They didn't speak. There was no need to do so.

In relatively quick order, Gavin pulled up to the Clarendon. He set the brake and hopped down.

While the tiger climbed into the seat to take the reins and presumably drive back for Ben, Gavin swung Sarah down from the vehicle.

"Your arm," she chastised but Gavin could barely feel his arm—not when compared to the other, more urgent feeling in another part of his anatomy.

He practically dragged her up the stairs to their floor. His anticipation was so great, the sound of the key in the lock was enough to put him over the edge.

And then they were inside.

Sarah moved first, throwing her arms around him, pressing her body against his, and pulling him down into her kiss.

Kicking the door shut, Gavin marveled that he had never imagined that a woman's desire could rival his own. The shy Sarah, the frightened one, the reserved, anxious woman was gone. In her place was the Siren.

Even if Gavin had wanted to resist her, he would have been powerless to do so.

She pushed off his jacket. He untied the ribbons to her bonnet so that he could taste her ear. Her shawl was on the ground at her feet and soon her dress followed.

She pulled out the tail of his shirt and then smoothed her hand across his muscles beneath it.

"I've been wanting to do that since you took off your shirt in that field," she said, her lips against his ear.

"It is wise you didn't or we would be doing this for all to see."

She laughed her agreement before kissing him again, deeply, fully, without reservations.

Sarah was more unclothed than he, so Gavin had to help. After all, men's fashions were more complicated than skirts and stockings.

As he explored her mouth, he unbuttoned his breeches. His manhood was a proud and ready being. He'd been waiting for years for this moment and he would no longer be denied.

Then Sarah took the lead. Ending the kiss, she took Gavin's hand and led him into the bedroom. "Sit," she said, gently pushing him toward the edge of the bed.

Gavin reached for her as he obeyed but she slipped from his grasp. Instead, she knelt in front of him. Her dress was unlaced and the bodice was dangerously loose and askew, revealing full breasts and a tantalizing glimpse of a nipple. He wanted to grab her by the arms and lift her up and on top of him. Instead, she took ahold of his left boot. She gave it a mighty pull and it slid down his leg. She reached for the other and did the same. Then she stood, holding her bodice in place with one hand. Ah, yes, she'd known where his eye had been the whole time.

"Let it go," he whispered.

She pretended to hesitate a moment and then released her dress so that it fell to her feet. She had not worn petticoats or small clothes this morning. There had been no time for leisurely dressing and the thought that she had been so completely naked under her dress during the duel shredded Gavin's last hold over himself.

He reached for Sarah and devoured her with his kiss as he brought her onto the bed beside him. Her hands held his waist, smoothed over his buttocks, pushing his breeches down. Gavin helped the best he could without losing this heady kiss.

Never before had he experienced this close connection with another person. Kissing Sarah was as natural and vital to him as breathing.

He rolled on top of her. Her legs—those long, lovely legs that had captured his imagination in the theater—opened to him, cradled him. He could feel her heat. He rose over her, placing himself against tight red curls. He was hard, beyond ready.

"Sarah—" he started, in this moment loving her so much, he needed to assure himself that this was what she wanted but she cut him off.

"Gavin, take me."

And that is what he did.

His manhood knew where to aim. His body

glided deeply inside as smoothly as if he'd been born to be there. Every pleasure sense pulsed with the joy of joining.

Sarah's hand pressed upon his hip. Her body curved to accept him, and Gavin found himself buried within her to the hilt. She was perfect, magic, tight.

Instinctively, he began moving. She eagerly matched his rhythm.

This was what Gavin had been waiting for.

Over the years, he'd heard men brag. They'd been descriptive. And, of course, there were the poets . . . but nothing could have prepared Gavin for the complete happiness he experienced being in *her* arms.

Her heat enveloped him. Her legs held him steady. He had worried that he would need to hold back, to be gentle, but he discovered that she would have none of that. She met the force of his thrusts and whispered for more. "Please, more, Gavin."

Angels could not sing such sweet music.

He felt her quicken. What a miracle a woman's body was. She tightened, pulled, and then came the hotness of her release—and he could hold back no longer. With one last thrust, he experienced his own release. The intensity of the moment robbed him of reason.

For a solid moment, they became one.

Nor did he think that at last he was a man.

What nonsense. Gavin had never had any doubts about his manhood or his place in the world.

No, what came to his mind was how blessed he was to share this moment with Sarah. They were complete, whole, one.

From the point where his path had crossed with hers, he'd been aware of her. Now, he understood why.

Every path of his life had been leading him to her.

Sarah could not move. She could barely breathe.

She'd thought she'd known what to expect in the coupling between a man and a woman. Now, she was stunned to realize that even with her years of marriage, she'd not had a clue.

Gavin had changed her into a creature of light, emotion, feeling. In his arms, she *was* the Siren.

Her body hummed from a sense of perfect fulfillment, and she wanted more.

He moved off of her and as a flower follows the sun, she turned to him, pressing her body along his.

His lips brushed her hair. She held him close, her hands on his back as she marveled at the differences between them. He was hard where she was soft and they had fit together perfectly.

Peace filled her being. She was safe with him. She could trust him. She believed in him. She kissed his shoulder. His skin was warm. She could feel the muscles move and flex beneath the smoothness of his skin. His scent set her heart pounding. She ran her hand across the bandage and wished she could heal him with her kiss.

When she shifted, he released his hold. She sat up, folding her legs under her on the mattress.

His gaze followed her every movement. He cupped her breast as if it fascinated him.

"Now what?" he asked, sounding as satisfied and serene as she felt.

"We could break our fast," she said as his thumb circled her nipple. She looked down the length of his tall body that filled the bed. He was stirring again, and the sight made her proud. Gavin acted as if he appreciated every inch of her.

"Or," she said, leaning so that her breast rested in his hand, "we could have another go at it. See if there is anything we missed the last time."

"I wouldn't mind the practice," he answered and slid his hand to her neck to bring her lips to meet his.

And practice they did. All that day and the next.

The room at the Clarendon became their sanctuary.

When she mentioned that her body was an old

one, a four-and-thirty one, he laughed and called her beautiful.

Beautiful.

Sarah had never thought of herself that way before. Her coloring was too strong, too out of fashion for true beauty—and yet, when she was with him, she believed herself lovely.

What truly amazed her was that when she decided to work on the task of copying the parts of her play for the actors, Gavin sat at the table next to her, helping. He hadn't been lying to her when he'd said he'd enjoyed reading the play and often asked perceptive questions about the characters.

And through it all, they made love. Delicious, soul-satisfying love.

However, they could not hide away forever.

Besides, they both had much to do. He had to return to his politics and she was determined to stage her play. Gavin encouraged her to do so. He told Sarah he admired her for being herself. Her spirit attracted him as much as her body.

His man Talbert was, of course, dismissed. Gavin had seen to the secretary and had sent letters demanding Lord Rovington's resignation as Chairman of the Committees on the day of the duel. He didn't appear to have any remorse over the action. Sarah understood he was the sort of man who would do what he believed must be done.

That meant that someday, he would end their liaison. However, for the first time in her life, Sarah did not want to worry about the future. She wanted to live this day and spend the night in his arms without doubts and fears.

She was now a mistress.

If she allowed herself the time to think deeply on the matter, she was embarrassed. This was the place she had told herself she would not go.

Still, she discovered that she lacked the will to give up Gavin.

And her feeling toward him had nothing to do with the clothes he purchased for her from Mrs. Hillsman or the house he purchased in her name not far from her old home on Mulberry Street and very close to the Bishop's Hill Theater. No, her feelings ran deeper than gifts.

Because of him, she had security. Because of him, she was living her dream.

She found herself anxiously waiting for the sound of his knock on her door. She adored the weight of his body upon hers and being curled up against his warmth. No matter where he went in the evening, he came to her bed for the night.

Sarah was learning what made him laugh and enjoyed sharing tidbits of her day that would make him smile.

Of course, he insisted she should have a maid

and a cook and a butler but when she protested, he settled for one maid to tidy the house. That was all she wanted. Sarah did her own cooking and her favorite moments were when he could join her for dinner. They would sit at her table in the kitchen before the hearth. She learned he liked his beef rare and his meals simple.

Her days were busy as well. She wanted the first performance to be in September. That didn't leave much time for casting the play.

Gavin acted as if he enjoyed listening to her share tales of her day. He always encouraged her, something she had never anticipated. All the other men in her life had been discouraging.

"I'm having difficulty finding a lead actress," Sarah confided over dinner one night. "The actresses who would be completely right are in other plays and the ones who have read for me lack a certain . . ." Her voice drifted off as she tried to choose the right word, which was also one of the problems. "The Widow Peregrine is a bold creature and very self-possessed. If she is played too strongly, the audience will not like her. So she needs to be soft; however, I want a certain intelligence to come through from her."

"Why don't you play the part?" Gavin suggested.

"I couldn't. I'm the manager."

"But many male managers are also lead actors. Isn't that what you told me?"

It was true. But could she do it?

"Frankly, Sarah, I can't imagine anyone else more perfect for that part."

"The work will be twice what I expected," she murmured. "She is a very involved character and in almost every scene. I'd have to learn the lines—"

"Lines you already know fairly well. I'll help you. We shall rehearse here. I'll read the other parts and it will all fall into place."

Fear wanted her to say no.

However, his confidence in her was contagious. "I could do it."

"I know you can. Where is the play?"

They started that very night with the opening scene. Gavin played the maid, a role that both made Sarah laugh and fall in love with him.

Yes, love.

Oh, love had been coming. Perhaps even before she'd discovered what it could be like between a man and a woman in his arms.

At first, she'd been suspicious of this fledgling emotion. After all, she'd believed she'd loved Roland. She wanted to think her feelings were due to the sex. The act was actually boring when one thought about it . . . but not with Gavin.

Each and every time was better than the last. Her passion didn't wane; it grew, almost in correlation with her respect for him.

He had only to look at her a certain way or touch her and she melted into his arms. He was a demanding, inventive lover and she discovered in herself that same yearning drive. They were well matched.

Granted he wasn't always with her. He was the Duke of Baynton. He had duties. There were affairs he attended where it would have not been the thing for her to go. However, he always came to her bed, no matter how late the hour, he returned to her.

And now that he was enthusiastically helping her to realize her dream, well, how could a woman not fall in love?

"Miss Charnock was disappointed you were not in attendance at Lord Trammell's rout last night," the dowager said to Gavin when he made his appearance one morning. She was already seated at the table. "In fact, I'm rather surprised to see you in the breakfast room this morning. It has been some time."

Gavin heard the censure in his mother's tone. He was not one to disappoint her. However, between his duties and obligations and living with

Sarah, he had not been home. Nor had he wanted to be. The only time he felt completely alive in his own life was with Sarah.

She fascinated him. Her mind was always busy. He discovered he had grown bored with the endless bickering of politics, arguments that rarely solved any problems. He enjoyed helping Sarah with her lines for the play. He found the challenges she faced in working with the actors interesting. He could even relate the trials she had managing her actors with his own difficulties with members of Lords and the Commons. Some of the solutions he and Sarah devised to assuage an actor's fragile pride also worked on members of those august bodies.

He discovered having a partner he trusted to hash over the difficulties and vagaries of his day was nice. The weight of his office seemed lighter when he shared with her. He had a sense of peace and contentment.

Therefore, no, he had not been dutiful in his courting of Miss Charnock. He hadn't thought of her until his mother mentioned her name.

His mother seemed to accurately read his mind. She looked to the footmen serving the room. "Please leave us."

Gavin knew he would not appreciate this discussion. He thought about leaving with the servants but that would be cowardly. Instead, he helped himself to the breakfast dishes on the sideboard.

Once he sat, his mother said, "You told your aunt and me that you were open to this courtship. The Charnock family has expectations of you."

But what if I don't wish to meet those expectations?

Instead of asking the question, he said carefully, "I've only spoken to her twice." He took a bite of buttered toast. He would prefer sharing his breakfast with Sarah. He'd had a very late meeting last night and, since he'd known she'd had a full day at the theater with the opening of her play right on the horizon, he had thoughtfully decided to spend the night at Menheim and let her have an uninterrupted night of sleep.

Besides, he needed to make an appearance in front of his mother sooner or later.

"You don't have to talk to her at all," the dowager answered. "You know how these things are done. Miss Charnock has been waiting patiently for your attention. More important, so has the rest of society. It is known that you are interested in her."

"Not because I put it about."

"You are not naïve, my son. The moment you walked with her in that garden, it was noticed. When you called upon her the next day, it was settled." She leaned forward, her hands in her lap.

"The world knows about your *mistress*, especially after you dueled over her." She said the word with a hint of disdain. "The two of you have not been discreet. Your father would never have approved. He trained you to be more circumspect. However, I am aware you have 'needs.' Over the years, you certainly have been better behaved than your brothers about the matter. I also understand that you have always honored the title and have striven to be all that the Duke of Baynton should be. I know you will not shirk your obligation to marry a young woman of *high* morals, *good* family, and a more than respectable *fortune*. You understand that your job is to breed an *heir*."

He did understand. Indeed, Gavin actually longed for children. They may be a way of forwarding the succession of the title but, for him, they were also a yearning. His father had been a harsh taskmaster. Gavin wanted not only to have a son but to raise him with more compassion. To let him be his own man—something his father had never allowed.

At the same time, he wanted Sarah.

He knew that now. He had not enjoyed having his bed to himself last night. He'd missed her presence.

Sarah could not have children. He pushed the thought from his mind, feeling disloyal.

"I see I have given you much to consider," the dowager said. She set her napkin aside and rose from the table, moving to the closed door. "I know you, of all my sons, will do what is right. What is expected."

Gavin found his voice. "And what if I refuse?"

Such a simple notion and he'd never thought of it until now. What if he disobeyed the order of things?

His mother stopped, met his eye and said. "You won't. It is in your nature to do what is right. I shall inform Mr. and Mrs. Charnock to arrange a betrothal party so the announcement may be made properly. As to your mistress, well, your father would not approve but I shall leave her to your own conscience."

She ended her statement with a tight smile, one that didn't reach her eyes.

In the past, Gavin would not have seen past that smile. In trying to understand, he was learning to understand others—and he realized, there was much he didn't know about his own mother. His father had taken up the room in his life, leaving his mother more in the background, even after his death.

The dowager opened the door and was ready to sail from the room, until Gavin stopped her by asking, "Did you love my father?"

She started as if his question had been completely unexpected, and it had. Gavin hadn't even known he would ask it. Her brows came together. "Love?"

"Aye, cupid's emotion. I believe it is part of the marriage vows."

"Why are you asking, Gavin?"

She scarcely used his given name. From the moment he had received his first title, a courtesy title, the Marquis of Trenton, she had referred to him by it. He'd been Trenton, my lord, Baynton, Your Grace, or "my son."

"I'm not asking. I'm wondering," he said. "After all, it is obvious Ben adores Elin. Jack would go to the ends of the earth for Charlene. I cannot see either of them with mistresses and I've started to wonder about Father? Did he live two lives?"

"Never. As far as I know, your father was one of the rare men who was completely faithful."

"So, he *loved* you?"

"I don't understand this question."

Gavin stood. "Not too long ago, you kept company with Fyclan Morris and I think you were the happiest I've ever known you." The financier Fyclan Morris was Elin's father and an important mentor to Gavin. Without him, he could not have restored the Baynton fortunes that his father, the old duke, had come close to ruining.

"I have respect for Fyclan," his mother answered. Now she was the one who trod carefully.

"Did you love him?"

With a sound of impatience, the dowager shut the door. "This is nonsense." And he would have believed her except for the second of raw emotion that swept her face to be quickly schooled away.

"Did he not return your regard?" Gavin pressed, on a mission now.

"In his fashion. What does this have to do with our discussion about Miss Charnock?"

"It doesn't, I suppose. And yes, I know my obligations . . . except recently, Mother, I feel as if I stand at the edge of an abyss and one step might destroy me. Not other men—*me*."

"I've never known you to be given to foolishness."

"Perhaps I never had a reason to before."

She frowned, took a deep breath, released it, and then said, "I've always admired Fyclan. When he and I kept company, I found I cared deeply for him . . . except he will always love his wife. She has been gone several years and still he loves her. Oh, he was kind and considerate when he was with me but the heart of him belonged to her and would never be mine."

There was a moment of silence and then she said, "In truth, I cared too much for Fyclan to be able to breathe in his wife's shadow. Lord Kent—"

she referred to her current escort "—is also a widower but he doesn't pine for what he once had. He holds me in high regard."

"Do you feel the same?"

"I am happy," she pronounced with a touch of defiance. "We suit each other. Fyclan will never let go of Jenny. Some men are that way. I will never be what she was to him. And now," she continued, opening the door, "I have appointments. I will let you know what date the Charnocks choose to announce the betrothal. Oh, and may I say, I wish you would hire a new secretary. It is tiresome communicating with you since you gave Talbert the sack."

"I shall, Mother."

He half expected her to flee the room then, but she didn't. Instead, she looked back at him. "Gavin, don't think overmuch on love. It has nothing to do with marriages of our class. Remember that, my son."

She left the room.

Chapter Seventeen

Don't think overmuch on love.

His mother's advice haunted Gavin.

She was right in that any discussion he'd ever heard about suitable marriage partners, love was never one of the qualities mentioned. A successful marriage was one that met the needs of the Great Houses and ensured the dynasties would be preserved.

In fact, he had never considered the true nature of the word "love" before—not relative to himself. He had an idea about what love looked like. He had given his blessing to Ben to marry Elin because they were in "love." He had stepped aside from Lady Charlene because she and Jack "loved" so deeply, they would defy convention.

Yes, he'd seen love. He'd not experienced it.

He now found himself trying to piece his thoughts about love together.

Ben and Elin served as a good example. He'd never known his younger brother to be so happy. Or productive. Ben's star was rising fast in the War Office. He was a respected, stable, and considered administrator, something he definitely had not been before Elin. She brought out the best in him. Even Ben, happily, gave her full credit for his success.

It was the same with Jack and Charlene. They belonged together. Gavin had been furious that his twin had claimed his bride. He had considered his brother's behavior traitorous. Everyone in society had known that Gavin had set his sight on Charlene.

And yet, once Gavin was in their company, he realized it would have been almost cruel to separate her from Jack, even if he could. He'd had to swallow his pride, let them marry; he had even paid for the wedding breakfast.

Because they were in love.

Late that afternoon, he found himself at the Bishop's Hill Theater. He took a chair in the rear of the theater.

Sarah did not know he was there. She was busy on stage with her actors. She was full of authority and exercised it very well, he had to note. He enjoyed watching her move on the stage. Her every gesture was grace.

His favorite moments were when a new idea struck her and her eyes came alive with possibility. Even at home, he would catch her standing, her mind mulling over a particular scene or bit of dialogue. He would watch her mentally chew on the problem, then gifting him with a smile of victory when she'd riddled it out to her satisfaction.

This afternoon, the actor playing the male lead Jonathan Goodwell did not like a line and Sarah changed it. Listening, Gavin had to admit the actor's wording was better. Gavin himself was not fond of admitting when he was wrong but Sarah was of a more open mind. She continually weighed what was best for her play, a trait Gavin had discovered that since knowing her, he had started to use in his political life to good success.

The actors were rehearsing the last scene. This was where Goodwell declares himself to the Widow. The actor playing the role was Thom Rawlins. He was a long, narrow man with a sharp chin and deep-set eyes.

Sarah had wanted a more dashing actor for the role but beggars could not be choosers. Gavin was as aware as Sarah that many of the prime actors in the city had chosen not to audition for *Widow* because they were not comfortable with a female manager.

He had offered to hire a male manager for her but Sarah was committed to serving as actress-manager and so she would.

Watching her, Gavin could tell she relished this dual role. His love liked being in charge—

His love.

The endearment caught his attention.

She *was* his love.

Many a night, after a bout of robust lovemaking, he would hold her and realize how blessed he was to have her in his life. Blessed, yes . . . wasn't that part of love? The blessing of love?

Nor did he have a desire to lose her. She was more than his lover; she was a confidant. He could speak his thoughts aloud and receive not only her wise counsel but also her loyalty. For the first time, he'd met someone who would never betray his trust—anymore than he would betray hers. There had even been times over the past weeks when she had understood what he was truly feeling before he could express it himself.

And he understood the same about her. *That* was the miracle.

In the past, Gavin had been so wrapped up in his ducal responsibilities, he'd rarely had a moment to think of anything or anyone else . . .

but he thought of her. All his waking moments. The grace of her visited his dreams as well.

Right now, observing her working, he knew she was frustrated with Rawlins. She claimed he was a lazy actor, always a bit slow with his responses or paying attention to the business on stage.

Only the other night, when Gavin had been saying Rawlins's lines to help Sarah practice hers, she had exclaimed with exasperation that she wished the actor had a bit of Gavin's ability. "You are a natural at this," she had declared.

"If I can't move the Money Bill forward, perhaps I shall turn to the stage," Gavin had teased in response. "Facing an audience will be vastly easier than Liverpool's disappointment." However, he'd been pleased by her compliment. He took pleasure in his escapade with the theater.

He took pleasure in Sarah.

She was not happy with how Rawlins crossed the stage to deliver his character's pronouncement of love for the Widow. She accused him of moving like a clod and not a man in love, something that made the other members of the company snicker. Apparently Rawlins was quite taken by the young woman playing the Widow's sister.

"Quiet, all of you," Sarah said in a voice that would have made a general proud. "We open in two days' time. We must pull together. Each of us can do a bit more. This play will be a success. It has everything Londoners like from their theater, but we need to give it our all."

Several heads nodded. Rawlins even managed to move with more grace.

And Gavin felt his chest swell with pride. His Sarah was a leader. She was clever, bright, and bold, a remarkable woman. She graced his table and his bed and he never wanted her to leave his side. It was that clear, that simple.

He loved her, and the knowledge was humbling because he actually needed her in his life.

Yes, Gavin must marry. If his mother and Dame Imogen believed the Charnock chit was suitable, he would not argue. But he would not give up Sarah. He couldn't.

Many men were more faithful to their mistresses than to their wives. He would be one. Sarah would lack for nothing.

His mind settled, Gavin left the theater to attend a meeting to negotiate with the Opposition to the Money Bill. It would be a late night. Apparently, Rov had not left London as everyone had anticipated in spite of his being disgraced in the duel. Jane had, thankfully, retired to the country but Rov stayed. It was said he whispered against Gavin but truly, what damage could he do? No decent door was open to him. The man was now beyond the pale.

The hour was late by the time he returned to the house he shared with Sarah. He let himself in, not expecting her to be awake.

Instead, he was surprised to see Sarah working away at her desk, crumpled and discarded sheets of paper on the floor around her chair. She looked up as he entered, the very picture of misery.

He crossed over to her. "Why are you awake? And what are you writing?" Looking down, he saw the names of the characters in *The Fitful Widow*. "You can't be rewriting your play. Not at this late date."

"I worry," she confessed. She was wearing her nightdress and her hair was down, the way he liked it. "I was thinking that the middle should have more power. Perhaps more drama."

"It has drama enough." He took her pen from her hand, setting it aside.

"But the part where Peregrine realizes Jonathan's true intentions is so slow."

"Not slow—*studied*," Gavin corrected. "Your audience will want to hear the nuance to every word. Isn't that what you told me last week?" He pulled her from the chair.

"But—" Sarah started to protest until Gavin silenced her with a kiss.

Her body quickly melted against his as if only he could give her strength. He ran his hand over her hair, her back, her hips.

He broke the kiss. "There is nothing wrong with your play," he said. "It will be a success."

"You never go to the theater."

"Only the occasional Shakespeare," he reminded her, savoring what had become a small joke between them. "But I have heard others speak who have seen *Widow*, and they all agree it is a brilliant piece of work. Trust your talent, Sarah. Your play will be the talk of London."

"It already is," she said. "Your connection to it has made it so."

"Good. I am proud to shine a light on such a lovely new playwright."

Her lips curved into a reluctant smile. She feared believing him. Gavin understood wanting something and yet fearing the outcome. "Be brave, my love."

She showed her appreciation for his faith in him with another kiss, and then another until they were on the carpet making love. Later, he carried her sleeping form up to their bed. Stretching out beside her, he realized how happy he was to be with her. He'd missed being beside her last night.

He felt more at home in this modest house than he did in the home of his childhood, Menheim. Then again, wherever Sarah was, there was where he would be happy.

He must not lose her.

Gavin was gone by the time Sarah rose the next morning. She felt rested and well loved. In the light of day, she realized he had saved her from immeasurable angst. Once she was in his arms, she could think of nothing other than him.

Of course, she was nervous about the opening of her play. One more day. That was all she had to prepare.

She knew that Colman and many of the other theater managers in town were very interested to see how she did. After all, most of them had turned down her plays. They hadn't refused her talent to help their own work, but she sensed that, territorial men that they were, they were not going to greet *The Fitful Widow* with open arms.

Sarah dressed quickly and went downstairs to see what she had to break her fast. Afterward, she hurried to the theater, ready for the hundreds of tasks scheduled for the day. One item she didn't have to worry about was her role. Gavin had rehearsed her so completely, she knew her part in every manner possible. One had only to throw out a line and Sarah could answer it. She knew this play better than anyone, save perhaps Gavin since he'd played every part rehearsing her lines with her. He'd even memorized most of them as well.

She was usually the first to the theater and especially so today. For a moment, she savored the quiet. Handbills had been passed out or tacked up where they may. Whether the house on the morrow would be a full one or almost empty, the die had been cast.

She knew there were some who said that Gavin had purchased all of this for her, and it was true. She'd said as much to him once. He'd answered that he was merely providing her the opportunity.

His faith in her seemed unwavering. Because of him, she'd found the courage to set aside doubts and to live her dream.

She prayed he would not be disappointed when the play opened, and yet, she knew he wouldn't be. *The Fitful Widow* was a good play. Her best. She'd been around the theater long enough to know what pleased an audience.

The day's rehearsals were in full costume. Things went wrong. They always did. Sarah was superstitious enough to believe if there were problems with the final rehearsal, then the play would be a success. She repeated that to herself every time a curtain didn't pull or an actor dropped a line.

That night she could have poured herself in bed. She did not expect Gavin until late. He'd sent word that he would not be home until later that evening.

She intended to wait up for him. She promised herself she would only close her eyes for a few minutes, just for a touch of relief. Instead, she fell into a deep sleep.

Sarah was a bit disoriented when she woke and realized it was still night. She reached over to Gavin's side of the bed. It was empty . . . and yet she sensed she was not alone. He was near.

Sarah had left a candle burning in the hallway. She pulled on a dressing robe, walked to the bedroom door and opened it. All seemed quiet in the house. Picking up the candle, she moved to the top of the stairs and stared down into the darkness. If Gavin was here, why did he not have a light burning?

"Gavin?"

There was no answer, and yet, she was certain of his presence.

She went down the stairs to the sitting room and that is where she found him. He sat in a patch of moonlight, sipping a glass of his whisky.

He looked up at her as she approached as if she

interrupted some deep thinking. "Why haven't you lit a candle?" she asked.

"I preferred the darkness," he answered. "Have you ever noticed how when it is truly dark you can almost imagine you have disappeared?"

His was an odd statement. Her every sense screaming that something was wrong, Sarah placed the candle on a side table and sat on the footstool close to his chair. "Do you wish to disappear?"

His sharp blue eyes met hers. He didn't answer.

"Gavin, what is wrong? Tell me."

His brows came together. His jaw tightened.

"Is it the Money Bill?" she asked. She knew he was frustrated by how long it was taking to drive this needed bit of legislation out of the Commons.

He shook his head. His mouth twisted in a mocking smile as if to say the Money Bill was nothing.

She reached for the glass in his hand and took a healthy sip. She placed the glass on the floor beside her, letting the warmth of the whisky settle through her. "Why are you down here alone?" She paused, reflected, and then asked, "What is it you don't want to tell me?"

He gave a start. "You know me so well."

"There is a reason you are not upstairs."

Gavin nodded. Then he said, "I must marry."

For the briefest, most glorious second, Sarah's heart leaped at those words, until she realized he didn't mean her. He was not upset because he was going to marry her. She was the mistress. An actress. Not the sort of woman a good man married.

She knew that. The world knew it. She had no right to feel hurt. Or deceived.

This moment was bound to come sometime. She just had assumed it wouldn't be so soon, that they would have more time together.

Or that perhaps it wouldn't come at all. She'd fooled herself into believing it would not matter.

But it did.

"Yes, of course," she murmured, surprised she could speak at all past the tightness in her throat.

"There are expectations," he said as if trying to explain what he couldn't accept. "I need an heir."

Those words were like tiny arrows to her heart. An heir, children . . . if he had asked for her soul, she would offer it up. But children were different. She would never be able to give him a child.

She found it hard to breathe, to think.

"I need to go to bed," she managed, anxious to leave the room before she betrayed herself. She stood, but then she had to ask, "Have you found someone?"

"I haven't been looking, if that is what you are asking. I've been here with you."

"And yet?"

"There is a suitable young woman. Her family is amenable to a match . . ." His voice drifted off, and then he sat forward. "Sarah, I don't want another."

Neither did she.

"When will you talk to her family?" she asked.

Gavin shifted in his chair, the set of his mouth grim. "Her father approached me today. He let me know he was pleased and told me he'd given the union his blessing. He did so in front of a number of witnesses. I was caught off guard."

"Have you even asked for her hand yet?"

He met her eye then and said, "My mother and aunt have made overtures. I called on the girl, back before we were who we are." There was a beat of silence and then he asked, "What of us, Sarah? I want *us*."

She had wanted "us," too, and now realized she had a decision to make. A painful one.

Sarah backed away, and yet she did not go far. She stopped at the edge of the circle of light. She had vowed that she would not end up like her mother. She'd tried marriage, and that had been a disaster. She'd attempted to be her own person, to make her own way . . . and she might have succeeded but she hadn't been doing well when she'd met Gavin.

So, she'd compromised herself. For love, she had bartered her principles.

And now he asked for her to continue on this way. Well, what had she expected? There was always going to be one ending and it would not be a happy one whichever way she chose.

However, she had not anticipated the temptation to be with him would be so strong. Or realize the cost . . .

He stood. "Sarah? Speak to me."

"And say what?"

"I need to know what you are thinking."

"I'm thinking that I've created this lovely little play in my head where everything was going to end well, but I see now that it won't."

"You know I care for you—" he started but she cut him off.

"Do you? Will you also care for her? The woman you will call wife? And what of your children? Don't they deserve your complete attention? You must understand, Gavin, I was married. I've been the wife of a faithless husband—"

"*Wait*," he said. "You cannot compare the marriage you had with my arrangement with Leonie Charnock. We barely know each other. She is an heiress, comes from a good family and—" He paused as if not knowing what else to say, so Sarah helped him.

"And is a good breeder. Because she is young, healthy." Dear Lord, as the truth of their conversation was sinking in, she felt as if her heart was being ripped in two. "Why does it hurt to speak those words? In fact, the pain is so great, I want to double over, and yet I can't. I'm caught in a web of my own making. I knew better than to let down my guard. *I knew.*"

"Sarah," he started again, taking a step toward her, but she placed her palm flat against his chest.

"I'm in love with you, Baynton. I love you. And instead of the joy those words should bring, I'm crushed because *how can I be so untrue to myself?*"

She would have run then, but he caught her before she could flee. She tried to push away. He held her fast, ignoring her struggles.

"Sarah, *listen to me.* I love you, too."

She shook her head. He mustn't. He couldn't. If she believed him, she would be trapped forever.

"If it could be another way, I would do it," he vowed.

She did not want to hear this.

"*I love you,*" he repeated. "Can you not understand? I love you. I can't live without you."

Hours ago, if someone had told her that he would be saying these words to her, she would have considered herself the most fortunate woman in the world. Now, they struck her with fear.

How could she leave?

How could she stay?

Placing both hands on his shoulders, she pushed, and he let go. She stumbled back. For a wild second, she looked around her at the house she had started to think of as her haven, and realized he had been what had made her feel safe. All of this was a shell without him.

He approached again. His arms came around her and this time, she did not fight. "I love you," he whispered, kissing her eyes, her cheeks, her lips. *"You,"* he repeated. "Whatever happens in my other life, you are the one I value. The one I cherish."

His other life.

She realized her own foolishness in believing she was his only life. Eventually, others—perhaps not his wife, but certainly his children—would take her place in his heart. The mistress was always expendable. Every fool knew that.

At last, she understood her mother.

Never before had Sarah felt so fragile in Gavin's arms.

She accepted his kisses but made no move to return them. Her response alarmed him. This was not the Sarah he knew. She was giving up on him, on *them*.

He needed her to believe that he would always be there for her. Then she would stay with him.

Slowly, he became more purposeful in his kisses. He knew what she liked. In spite of herself, he felt her respond and he could have sighed his relief. Instead, he swung her up into his arms and carried her to their bedroom.

She held on to him, her arms around his neck, her face buried in his shoulder.

In the darkness, they undressed as they had countless times before. Sarah was kissing him now with a fervent passion, as if she, too, did not want to let him go.

He laid her on the bed. *Their* bed. He could not imagine her not being here. He lived for the moments he was with her like this.

Her body opened to him. Gratefully, he slid into her. Nothing felt better in his arms than his Sarah. His lovely, vibrant Sarah.

Gavin began moving, wanting this to be good for her, reassuring her in the most intimate of ways of the depth of his love for her. Whatever he could do to honor her, he would. It was that simple. She held his heart—

He tasted her tears upon her cheek.

She'd been giving, but also quiet, and now he understood why.

However, God help him, he could not stop. No now.

Gavin drove both of them then. He was demanding and hard. She must trust him. He would do all he could for her. She needed to have faith in him . . . and yet, he, too, knew this would not work

Some women flaunted their independence They didn't need the solace of husbands or lovers Sarah was not one of them.

In turn, there were men who easily separated the threads of their lives. They had no difficulty giving pieces of themselves to many others and appeared at peace with the matter.

Gavin was not that sort. Nor should Sarah accept a lesser place in his life.

He recognized the fact as he felt her release and carried her with him on his own. This was no mere act of animal mating. It never had been for the two of them. When Gavin held her, when he was this connected to her, it was as if their souls merged. They were one.

In this moment of complete fulfillment, he understood her almost better than he did himself.

For long moments, they held each other.

And then she said, "I shall shut down the play."

"No, it opens tomorrow evening. You can't stop now. Your play is important."

She was quiet, and then whispered, "No, Gavin, nothing is important now."

"Trust me, Sarah." It was his last plea.

She turned to him then. "I can't be that other woman, Gavin. I know what that life is like and I won't live it."

He sat up abruptly, ran a hand through his hair. His heart was a heavy stone in his chest. He knew she had made up her mind.

She didn't say a word as he dressed.

He stood at the foot of the bed, waiting for her to call him back, and knowing she wouldn't. The mattress they shared now appeared cold and empty save for her glorious hair spread across the pillow.

"You will open the play," he said. "It is your future, Sarah. You must take the chance."

On those words, he left.

As he reached the top of the stairs, he heard the sound of her crying. His strong, resilient Sarah. She was broken.

And yet, she would survive. They both would. They had no choice.

He left the house as if the hounds of hell were after him, and perhaps they were.

Chapter Eighteen

Gavin did not go home to Menheim. Instead, he walked. There was an hour or so before dawn but time had ceased to matter. He didn't even care where he traveled.

Eventually, he found himself in front of his club. He went inside, nodded to the steward, and made his way to the dining room. He had some idea to break his fast. He wasn't hungry but he knew he must go through the motions.

Today would be a long day. There were his usual duties, and then, of course, he would attend Sarah's play. He'd purchased the most expensive box in the theater. She'd wanted to give it to him for free, but he'd insisted on paying.

She might have protested further; however, her friend Lady Baldwin, herself a former actress, was managing the seat tickets. She'd been happy to accept Gavin's money.

Now, he didn't know how he was going to live through the evening. He'd been seated close to the stage. He'd be able to see her every gesture and know that she was leaving him.

He would do it for Sarah. Their liaison was so well known, his not being there would be noticed. Her play should not suffer because of their personal relationship.

Gavin sat at his usual table by the window. A waiter approached but he waved him away. He wasn't ready to interact with anyone yet and it was too early in the morning for a whisky. God, what he would give to climb in the bottle and never come out—

"Good morning, Your Grace," the familiar voice of Fyclan Morris said. "May I join you since it seems the two of us are the only ones up at this hour?"

"Yes," Gavin answered, not particularly welcoming.

If Morris heard the curtness in his voice, he gave no indication but pulled out a chair, resting the cane he used against the wall. "Stout," he said, giving his order to the waiter. "And one for His Grace as well." The waiter bowed and left.

Fyclan gave Gavin an assessing look. Gavin knew he did not look his best and why should he

"You are not usually in here this early," Fyclan said, his soft Irish brogue coloring his words "And you have the look of a man who has lost his moorings."

Gavin didn't answer. He had nothing to say.

Morris continued as if they were involved in a spirited conversation. "I'm always up early. First light. I don't like dining at home. Too lonely now without Jenny."

Gavin's life would be "too lonely" now without Sarah.

The waiter returned with their drinks. Morris took a healthy sip of his and said, "Good news about Ben and Elin, isn't it? Twins!"

That statement pulled Gavin out of his dark thoughts. "What?"

"You have not heard? Elin and Ben told me yesterday. Your brother had said he was going to search you out. I hope I haven't upset their plans by tipping the teapot. When they tell you, please act as if you are hearing the news for the first time."

"I will, I will, but now that it is out, tell me all."

"There is not much to say. The midwife told them she is certain Elin is having twins. She believes she can feel the movement of two wee bodies inside Elin when she places her hands on her. It is a bit of a surprise because I didn't believe Elin was showing that much. However, with the fashions the way they are, how can anyone tell if a woman is carrying or not? I know she has found moving difficult. However, the midwife cautions we could be surprised with only one, but she claims she is rarely wrong."

Gavin sat back, a bit stunned. Twins, well, it was possible. They ran in the family. He was a twin.

He also felt more than a touch of envy.

"Here is to healthy babies," Morris said, raising his glass in salute.

Gavin joined him.

Morris set down his tankard. "I understand from your mother that we shall be wishing you happy relatively soon. She said you are making a match with the Charnock heiress." He nodded to the waiter that he was ready to order his breakfast.

No, not happy. And the realization that he and Leonie Charnock were becoming common gossip made Gavin unhappier. His chest grew tight as if steel bands wrapped around him, making it difficult to breathe.

As if from a distance, he heard Morris ask, "Will you have the beefsteak as well?"

Gavin frowned at him, momentarily confused,

then nodded when he realized they were ordering food. The waiter left.

Morris leaned forward. "Are you feeling quite well?"

No, nothing in his life would ever be "well" again. "I'm fine."

The man across from him nodded but the look in his eye said he didn't believe Gavin—and suddenly Gavin needed to bolt. He wanted air and to be away from Morris's keen sensibilities. The man was known for his careful observation.

Gavin pushed back on his chair, but Morris leaned forward. "Wait. Give me a moment of your time."

"I don't know that I have a moment," Gavin replied brusquely. After all, he was a busy man. Few questioned him.

Morris was not of that number. "What is the matter with you? Are you ill?"

Gavin almost nodded his head yes and yet it was not in his nature to lie. "I have matters on my mind."

"You don't want to marry Miss Charnock?"

Warily, Gavin asked, "What makes you say that?"

"Well, you were grim when I first sat with you but you turned positively white when I mentioned her."

"She is an admirable young woman."

"I'm certain she is, but we aren't talking about her."

A party of four gentlemen took a table not far from theirs and there were other club members coming in the door. Gavin settled back in his chair. He knew most of those men. If he walked across the room, they would expect his attention or be offended. He was better with Morris.

"I accept the marriage," Gavin said. There, that should be it.

However, to his surprise, it wasn't.

Morris had given him careful scrutiny and Gavin was becoming aware he didn't look his best. His appearance was exactly that of a man who'd had little sleep and had spent a good portion of the night wandering in an attempt to quiet his thoughts.

"Tell me about it," Morris said quietly.

"About Miss Charnock?" Gavin answered, denying what his friend was asking.

"Don't treat me like an old fool. I respect you, Baynton. I pray you respect me as well."

"There is not much to say," Gavin demurred.

"You are in love."

The direct and very accurate response blasted through Gavin's defenses.

He looked to Morris, tempted to deny the statement. After all, men in love were weak . . .

and he would be seen as the weakest of all—a man in love with his mistress.

And yet, God help him, he was.

"She won't stay with me," Gavin confessed and with those words, the tightness in him seemed to spring open.

He plunged ahead, the words tumbling out of him in mad confession. "I all but forced her to become my mistress. I had to have her, you see. From the moment I saw her back when I was courting Lady Charlene, I noticed her. Me, who was always too busy to think about women. I didn't have the time."

"I understand. You and I have much in common. I remember those days when I was building my fortune and my career. It takes great energy."

"I have no energy for anything right now," Gavin admitted. "I told her last night that I was going to offer for Leonie Charnock. I explained that I needed an heir, that my marriage would be nothing more than a business arrangement." He met Morris's eye. "I love Sarah. I can't imagine my life without her. I'm a fool, aren't I?"

"Why? Because you are in love?" Morris leaned back in his chair. "That is the state man was born to be in. Until I experienced it with Jenny, I, like you, thought it made me appear weak. Now I know, I was strongest with her. I had no life before her. It was all work and selfish thoughts. I believed money made me rich. She taught me what riches truly are."

"And that was?"

"Having her in my arms. Hearing her laugh. Seeing her smile, or even cry. She made me feel like I mattered."

Gavin fell back in his chair. "With Sarah, I am myself."

"It is a gift."

"Will I not find that with Miss Charnock?"

Morris shrugged. "You tell me." He smiled at the server who delivered their food. The plates were set before them. Morris waited until they were alone again to say, "Eat. Food will help."

"I have no appetite. I've lost her, Fyclan. Sarah is a proud woman. I feel as if I have betrayed her. *I have.*"

"Then don't marry the Charnock heiress."

"I must. I haven't spent that much time with her, but my mother and my aunt have made inquiries. Her parents have approved the match. There are expectations."

"Ah, yes, expectations." Fyclan began cutting his meat. "The bane of a civilized society."

"I'm not just anyone. I'm a duke—"

"Because you were born first and had the luck of a certain set of parents. I've worked with the peerage all my life, Baynton. Men who feel it beneath them to dirty their hands. Or who play at politics to make themselves feel important. Worse are the ones who don't do anything but gamble and socialize. And then there are the good ones." Fyclan pointed at him with his knife. "I would have been proud to have had you for a son-in-law. You worked hard to turn your family's fortunes around. I know what a struggle it was. And I should state, I am pleased with your brother. Lord Ben makes Elin happy. Your father may have been a rigid man but he turned out sons with initiative and drive."

"I know." Once again, Gavin experienced the tightening in his chest. "I understand what I should do."

"Do you?" Fyclan set the knife aside. "Your father was a good one for saying one thing and doing the opposite himself. What does that tell you?"

"That he was the man he was."

"No, it should tell you that those responsibilities and expectations people talk about are subject to interpretation. Jenny's father didn't approve of me. He felt I wasn't good enough because I didn't have a title before my name and because I was Irish. He was wrong. So, the question I ask, do you believe people who would look down their noses at your Sarah are wrong?"

"Absolutely." Gavin leaned forward. "She is the

bravest woman I know. I have learned from her how difficult it is for a woman to survive alone, but she has. She even did what she must to rescue her niece from, well, an unspeakable fate. She has overcome odds that would break any dozen men I know."

God, just thinking about Sarah, about his admiration for her and all that she had brought into his life the last two months and how people might perceive her made him a bit crazy. He wanted to pick up chairs, throw them, and rail against the injustice of narrow minds. "If I was a boot maker or a deacon or any number of working occupations, I'd ask her to be my wife and be humbled if she answered yes."

"But you can't ask her as a duke?"

"You know that I can't."

"Why not?"

Gavin frowned at Fyclan. "She is an actress. People know her as my mistress. It is not done."

Fyclan shrugged. "Of course it has been done. There has been a mistress or two who has married her man and gone respectable."

"None that I know. Or that my family knows."

"Yes, but what is the purpose of being the most powerful duke in England if you can't do exactly as you wish?"

"She can't have children, Fyclan."

That statement stopped him. "You know this?"

Gavin nodded. "It isn't just that I need an heir for the title, I always imagined myself with children. I want them."

"And you are certain she can't have them?"

"Sarah is certain."

"Damn. Now I understand. I'm sorry, my friend. That is a facer . . . however, we can't always order our lives."

"We can for what is in our control."

"Whether or not we have children is far from under our control." Fyclan took a drink of his stout and set the glass down, studying it a moment before saying, "Jenny wanted a cartload of children, but her heart was not strong. The doctors warned us there was a danger to her heart if she should be pregnant. I loved Jenny, Baynton. From the moment I set eyes on her, I knew she was the one and I would have happily foregone children to keep her well—but she didn't agree. She said her arms felt empty without a child."

Gavin could understand that sentiment.

"So, we tried. There were some miscarriages. It was as if Jenny's body was protecting her, and then we were blessed to have Elin, and very lucky." He spoke as if living a happier time in his mind. "When I said as much, Jenny had laughed at me. She teased me for not believing in my gypsy gran."

"Your gypsy gran?"

"Aye, she had the gift of sight. She could see the future."

"You don't believe that."

"When I was a lad I did. None of us questioned her because she was often right. She predicted that my children's children would be peers. Dukes, she said. But I loved Jenny. I knew about her heart and I loved her all the more, Baynton. She was light to my dark. A joyful, giving woman. I didn't care about the prophecy when I was with her. My heart, even my soul was hers. Still are." His eye had gone misty and he looked away for a moment to gather himself.

"You can imagine how excited I was when your father suggested a match between you and Elin," Fyclan continued. "Jenny was elated. I'd given up the prophecy as nonsense. Jenny believed. She was proud our daughter would be a duchess, that Gran's words would come true. And then, Elin bypassed you to fall in love with your brother."

"They are truly made for each other."

"Aye, they are. I also feel Jenny has given them her blessing. I have a sense of peace about it, especially since you were more than decent about the whole situation."

What choice had he had? Gavin frowned at the now cold beefsteak on the plate in front of him.

"What I'm trying to say, Your Grace, is that love must have its way. My grandchildren may be peers or not. My daughter is happy and that is all that matters to me."

Fyclan sat forward. "You have asked my advice in the past. You have not asked it now but you will receive it. You need to decide what you can live with. Years from now, when you have your children around you, will you be happy? Or will you think of your actress and have regrets? Don't live a life with regrets, Baynton. It is not worth it, even if you do have a ducal title."

Gavin could have told him that he'd been schooled in regrets. His father had burned into him an understanding that the good of the title took precedence before all else.

However, they were interrupted by Lord Naylor and Mr. Dinwiddie, who had spied Gavin at his breakfast, and begged a moment to discuss the difficulties of the Money Bill.

The damn Money Bill.

Fyclan took his leave then. He had no desire to listen to men chew over politics.

Gavin never did eat his breakfast. He heard what they had to say and then returned home to be cared for by his valet. He had a busy schedule set by his new secretary, Andrew Riffey, an eager, experienced gentleman sent over by an agency.

"Your mother asked that you call upon Miss Charnock this afternoon. She intends to join you on the visit."

Gavin knew what was expected, and then he thought of his conversation with Fyclan.

He had no desire to call on Leonie Charnock, who was a lovely woman. He especially did not want to see her this day, hours before he was to watch Sarah's triumph on the stage. He did not wish the distraction.

Sarah would be a success this evening. Gavin enjoyed *The Fitful Widow* and he didn't like anything on stage. He knew Sarah was an uncommon talent. London would embrace her. Tomorrow he would do his duty and call on Miss Charnock.

Tonight, he was going to celebrate Sarah's accomplishment.

"Delay the call," he told Riffey.

"Until when, Your Grace?"

The word "tomorrow" was on the tip of his tongue, but Gavin held back. "When I decide," he said.

"Yes, Your Grace." Riffey left Gavin's study.

Gavin poured a whisky and silently counted, *one, two, three—*

His mother burst into his office. "What do you mean you will not go with me to call on Miss Charnock?"

"Exactly what you just said. I will not go. Not today."

"It is because of this actress, isn't it?" the dowager charged.

"Partially."

"Can you care for her so much that you would insult one of the leading heiresses in this city? Are you that much of a fool?"

Gavin considered his mother's question and answered, "Quite possibly."

The dowager practically stamped her foot in frustration. "This will not do—"

"It *must*," Gavin answered. It wasn't the son who had interrupted her; it was the duke. Fyclan had been right. What *was* the purpose of being a powerful duke if he couldn't do exactly as he pleased?

He moved over to his desk and sat down, placing his glass to the side. He expected his mother to stomp out.

She didn't.

Instead she took the chair in front of his desk.

Gavin wanted to ignore her. He also knew she wouldn't let him.

"Why have you made this decision?"

Because I've lost the only person who means anything to me, Gavin almost responded, but didn't. "I do not have time."

"Yes, but I imagine you have time for the theater this evening. Isn't tonight the opening of your paramour's play? Oh, don't look so surprised. Of course I know this. All of London is gossiping about it. Did you truly imagine I would not know of your involvement? I've received more questions than you can imagine about this play. Eyebrows have been raised. Not just about this woman being your mistress but that you are supporting her play."

"And why is that? Do they not think a play is a wise investment?"

"Do you?"

"As a matter of fact, I do. Mrs. Pettijohn is very talented. It has been my honor and privilege to support her."

"Baynton, it is not done. A woman is not a theater manager."

"This one is." He picked up his drink.

The dowager eyed him in the way only a mother could. "You are done with her, aren't you?"

Gavin set the whisky down without a taste. "Actually, she is done with me."

His mother's chin lifted in affront. "Done with you? Is she mad?"

"She may well be the sanest person I know."

He could feel her scrutiny as if she weighed his words for what he had not said. In that moment,

Gavin could look anywhere save his mother's eyes. He would be a disappointment to her. He knew her thinking. And yet, God help him, his heart was broken.

Yes, his heart. He'd often wondered if he had one. While other men did fanciful and foolish things over women, Gavin had focused on duty and responsibility. He'd thought those men deluded for their lack of sound reason.

Now Gavin wished he was not so responsible, so chained to family honor and expectations.

His mother rose majestically to her feet. "I shall go with you this evening."

"You don't like the theater."

"I do not, save for the occasional Shakespeare. However, this play is your investment. And you are my son. I consider it a show of family solidarity."

"There is no need for that."

"Then understand *I* need to be there this evening."

"For what reason?" he asked carefully.

"My own purpose. We women have a feeling about these things. Imogen will also attend. You may need the two of us."

"Lest I do something foolish? I told you—"

"We will be there, Baynton." And with that, she sailed from the room.

Chapter Nineteen

Sarah woke with a groggy brain and with eyes so swollen they hurt to open.

Today her play opened. She'd dreamed of this day, worked for it—and instead of elation, she looked to the empty side of her bed and didn't know if she could move.

Then again, the one thing she had learned over her years is that to survive, a woman never gives up.

She crawled from the bed, shoved her hair back, and walked to the washbasin. She splashed cold water on her face. Her reflection in the glass was not good. She looked old, defeated.

In her plays, Love always won . . . but not in life—not for her.

It had been a blessing that Charlene had found love and been happy. Perhaps that is why Sarah had let down her guard, had started to let herself hope?

"What a terrible word—'*hope*,'" she muttered to her reflection.

He said he loved you, the devil's angel said in her head. *He claimed you would always have his heart. It is yours and will never go to another woman.*

Sarah dropped her hands into the basin's cold water, holding them there, appreciating the feeling of something other than pain, denying that ache inside her that begged her to settle for what crumbs Baynton offered.

But she knew better. She'd watched her mother trust one lover after another. In the end, people moved on with their lives. The woman who won was the one with the commitment.

A commitment Baynton was not free to make.

"I will overcome this," she assured herself. "My play will be a success and I will go forward without him."

And Gavin could have his little wife who was barely out of the schoolroom and his hundreds of horrid children. Sarah would not only survive, she was determined to thrive.

With that mind-set, she arrived at the theater shortly before one. Already, as with any opening night, members of her company were at work. Costumes were being carefully inspected. Bits of stage business were being rehearsed. The workers tested the ropes that pulled the set pieces and finishing touches were added to the scenic curtain of a country village.

There were hundreds of small tasks to keep Sarah's mind busy and off of Baynton. She helped realign the bench seats in the pit. She personally swept the boxes and was thankful that Geoff and Charles knew how to spend money and had good taste because the cushioned chairs and appointments of the boxes could have rivaled the finest theaters.

Her dear, dear friend Lady Baldwin came early as she had promised to help with selling seats. Having been an actress, she understood what was important. Lady Baldwin was as tall as she was wide and adored flamboyant feathers in her turban and bold prints.

Sarah had never been so happy to see anyone. She confided in Lady Baldwin that she and the duke were no more. Her ladyship enveloped her in a hug.

"I'm so sorry," she told Sarah. "I had hoped you would be like my Bertie and me." Her late husband Bertie had been one of the king's closest advisors. "I had believed you would make a lovely duchess."

"I didn't want a title," Sarah said. "I just wanted him."

"I know, dove," Lady Baldwin commiserated. "But a title is never a bad thing, either."

Her common sense sparked a laugh out of Sarah.

"Very good," her ladyship said approvingly. "That is the spirit I want from you. No moping. Not now. We have a play to stage—and one that has all of London buzzing."

She was right. Seat sales were brisk. In fact, people were clamoring for even the most expensive boxes.

Usually first nights, especially in new theaters, were not well attended. Sarah had been worried that no one would show. Now it seemed as if all the fashionable world would be in attendance.

She was certain it was because of Baynton. London knew what he was doing for her and now wished to know if he had purchased a pig in the poke. Sarah was determined to prove all critics wrong.

Of course, Gavin would be in attendance. She knew he would not stay away.

Standing in the wings of the stage she would grace in a few hours as the Widow Peregrine, Sarah looked up at the finest box in the house where he would be sitting. She could well imagine him there. For a second, her throat tightened and tears threatened. If she allowed herself, she could have a complete breakdown—

"Mrs. Pettijohn," Lady Baldwin said in an offi-cious tone, "we are completely sold out and there are still more who want to come in. What shall we do? I suggest we add more benches in the pit. Sir John Dawson said he'd be willing to sit there if it means he may have a ticket."

"No, it is already a crush as it is. Please offer my apologies and beg him to return tomorrow."

"All right, but I believe you are making a mis-take. One extra bench will not hurt."

Sarah glanced out at the people already mill-ing around for seats in the pit. "It is never wise to overstuff a theater. I've seen what happens when fights are started."

"Very well," Lady Baldwin replied and then gave a giddy laugh. "This is all so exciting." She hurried off to deliver the bad news to Sir John.

Time before a show always seemed to travel slow and fast, all at once. Sarah had spent the af-ternoon fearing the moment the curtain would be drawn and impatient for it as well.

She went to wardrobe to put on her costume. Elsie, the wardrobe mistress, helped her dress. When they were done, Elsie, in the most casual manner possible, said, "I haven't seen Thom."

"He should have been here an hour ago." Curs-ing the lead actor under her breath, Sarah went in search of him. It was quite possible he was busy having a flirt with the actresses or mingling with the audience.

"Rawlins just arrived," Billie, the watchman at the back door, said. "He asked after you."

"I pray he is changing into his costume," she muttered. She charged off in the direction of the dressing room and there she did find Thom, but he wasn't in costume.

Instead, he was talking to the gathered members of the company who listened intently. This was a strange scene to Sarah with only fifteen minutes to the performance. The actors were so absorbed with what Thom was saying, they didn't notice her at first.

Something was happening here and she was not certain what.

Then someone caught sight of her in the door and nudged another and soon Thom realized he was losing his audience. He turned and faced Sarah.

"Why aren't you in costume?" she asked.

He swallowed. "I will not go on, and before you become angry, you need to listen to me. We should cancel the performance."

"I will not. We have a curtain in fifteen minutes."

"Sarah, someone is determined to sabotage your play."

"What?"

"That is right. I have been warned by a person
trust that there will be men here tonight who
wish to ruin you. They are intent on ridiculing
ou and destroying your play. They have cabbage
heads and rotten apples to throw at any of us who
step on stage. They plan on making an example of
ou for what you are doing."

"And who would do such a thing? Colman and
the other theater managers?" She knew they were
critical and did not wish her well, but to be vio-
ent? Actors did not toss things at other actors on
the stage. It was just not done.

"The name I was given was Rovington. A man
called Rovington is said to have hired men to
embarrass you. He is determined to shut your
play down. I'm sorry, Sarah, I won't go on. I've
been in front of a crowd like that before. A man
can be seriously injured and if I can't work, then
what happens to me? It does nothing for my
reputation in the theater. My advice is to delay the
opening—"

"Is that what you are being paid to say?" Sarah
accused, stepping forward. The mention of Lord
Rovington did shake her, but she could not afford
to let Thom frighten the other actors. She had a
full house. It would be a nightmare to account for
all and return money.

"Paid?" Thom blustered as if offended but, as

was so often the case in his acting on stage, hi
response was not truly convincing.

"Yes, *paid*," she snapped. "Was this part of
plot from the beginning or did someone approacl
you recently, about the time you started show
ing up late for rehearsals?" She didn't wait for a
answer. She suddenly knew the truth. Thom hac
been planted in their midst to disrupt her play
"Go. *Leave*. We don't need you."

"Sarah, trust me, you do not want to go ou
there. If you show your face—"

"*I said leave*." If she'd had a stick in her hand
she would have chased him with it. Thom ap
peared affronted, and then dashed out the doo
like the coward he was.

She turned and addressed the other actors. "
know Lord Rovington. He is a scoundrel, a mai
without honor. It is also possible that he would do
what he could to upset this night, but we won't le
him."

She spoke as a general rallying the troop:
because that is what the cast needed. No acto
wanted to play before a hostile crowd. "We also
don't know if anything Thom said is true. I
actually sounds quite fantastic," she continued—
and then seeing Lady Baldwin by the door where
she had apparently been listening, drew her friend
into the conversation. "Does it not, my lady?"

Lady Baldwin did not sound terribly confident as she chimed in loyally, "The seats are filled. Everyone is expecting a good evening." She stepped back.

"Marcus," Sarah said to a young man standing to the back of the group. "You are Thom's understudy. Tonight is your opportunity to shine upon the stage." He was of middling height with lank brown hair and a huge nose—not exactly the characteristics Sarah had imagined for her romantic hero Jonathan Goodwell, but she had never expected Thom to not go on.

Instead of stoutly agreeing, Marcus shook his head. "I don't know, Sarah. Thom is right about the risk going out there. I don't know that I can play the part, what with worrying about a cabbage being thrown at my head. Those things can be as hard as a rock."

"You must," she insisted. "Without you, we don't have a play."

"Perhaps that might be for the best," Louisa, one of the actresses, suggested. Several heads nodded.

Sarah could not let her show close. "We don't know that Thom is telling the truth."

"When was the last time there was a theater this full for new play *and* a new manager?" Louisa said. "Sarah, it may be a trap. We will all be ruined—"

Sarah jumped up on a chair. "*Not* if we keep our heads. What if the excitement is because word has spread about the play? What if everyone is here to be the first to witness our triumph?"

"Are you talking about a *London* crowd?" one of the actors scoffed. By the looks on their faces, the other actors agreed with him.

"I can't do it," Marcus said. "I'm out." He flew from the room. Sarah tried to step in front of him but he dodged her.

"That is it," Louisa said. "Without Thom or Marcus, we can't put on the play—"

"Or *I* can play the part," said a familiar male voice from the doorway.

The Duke of Baynton stepped forward from where he had obviously been listening outside the door.

Sarah stared at him, a thousand different emotions assailing her at once. She wanted to fly into his arms, she wanted to hurl things at him, she wanted to embrace him . . . His presence threw her off. He looked so noble and handsome standing there.

And what was she? A failure. He was right to choose the young, lovely heiress. Sarah would never be anything.

"I know the role," Gavin said as if interpreting her silence for doubt. "I have the lines memorized and I believe I've seen enough of the rehearsals to have a general idea of where to move."

"But you have never been on stage," Sarah reminded him. "It won't work. It can't work. We are done."

Lady Baldwin voiced all the actors' opinions when she said, "Why won't it work? His Grace would be perfect for the part. And this Rovington would not dare to throw anything at the Duke of Baynton."

"Rovington?" Gavin asked.

"Yes," Lady Baldwin, always the chatterbox, said. "We have learned he has paid men to ruin the play. He wants to ruin and disgrace Sarah."

That was not true. Rovington was after Gavin and he and Sarah knew it.

"I am definitely playing the role," Gavin said. "And," he continued, raising his voice to include the others, "I will double your wages for this evening. You will have earned it if Rovington and I come to blows."

A cheer went up among the actors.

Sarah did not join them. She wanted to run from the room, from London, perhaps even from England.

Gavin came to her. "Sarah, don't back down now," he said in a voice only the two of them could hear. "You have more courage than this."

"Do I?" She could almost laugh but the sound would be too bitter. Her actors already were con-

tinuing to prepare for their parts. The matter wa
solved. Her play would go on.

Gavin had watched her struggle with her emo
tions. He understood why she did not want to rely
on him. Besides their argument last night, she wa
not one to ask for help, especially *his* help.

And yet he was not sorry for this opportunity.

He had come backstage to wish her well. The
moment he'd set eyes on her, he'd realized he
would be a fool to lose her. His Sarah had more
spirit in her small finger than a battalion of men
had in their whole bodies.

The weight of the play was on her shoulders
But he was here now. He'd not let Rovington or
anyone harm her.

She sized him up. "Your breeches are fine for
the part as is your shirt. We will have to use your
jacket as well." He had on a well-tailored coat of
marine superfine. "Tie a less complicated knot in
your neck cloth."

Gavin obeyed. While he did, she took a painted
wooden sword from one of the other actors. "Wear
this."

Gavin buckled the sword on and stepped back

"Better," she snapped. She handed him the

ctor's tricorn hat. Her gaze had not met his since
e'd come backstage and volunteered for the part.
here was definitely a divide between them.

As they walked to the stage, Sarah said, "You
now the lines, but saying them is different when
ne is in front of an audience. If you become lost,
ook to me and I'll mouth the words to you."

"Yes, ma'am."

Her back straightened at his humble response,
ut she ignored it.

"You enter through the door on the opposite
de of the stage," Sarah directed and pointed him
n the right direction while she took her place on
ne stage. The curtain had not yet been opened
nd he crossed to the other side.

The sounds of the audience were quite audible.
avin could imagine them restless. It was past
me for the play to start. He had been part of that
rowd. He'd seen more than a few people he knew.

He thought of his mother and Dame Imogen
n his box. This was not going to go over well . . .
nd yet, he was excited. Thrilled actually. He was
bout to test his mettle on the stage.

Gavin had not noticed Rov when he'd been out
here, but that didn't mean the man wasn't there.

After a nod from Sarah that all were in their

places, Lady Baldwin stepped out in front of tl curtain. Gavin listened to her welcome the aud ence and then announce a change in the playe "The male lead will be played by—" she pause dramatically "—the Duke of Baynton."

Her announcement was met with a stunned s lence followed by twitters of interest.

Lady Baldwin retreated behind the curtain. did see some cabbages, Sarah," she warned.

"You did?" Sarah squared her shoulders. was hoping that Thom was wrong."

"It is hard to hide the cabbages. The small frui and vegetables they can sneak in but with cabbag there is that tell-all bulge."

"Is it sporting to throw cabbages back?" Gavi wanted to know. The male actors laughed an nodded at the thought.

Sarah was not so amused. "Not unless yo want to start a riot."

"Then you'd best be a good dodger, Your Grace one of the lads said.

That was met with good-natured laughing an a bit of the tension broke.

Lady Baldwin vanquished the rest when sl said, "Oh, and, Your Grace?"

"Yes?"

"Is your mother, the dowager, in your box?"

"She is. With my aunt."

"Well, when I made the announcement, one of them swooned. I'm not certain which."

"Thank you, Lady Baldwin." There would be the devil to pay for this, and Gavin felt himself smile.

"Oh, don't worry, Your Grace," Lady Baldwin said. "The woman with her, an older woman, called for sherry, so all should be fine."

Gavin could only imagine the picture of his mother and Imogen fortifying themselves with sherry throughout the play. He'd have to carry them both home. Now he grinned outright and the other actors joined him.

Only Sarah was all business. She snapped her fingers. "Enough talk. To your places." She gave a sign, and the curtain opened.

Gavin could see the audience from where he waited although they could not see him, he didn't think. The actress named Louisa stood beside him. She played the Widow's nosy sister. It was a choice part. She now advised Gavin to never look at the audience, especially when one is on stage.

Sarah said the opening lines and the play was on. Louisa knocked on the door and entered the stage. Gavin hung back. It would be some time before Jonathan Goodwell would be called upon. It gave him the opportunity to watch the other actors work.

Sarah was a marvel. She had donned Peregrine's persona and seemed completely at ease.

At one point, someone from the pit yelled, "Why don't you dance naked for us, Siren?" However, before Gavin could think to react, the audience itself shushed the person who had shouted.

They were already involved in the play.

However, Gavin *had* to see who had called out. Against Louisa's advice, he edged to where he could look out and there was Rovington.

His Lordship did not look completely like himself. Rov wore a white bagwig and what appeared to be a cobbler's coat. Damn the man. Did he not think he would be recognized?

Gavin had half a mind to leave his post, make his way into the audience and pull the wig off the scoundrel's head.

Unfortunately, it was time for him to go on stage. He heard his cue to knock on the door as Louisa had done.

The Widow said, "Please enter."

Gavin walked through the portal and was met with enthusiastic applause. Gavin was stunned.

Sarah took a step close to him. Out of the side of her mouth, she said, "Bow. Acknowledge them."

Gavin obeyed. He made a courtly bow and earned a few cheers. Then audience grew quiet, signal for the play to continue.

However, before Gavin could deliver his first ne, Rov's voice shouted out, "So now do we have e opportunity to watch him poke her in front of s?" His comment was met with a few ribald laughs.

Sarah edged close. "Ignore him."

"Show us your legs, lovely Sarah," Rovington alled and started clapping. A scattering of others ok up clapping, and Gavin knew if he didn't ddress Rov, the situation would grow worse. ither way, Sarah's play would be ruined. All eople would remember on the morrow would be ovington's crude comments.

Gavin walked to the edge of the stage.

The crowd grew silent. "Lord Rovington," avin acknowledged, "I see you in disguise."

Heads turned, searching for Rov. Some spied im.

Gavin placed his hand on the hilt of his wooden word. "Are you asking for a rematch?"

The word of their duel had spread. Many in his room knew that Rov had disgraced himself. Most believed that by firing before the count, he ad attempted murder, and now Gavin was call-ng him out by name. This was the sort of drama heatergoers liked.

Knowing he held the attention in the room, avin challenged quietly, "Or is there nothing of e gentleman left in you?"

Rov stood. He pulled off the wig. "You are terrible actor, Your Grace."

"But I am an excellent swordsman. Far bette than I am a marksman."

"Go on with your play."

"No," Gavin said easily. "We shall settle this be tween us. You came this night to destroy what th woman has created. You wish to make a mocker of not only the cast, but all those in this room wh have gathered for the enjoyment of a play. Let u you and I, give them entertainment, Rovingto The sort they will not forget soon. Mrs. Pettijohr fetch another sword. I've challenged his lordship

"Are you mad?" Rov demanded.

"Is it madness to do what is honorable?" Gavi asked. He held up his wooden sword and the smiled down at Rov. "I think not. But let us as our audience. My friends," Gavin spoke to thos in the boxes and in the pit, "Lord Rovington ha come disguised to start a riot. He thinks to strik out at me by making a mockery of Mrs. Pettijohr a woman I sincerely admire."

Gavin had not looked over to the box where hi mother sat. He knew she would not be pleasec but he was enjoying himself. This was far mor fun than addressing Parliament.

"Now I ask you," Gavin continued. "Should not avenge her good name?"

Heads nodded. Fans fluttered. There was murmuring through the audience. "Yes," one woman called out. It may have been Lady Baldwin. Gavin was not certain; however, the emphatic word was soon echoed and then the crowd began clapping and calling for a duel with wooden swords between Rovington and Gavin.

Gavin took the sword that Sarah had taken from one of the other actors. Her expression was worried.

"I know what I'm doing," he promised.

"That's what I fear," she answered and Gavin couldn't help himself—he had to kiss her on the forehead, right there in front of everyone. It was a playful gesture. An affectionate one.

He held the wooden sword out. "Lord Rovington, you came here with cabbages to toss at this stage. Now let us see if you are man enough to fight in the open and to be judged by your peers."

Rov made his way down the bench to the aisle. People moved out of his way. Necks craned to watch his progress. They expected him to go to the stage. Instead, he stood in the aisle a moment, his head high, his shoulders back, and then he said, "I shall not play the fool, especially in front of your whore."

On those fine words, he pivoted and started to walk out of the theater.

But Gavin would not let him off, not after call ing Sarah that name.

Gavin hefted the wooden sword in his hand With a strength that would have made hi Norman ancestors proud, he threw it at Rov's re treating figure.

The sword turned like a knife in the air. The fla of it hit Rovington's back; the hilt thumped him i the head. Rov went down like a sack of bricks.

There was a stunned silence in the theater. Th closest man to Rov's prone figure leaned over i his seat and inspected him. "He is out cold," h reported. He looked him over again. "He'll com to. His head will ache though." The statement wa met with laughter.

"Good," Gavin said. "Remove him from thi place."

Several men jumped up to do as he bid. Rov ington was carried out of the Bishop's Hill to th sound of catcalls and hoots of derision.

Gavin addressed the audience. "There are me here whom I believe Lord Rovington hired to dis rupt this play. I advise them to mind their man ners. Or, I shall deliver to them the same treatmen but with less respect. Am I understood?"

No one answered, but Gavin knew his messag was clear.

"Very well," he said. "Let us continue with th

ay." He went back over to the door on stage,
xited it, knocked, and made his entrance.

Once again he was greeted with applause and
was louder and wilder than before.

Gavin wondered what Sarah was thinking. He
ad no way of knowing because she delivered her
ne and off they went in their parts.

Just as they had for so many evenings.

Only this time, there was a difference. They
ore the costumes and they were surrounded by
theater full of people who wanted them to be
ho they were, the Widow Peregrine and Jonathan
oodwell. The mantle of Duke of Baynton slipped
way.

Gavin found himself responding to Sarah's
haracter in a way that was meaningful and real
only for this moment on stage.

The audience became involved. They laughed at
ll the right moments. They grew serious when the
haracters had need of introspection and doubt,
nd Gavin could feel them rooting for his charac-
r to win the Widow, to succeed in his pursuit of
ove. To be the noble hero who was still just a man.

And isn't that what he wanted for himself?

Yes, he had worked hard to build his reputation
ut after everything was said and done, he was
nly a man—one who hadn't realized how lonely
e'd been until Sarah.

Now, acting with her, saying the words she ha
written, he knew there would never be anothe
woman for him.

Ever.

It was exactly as Fyclan Morris had said—sh
was his destiny. The One.

They came to the end of the play.

Gavin had managed fairly well, if he said s
himself. There had been a misspoken sentenc
here and there, a forgotten line or two, but Sara
had easily covered his mistakes.

He was also aware that in spite of the actin
there was a tension about her. He'd hurt her tha
deeply when he'd spoken of his duty to marr
Leonie Charnock.

She might not ever forgive him for the hurt.
was more than being proud. To those who didn
know her well, Sarah seemed a strong womar
But Gavin had learned the other side of her. Whe
she loved, she gave all . . . and she loved him.

The moment came when Goodwell was to dro
to one knee and profess his undying love for th
Widow.

Suddenly Gavin knew this might be his onl
chance to plead his case. Once they left this stag
Sarah would be gone from him.

But right now, he had her, and he did not war
to lose her.

So, when the moment came, Gavin didn't speak Jonathan Goodwell.

He took Sarah's hand and instead of saying, Dear Peregrine, will you do the honor of marrying me," he said, "Sarah Pettijohn, will you be my wife? Will you be my duchess?"

She blinked, startled.

The audience was equally confused, but then e felt them understand, and listen close with nterest.

Sarah frowned and then did what Gavin had nticipated she would do. She hid behind her haracter. "Thank you, Mr. Goodwell. You do me reat honor—"

"*Sarah*, I am not acting. I know that once you alk off this stage, then we will be done and I annot let you do that, not without telling you hat I truly feel. I'm no poet. I have no flowery peech. I'm not gifted with words the way you re. I've never spoken of love to any other woman efore you. In truth, I believed love was a myth. It vas for other people, not dukes. You have taught ne different. Now, I am not embarrassed to say I eed you. I don't want my days to go on without ou. Please, Sarah, I am on bended knee," he said, neeling in front of her. "I love you and am offerng all I have to you. Please, marry me."

The theater was dead quiet.

Everyone, including Gavin, waited for her answe[r]

She looked down at him and he could read th[e] struggle in her eyes. She did love him. He kne[w] that.

But instead of giving him the answer he wante[d] she whispered, "I can't marry you, Gavin. Don['t] you understand? I mustn't."

Nothing had been more wrenching to her sou[l] than to turn Gavin down.

He was the noblest, most gallant of men. He['d] protected her from Rovington and his hench men . . . *and* he'd taught her to trust again. He['d] made her believe this thing called love did exi[st] and it was grander than her imagination coul[d] ever have pictured.

And now, she must refuse him.

Not just Gavin but everyone in the theater, eve[n] the actors in the wings, had wanted her to say *ye[s]* He wanted *her*, the bastard daughter of a falle[n] woman. Gavin's love had lifted her to height[s] she could not have anticipated and she knew sh[e] loved him too much to accept.

"I can't give you children," she said, explain ing not just to him but to all who listened. "I lov[e] you too much to deny you something you wan[t,] something you need." She pulled her hand fro[m] his. "I'm not worthy of you."

She would have run then. She took a step but he was upon her, his arms around her. Tears burned her eyes.

She struggled against him. She dared not look at him, but he held her close and whispered in her ear, "Children mean nothing to me if I can't have you."

Sarah ceased resisting.

"Do you hear me, love?" he said, the sound of his voice humming through her body. "You are the one I choose. I was meant to love you, Sarah."

Tears streamed down her face. She couldn't stop them. "You could discover you are wrong, that children are more important," she said, praying he meant what he said.

"Sarah, there are no guarantees that if I married someone else that I'd have sons with her or even a son. It is one of the risks of life. However, I do know, with complete certainty, that I love you. You make my life interesting. In truth I was a bit of a bore until I met you. Staid and tedious. I don't want to go back to being that man. Save me, Sarah. Marry me."

How could she resist?

He was right, he did need her.

And she wanted him. He'd won past her defenses. He'd claimed her heart and there would be no other.

Her answer was to throw her arms around his neck. "Yes," she said. "Yes and yes, and *yes.*"

He lifted her up, swung her around—and the audience came to its feet with approving applause. Gavin kissed her then, right there on the stage—and the cheers grew louder.

Sarah knew that no one in the theater tonight would forget this performance. She never would.

His arm around her, Gavin waved at the crowd and both he and Sarah basked in the goodwill.

"Even my mother and great-aunt are clapping," Gavin said in Sarah's ear.

"We shall see how they feel in the morning," she said.

He laughed and then promised, "It doesn't matter how they will feel. I love you now, I will love you on the morrow, I will love you forever."

And then, to the audience's cheers, he kissed her again before the curtain closed.

And so . . .

Gavin's mother and Dame Imogen surprised him—they approved of his marrying Sarah.

"Your proposal on stage was the most romantic thing I have ever witnessed," the dowager told him. "And Sarah's willingness to sacrifice her happiness for you, well, it robbed me of breath."

"I've also done a bit of investigation into Mrs. Pettijohn's heritage," Dame Imogen said. The three of them were in Menheim's sitting room, the day after Gavin's theater debut. "She may be from the wrong side of the blanket but her bloodlines are impeccable."

"Really?" Gavin asked.

His great-aunt looked down her nose at him. "Am I ever wrong?"

"Never," he admitted, and did not add how thankful he was for her approval.

"Her father, Lord Twyndale, is descended from the Conqueror himself. Through him, she is related to the most noble houses in Britain. Furthermore, we've been needing what she will bring to us. There are holes in our ancestry."

"And she will be a graceful duchess," his mother noted. "Her coloring is quite dramatic."

"She is beautiful," Gavin said.

"Yes," Dame Imogen concluded, "she will make a fine appearance next to you in your portraits. Besides, she has lovely manners."

Gavin knew there could be no higher praise.

"But what of children?" his mother asked. "I like her, my son. I know your mind is set, still, I must mourn a bit."

"Well, now that we know Ben and Elin are having twins, there will be heirs," Gavin said. "If not Ben, then a child of his."

"You are not a little sad?" the dowager said.

Gavin laughed. "I will have Sarah for my wife and I need nothing else."

And so, with the blessing of his family, Gavin Whitridge, 5th Duke of Baynton married Mrs. Sarah Pettijohn on a lovely October day in London. The wedding breakfast was the most coveted invitation of the year.

Afterward, Gavin took his bride to Trenton, his family estate. *The Fitful Widow* was a grand success; however, with all the gossip about that fateful night at the theater, Gavin wanted his wife to himself and she was happy to comply.

Ben and Elin were already there. She was huge with child and everyone, including her father Fyclan Morris who lived on the property next to Trenton, was anxious for the arrival of the babies.

Gavin discovered each day of his married life was better than the last. Sarah had set aside her doubts. "I've found my place in the world," she told Gavin.

"And it is in Trenton?" he asked.

"No, it is by your side."

He was the most fortunate of men.

On a stormy day in early November, Elin went into labor and Henry Morris Whitridge and Jennifer Anne Marie Whitridge made their entrances to the world.

Gavin paced the floor with Ben and Fyclan. The sound of the babies' crying was sweeter than the herald of angels. He was as elated as the other men.

Sarah was the first out of the birthing room. She was misty-eyed. "Ben, Elin is asking for you."

He hurried inside.

"You as well, Fyclan," Sarah said.

Gavin had never seen his old mentor look so proud.

"Your gran's prophecy has come true," Gavin said. "Furthermore, Henry will someday be a duke."

"If it is God's wish." Fyclan took a step to the door and paused. "I'm just proud to have another Jenny in my life. A different one but I pray she has her grandmother's spirit."

"I'm certain she will," Gavin answered and Fyclan went into the birthing room to pay his respects to his grandchildren.

Sarah looked to Gavin and said, "Their births were the most incredible thing to witness. True miracles they are. And I'm so happy I could be present for it."

He took her in his arms, knowing what she did not say. For a long moment they held each other. "I want to be enough for you," she whispered.

"You are. Am I all that you want?"

"Yes, a thousand times yes," she told him . . . but they both knew that however much they meant to each other, they recognized what they could not have.

Around Christmas Day, a letter arrived from Charlene and Jack. What with the American war, it was hard to receive letters. They sounded well and Charlene shared that come the spring, Sarah would be a great-aunt. If Charlene and Jack had received Sarah's letter about her marriage to Gavin, it was not mentioned.

"Another child," Sarah said.

"It is all good," Gavin answered.

She reached for his hand. "Yes, very good. I could not love anyone more than I do you."

He lifted her hand to his lips and kissed the back of her fingers. "My duchess."

She smiled, but there was a wistfulness in her expression, one he wished he could dispel.

Gavin had thought to stay in Trenton until January but Sarah seemed so happy there, he extended their stay. She still wrote, but she hadn't said anything about staging another play. It was as if her dream had been realized. Gavin knew she now longed for what she could not have.

Sarah was very active in helping Elin take care of the babies. In fact, everyone in the family wondered what they'd done before for entertainment since most of their evenings were spent watching Henry and Jenny develop into interesting little people.

Of course, Gavin was often called to London. He did manage to see the Money Bill through and the prime minister was pleased. Eventually, he knew he and Sarah would have to return to Menheim. His wife was embraced by London society, even by the sticklers. Dame Imogen's approval had ensured if not their acceptance then their tolerance.

Yes, life could not be better, or so Gavin thought until one day when he was making his return to Trenton from London.

He had stopped at a small inn for the night. It was out of the way and one he used often when he traveled. The establishment was run by a cheery family by the name of Lodenberry.

Gavin was so accustomed to their goodwill and friendly greeting, he noticed that Mrs. Lodenberry was not her usual self when he arrived. Her eyes were red and her face pinched as if she'd been crying.

"Is something the matter, Mrs. Lodenberry?"

She gave him a piteous look and apologized, "I'm sorry, Your Grace, we've had sad news here. A young man and his wife died last week. They left three children orphaned and without relatives. Six, five, and a wee newborn. The parson is taking them to the foundling home today. Mr. Lodenberry and I offered to take the boys but they will not leave their baby sister. I can't take on a baby. I can't. I have my hands full with my own brood and this inn. But who knows what will become of those poor motherless children? Who knows?" She started to weep again.

An idea formed in Gavin's head. "Where is the parson?"

He followed her directions and was in short

order introduced to two charming boys who were both grieving the loss of their parents and wise enough to be fearful for their own futures. They gathered protectively around their sister, a ginger-haired baby.

It was the red hair that settled the matter for Gavin.

Since there was no one to take charge of Andrew, Wills, and their sister Merriam, Gavin did.

He practically flew home and nothing gave him greater pleasure than to place Merriam in his wife's arms. A sense of contentment spread across Sarah's face, especially when Merriam, who had to be the happiest baby Gavin had ever met, smiled up at her.

"She's precious," Sarah said. She looked to the boys. "Come and sit here," she invited. "Tell me about yourselves."

The boys were happy to do so . . . and that is how Sarah and Gavin created the family they both had longed for. Nor did they stop with their initial three. Over the years, they adopted a total of nine children.

Children of their heart—that's how Gavin and Sarah referred to their brood. No, the boys could not inherit a title, but they received educations and love and isn't that all any child needed?

Better yet, Gavin's days were filled with the

right sort of priorities. Yes, he still wielded power, but he gave time to his own life as well.

And his favorite nights with his family?

Those were the evenings, when his children staged a play. He and Sarah were the audience, and there was a curtain made of a blanket and costumes scavenged from family trunks in the attic and, of course, wooden swords.

Author's Note

Dear Readers,

Lest you accuse me of imitating a Shakespearean play where everything turns out for the best in defiance of convention, and sometimes common sense, let me assure you that many an actress has married a lord, even during the Regency. Bold and talented women have always attracted men. Conversely, many a man has landed one of those women because he had a title before his name and/or a good deal of money in his pocket. Of course, Sarah would never be so crass. Her love for Baynton is as genuine as his devotion to her. It is just her good fortune he is not a ditch digger.

Names in history that come to mind are

Miss Anastasia Robinson, an opera singer, who secretly married the 3rd Earl of Peterborough in the early 1700s. Everyone assumed she was his mistress and for ten years they kept their marriage a secret until right before his death.

Then there was Miss Harriet Mellon who starred on Drury Lane's stage and captured the hearts of *two* powerful men. The first was the wealthy banker Thomas Coutts who left his entire fortune to her upon his death. The second was the 9th Duke of St. Albans who was twenty-three years her junior. Frankly, I wouldn't know what to say to a man that much younger than myself. She was fifty years old when they married and he was practically a lamb chop. However, please note, this may have been a case where *her* money was the attraction, although Harriet was a renowned beauty.

Another I will tell you about is Louisa Brunton. She was quite successful on the Regency stage and came from a family of actors. She married the 1st Earl of Craven in 1807 and her days treading the stage were done.

Finally, let me share a bit about female playwrights. Women have been scribblers since time began—we just haven't received much credit for it.

In the 1600s and 1700s, it was not unusual for female playwrights to be titled women whose work was produced because of their husbands' largesse. In 1812, Sarah is fortunate that Baynton would finance her theatric endeavors because then, like now, who you know is everything.

Known female playwrights during the Regency, include Marie-Thérèse De Camp who had married into the Kemble family. The Kembles were one of the leading stage families of the day. Marie-Thérèse's plays and light farces were relatively successful. Wherever the family managed a theater—Drury Lane or Covent Garden—that is where her plays were staged.

Another successful playwright of the day was the Scot Joanna Baillie who is noted as a protégé of Sir Walter Scott. She was considered, even back in the 1800s, the leading Scottish playwright of *any* gender.

Sir Walter helped produce her play *The Family Legend*. Staged in 1810 at the Theatre Royal in Edinburgh and then Drury Lane in London in 1815, it is a tale of clan rivalry, deceit, revenge, lost loves, a secret baby . . . and, unfortunately, is a tragedy.

If only she'd added a little romance and

that happily-ever-after . . . then maybe we'd be making movies of her work as we do Austen's.

Happy reading, my friends,
Cathy Maxwell
April 12, 2015